It Starts with Us

It Starts with Us

Colleen Hoover

SIMON &
SCHUSTER

London · New York · Sydney · Toronto · New Delhi

First published in the USA by Atria, an imprint of Simon & Schuster, Inc., 2022
This edition published in Great Britain by Simon & Schuster UK Ltd, 2022

1 3 5 7 9 10 8 6 4 2

Simon & Schuster UK Ltd
1st Floor
222 Gray's Inn Road
London WC1X 8HB

Simon & Schuster Australia, Sydney
Simon & Schuster India, New Delhi

www.simonandschuster.co.uk
www.simonandschuster.com.au
www.simonandschuster.co.in

A CIP catalogue record for this book
is available from the British Library

Hardback ISBN: 978-1-3985-1816-2
Trade Paperback: 978-1-3985-1817-9
eBook ISBN: 978-1-3985-1818-6
Audio ISBN: 978-1-3985-1819-3

Printed and bound in Great Britain by CPI Group (UK) Ltd, Croydon, CR0 4YY

This book is for the brave and bold Maria Blalock

Dear reader,

This book is a sequel to *It Ends with Us* and begins right where the first book concluded. For the best reading experience, *It Starts with Us* should be read second in the two-book series.

After releasing *It Ends with Us*, I never imagined I would one day be writing a sequel. I also never imagined that the book would be received as it has been by so many. I am so grateful to all of you who found Lily's story to be as empowering as I find my own mother's.

After *It Ends with Us* gained momentum on TikTok, I was inundated with requests for more Lily and Atlas. And how could I possibly deny a community that has changed my life? This novel was written as a thank-you for the tremendous support, and because of that, I wanted to deliver a much lighter experience.

Lily and Atlas deserve it.

I hope you enjoy their journey.

All my love,
Colleen Hoover

It Starts with Us

Chapter One
Atlas

The way *ass whole* is misspelled in red spray paint across the back door of Bib's makes me think of my mother.

She would always insert a brief pause between syllables, making it sound like two separate words. I wanted to laugh every time I heard it, but it was hard to find the humor in it as a child when I was always the recipient of the hurled insult.

"Ass . . . whole," Darin mutters. "Had to be a kid. Most adults know how to spell that word."

"You'd be surprised." I touch the paint, but it doesn't stick to my fingers. Whoever did this must have done it right after we closed last night.

"Do you think the misspelling was intentional?" he asks. "Are they suggesting you're so much of an asshole that you're a whole *entire* ass?"

"Why do you assume they were targeting *me*? They could have been targeting you or Brad."

"It's your restaurant." Darin takes off his jacket and uses it to pry a large shard of exposed broken glass out of the window. "Maybe it was a disgruntled employee."

"Do I have disgruntled employees?" I can't think of a single person on payroll who would do something like this.

The last person I'd had quit was five months ago, and she left on good terms after getting a college degree.

"There was that guy who did the dishes before you hired Brad. What was his name? He was named after some kind of mineral or something—it was super weird."

"Quartz," I say. "It was a nickname." I haven't thought about that guy in so long. I doubt he's holding a grudge against me after all this time. I fired him right after we opened because I found out he wasn't washing the dishes unless he could actually see food on them. Glasses, plates, silverware—anything that came back to the kitchen from a table looking fairly clean, he'd just put it straight on the drying rack.

If I wouldn't have fired him, he would have gotten us shut down by the health department.

"You should call the police," Darin says. "We'll have to file a report for insurance."

Before I object, Brad appears at the back door, his shoes crunching the broken glass beneath his feet. Brad has been inside taking inventory in order to see if anything was stolen.

He scratches the stubble on his jaw. "They took the croutons."

There's a confused pause.

"Did you say 'croutons'?" Darin asks.

"Yeah. They took the whole thing of croutons that were prepared last night. Nothing else seems to be missing, though."

That wasn't at all what I was expecting him to say. If someone broke into a restaurant and didn't take appliances or anything else of value, they probably broke in because they were hungry. I know that kind of desperation firsthand. "I'm not reporting this."

Darin turns to me. "Why not?"

"They might catch whoever did it."

"That's the point."

I grab an empty box out of the dumpster and start picking up shards of glass. "I broke into a restaurant once. Stole a turkey sandwich."

Brad and Darin are both staring at me now. "Were you drunk?" Darin asks.

"No. I was hungry. I don't want anyone arrested for stealing croutons."

"Okay, but maybe food was only the beginning. What if they come back for appliances next time?" Darin says. "Is the security camera still broken?"

He's been on me to get that repaired for months now. "I've been busy."

Darin takes the box of glass from me and starts to pick up the remaining pieces. "You should go work on that before they come back. Heck, they might even try to hit up Corrigan's tonight since Bib's was such an easy target."

"Corrigan's has working security. And I doubt whoever it was will vandalize my new restaurant. It was a matter of convenience, not a targeted break-in."

"You *hope*," Darin says.

I open my mouth to respond, but I'm interrupted by an incoming text message. I don't think I've ever reached for my phone faster. When I see the text isn't from Lily, I deflate a little.

I ran into her this morning while I was running errands.

It was the first time we've seen each other in a year and a half, but she was late for work and I had just received the text from Darin informing me we had a break-in. We parted somewhat awkwardly on the promise that she would text me once she got to work.

It's been an hour and a half since then, and I still haven't heard from her. An hour and a half is nothing, but I can't ignore the nagging in my chest that's trying to convince me she's having doubts about everything that was said between us in that five-minute exchange on the sidewalk.

I'm definitely not having doubts about what *I* said. I might have gotten caught up in the moment—in seeing how happy she looked and finding out she's no longer married. But I meant every word I said to her.

I'm ready for this. *More* than ready.

I pull up her contact info in my phone. I've wanted to text her so many times over the last year and a half, but the last time I spoke to her, I left the ball in her court. She had so much going on, I didn't want to complicate her life even more.

She's single now, though, and she made it sound like she was finally ready to give whatever could be between us a chance. However, she's had an hour and a half to think about our conversation, and an hour and a half is plenty of time to form regrets. Every minute that passes without a text is going to feel like a whole damn day.

She's still listed as Lily Kincaid in my phone, so I edit her contact info and change her last name back to Bloom.

I feel Darin hovering, looking over my shoulder at my phone screen. "Is that *our* Lily?"

Brad perks up. "He's texting Lily?"

"'*Our* Lily'?" I ask, confused. "You guys met her once."

"Is she still married?" Darin asks.

I shake my head.

"Good for her," he says. "She was pregnant, right? What did she end up having? A boy or a girl?"

I don't want to discuss Lily because there's nothing to discuss yet. I don't want to make it more than what it might be. "A girl, and that's the last question I'm answering." I focus on Brad. "Theo coming in today?"

"It's Thursday. He'll be here."

I head inside the restaurant. If I'm going to discuss Lily with anyone, it'll be Theo.

Chapter Two
Lily

My hands are still shaking, even though it's been almost two hours since I ran into Atlas. I can't tell if I'm shaking because I'm flustered or because I've been too busy to eat since I walked in the door. I've barely had five seconds of peace to process what happened this morning, much less eat the breakfast I brought with me.

Did that actually just happen? Did I really ask Atlas a series of questions so awkward, I'll be mortified well into next year?

He didn't seem awkward, though. He seemed very happy to see me, and then when he hugged me, it felt like a part of me that had been dormant suddenly sprang to life.

But this is the first moment I've had to even take a bathroom break, and after looking at myself in the mirror just now, I kind of want to cry. I'm splotchy, I have carrots smeared across my shirt, my nail polish has been chipped since, like, January.

Not that Atlas expects or wants perfection. It's just that I've imagined running into him so many times, but not one of those fantasies starred me bumping into him in the middle of a hectic morning, half an hour after being the target of an eleven-month-old with a handful of baby food.

He looked so good. He smelled so good.

I probably smell like breast milk.

I'm so rattled by what our chance encounter might mean, it took me twice as long to organize everything for the delivery driver this morning. I haven't even checked our website for new orders today. I give myself one last look in the mirror, but all I see is an exhausted, overworked single mom.

I make my way out of the bathroom and back to the register. I pull an order from the printer and begin making out the card. My mind has never been more in need of a distraction, so I'm glad it's been a busy morning.

The order is for a bouquet of roses for someone named Greta from someone named Jonathan. The message reads, *I'm sorry about last night. Forgive me?*

I groan. Apology flowers are my least-favorite kind of bouquets to assemble. I always end up obsessing over what they're apologizing for. Did he miss their date? Did he come home late? Did they fight?

Did he hit her?

Sometimes I want to write the number for the local domestic violence shelter on the cards, but I have to remind myself that not every apology is attached to something as awful as the things that were attached to the apologies I used to receive. Maybe Jonathan is Greta's friend and he's trying to cheer her up. Maybe he's her husband and he took a prank a little too far.

Whatever the reason for the flowers, I hope they mean something good. I tuck the card into the envelope and stick it into the bouquet of roses. I set them on the delivery shelf and am pulling up the next order when I receive a text.

I lunge for my phone as if the text is about to self-destruct and I only have three seconds to read it. I shrink when I look at the screen. It's not from Atlas, but rather from Ryle.

Can she eat French fries?

I shoot a quick response. **Soft ones.**

I drop my phone onto the counter with a thud. I don't like for her to have French fries too often, but Ryle only has her one to two days a week, so I try to make sure she gets more nutritious foods when she's with me.

It was nice not thinking about Ryle for a few minutes, but his text has reminded me that he exists. And as long as he exists, I fear that any type of relationship, or even a friendship between me and Atlas, *can't* exist. How will Ryle take it if I start seeing Atlas? How would he act if they ever had to be around each other?

Maybe I'm getting ahead of myself.

I stare at my phone, wondering what I should say to Atlas. I told him I would text him after I opened the store, but customers were waiting before I even unlocked the door. And now that Ryle has texted, I've gone and remembered Ryle exists in this scenario, too, which makes me hesitant to text Atlas at all.

The front door opens, and my employee Lucy finally walks in. She always seems so put-together, even when I can tell she's in a bad mood.

"Good morning, Lucy."

She flicks hair out of her eyes and sets her purse on the counter with a sigh. "Is it?"

Lucy isn't at her friendliest in the morning. It's why my other employee Serena or I usually work the register until at least eleven, while Lucy puts arrangements together in the back. She's much better with customers after a cup or five of coffee.

"I just found out our place cards never arrived because they were discontinued, and it's too late to order more. The wedding is in less than a *month*."

So much has gone wrong leading up to this wedding, I have half a mind to tell her not to go through with it. But I'm not superstitious. Hopefully she isn't, either.

"Homemade place cards are in style," I offer.

Lucy rolls her eyes. "I hate crafting," she mutters. "I don't even want a wedding now. It feels like we've been planning it for longer than we even dated." *That's accurate.* "Maybe we'll just call it off and go to Vegas. You eloped, right? Do you regret it?"

I don't know which part of all that to address first. "How can you hate crafting? You work at a flower shop. And I'm divorced; of course I regret eloping." I hand her a small stack of orders I haven't gotten to yet. "But it *was* fun," I admit.

Lucy goes to the back and starts on the rest of the orders, and I go back to thinking about Atlas. *And Ryle.* And Armageddon, which is what the two of them in my brain at the same time feels like.

I have no idea how this is expected to work. When Atlas and I ran into each other, it was as if everything else faded away, including Ryle. But now Ryle is beginning to seep back into my thoughts. Not in the way thoughts of Ryle *used* to occupy my mind, but more in a way that feels like a roadblock. My love life has finally been on a straight path with no bumps or curves, basically because it's been nonexistent for well over a year and a half, but now it feels like there's nothing but rough terrain and obstacles and cliffs ahead.

Is it worth it? Of course *Atlas* is worth it.

But are *we* worth it? Is us potentially becoming a thing worth the stress it would inevitably bring to all the other areas of my life?

I haven't felt this conflicted in so long. Part of me wants to call Allysa and tell her about seeing Atlas, but I can't. She knows how Ryle still feels about me. She knows how he'd feel if I brought Atlas into the picture.

I can't talk to my mother because she's my mother. As close as we've become lately, I'd still never freely discuss my dating life with her.

There's really only one woman I feel comfortable talking to about Atlas.

"Lucy?"

She appears from the back, pulling an earbud out of her ear. "Did you need me?"

"Can you cover me for a while? I need to go run an errand. I'll be back in an hour."

She makes her way behind the counter, and I grab my purse. I don't get a lot of alone time now that I have Emerson, so I occasionally steal an hour here and there during the workweek when I have someone to back up my absence at the shop.

Sometimes I like to sit in my thoughts, and it's impossible to do that in the presence of a child because even when she's asleep I'm in mom mode. And with the constant flow of traffic at work, it's rare that I can find a stretch of peace without being interrupted.

I've found that being alone in my car with my music on, and occasionally a slice of dessert from the Cheesecake Factory, is sometimes all it takes to sort through the knots in my brain.

Once I'm parked with a clear view of Boston Harbor, I lean my seat back and grab the notepad and pen I brought with me. I don't know if this will help as much as dessert sometimes does, but I need to release my thoughts in the same way I've done in the past. This method has helped before when I need things to fall neatly into place. Although this time, I'm just hoping it helps things not to fall completely apart.

Dear Ellen,

Guess who's back?

Me.

And Atlas.

Both of us.

I ran into him on my way to meet Ryle with Emmy this morning. It was so good to see him. But as reaffirming as it was to see him and to know where we both stand at this point in our lives, it ended a bit awkwardly. He was having a minor emergency with his restaurant and was in a hurry; I was late opening the store. We parted on the promise that I would text him.

I want to text him. I do. Especially because seeing him reminded me of how much I miss the feeling I get when I'm around him.

I didn't realize how lonely I'd been feeling until those few minutes with him this morning. But since Ryle and I divorced . . . oh, wait.

Wow. I haven't told you about the divorce.

It's been way too long since I've written to you. Let me back up.

I decided my separation from Ryle should be permanent after giving birth to Emmy. I asked him for a divorce right after she was born. I wasn't attempting to be cruel in my timing, I just didn't know which choice I was going to make until I held her in my arms and knew with every fiber of my being that I would do whatever it took to break the cycle of abuse.

Yes, asking for a divorce hurt. Yes, I was heartbroken. But no, I don't regret it. My choice helped me realize that sometimes the hardest decisions a person can make will most likely lead to the best outcomes.

I can't lie and say I don't miss him, because I do. I miss what we sometimes were. I miss the family we could have been for Emerson. But I know I made the right decision, even though I sometimes get overwhelmed by the weight of it. It's difficult because I still have to interact with Ryle. He still possesses all the good qualities I fell in love with, and now that I'm no longer in a relationship with him, it's rare I see the negative side that ultimately ended our marriage. I think that has to do with the fact that he's on his best behavior. He had to be agreeable and not put up too much of a fight because he knew I could have reported him for all the incidents of domestic violence I experienced at his hands. He could have lost a lot more than his wife, so when it came to the custody arrangement, things were more amiable than I expected them to be.

That may have been more because I put up less of a

fight than he did. My lawyer was very straightforward when I said I wanted sole custody. Unless I was willing to drag the dirtiest parts of our rock bottom into a courtroom, there wasn't much I could do to prevent Ryle from getting visits with Emerson. And even if I were to bring up the domestic violence, my lawyer said it's very rare that a willing, successful father without a record, who provides financial support, would have any sort of rights removed.

I was looking at two options. I could choose to press charges and drag this through the courts, only to be met with a very possible joint custody arrangement. Or I could attempt to work an agreement out with Ryle that would satisfy us both, while preserving our coparenting relationship.

I guess you could say we came to a compromise, even though there isn't an agreement in the world that would make me feel comfortable with sending my daughter off with someone I know possesses a temper. But all I can do is choose the lesser of two evils when it comes to custody and hope that Emmy never sees that side of him.

I want Emmy to bond with her father. I've never wanted to keep her from him. I just want to ensure she's safe, which is why I begged Ryle to agree to day visits for the first couple of years. I never told him outright it's because I don't know that I fully trust him with her. I think I might have blamed it on my breastfeeding situation and the fact that he's on call all the time, but deep down I'm sure he knows why I've never wanted her to stay with him overnight.

The past abuse is something we don't talk about. We

talk about Emmy, we talk about work, we plaster on smiles when we're in the presence of our daughter. Sometimes it feels forced and fake, at least on my end, but it's better than what this could have been had I taken him to court and lost. I'll fake a smile until she's eighteen if it means I don't have to share custody and potentially expose my daughter to the worst parts of her father on a more regular basis.

It's been working out okay so far, if you don't count the occasional gaslighting and unwanted flirtation from him. As clear as I've made my feelings during this divorce, he still has hope for us. He says things sometimes that indicate he hasn't fully let go of the idea of us. I fear that a huge part of Ryle's cooperation rests on the notion that he'll eventually win me back if he's good enough for long enough. He has it in his head that I'll soften over time.

But life isn't going to happen his way, Ellen. I'm ultimately going to move on, and if I'm being honest, I hope I end up moving on in Atlas's direction. It's too soon to know if that's a possibility, but I know for a fact I'll never move back in Ryle's direction, no matter how much time passes.

It's been almost a year since I asked Ryle for the divorce, but it's been almost nineteen months since the fight that ultimately caused our separation. Which means I've been single for over a year and a half.

A year and a half of separation between potential relationships seems like plenty of time, and maybe it would be if it were anyone other than Atlas. But how can I possibly make this work? What if I text Atlas and he invites me to lunch? And then lunch goes wonderful, which I'm sure it would, and lunch leads to dinner? And dinner leads to us *falling right back into step with where we left off when we were younger? And then we're both happy and we fall back in love and he becomes a permanent part of my life?*

I know it sounds like I'm getting ahead of myself, but it's Atlas we're talking about here. Unless he had a personality transplant, I think you and I both know how easy Atlas is for me to love, Ellen. That's why I'm so hesitant, because I'm scared it will work out.

And if it works out, how will Ryle feel about my new relationship? Emerson is almost a year old, and we've gone this whole year without too much drama, but I know that's because we've found a good flow that nothing has interrupted. So why does it feel like any mention of Atlas will cause a tsunami?

Not that Ryle deserves the concern I'm currently feeling over this situation, but he has the potential to make my dating life a living hell. Why does Ryle still occupy an entire wall in my many layers of thoughts? That's what it feels like—as if these wonderful things happen, but as they start to sink in, they eventually reach a part of me that is still making decisions based on Ryle and his potential reactions.

His reactions are what I fear the most. I want to hope that he wouldn't be jealous, but he will be. If I start dating Atlas, he'll make it difficult for everyone. Even though I know divorce was the right choice, there are still consequences to that choice. And one of those consequences is that Ryle will always look at Atlas like he's the thing that broke up our marriage.

Ryle is the father of my daughter. No matter what man

comes and goes in my life from this point forward, Ryle is the one constant that I'll always have to appease if I want the most peaceful experience for my daughter. And if Atlas Corrigan is back in my life—Ryle will never be appeased.

I wish you could tell me what decision to make. Do I sacrifice what I know will make me happy for the sake of avoiding the inevitable disruption Atlas's presence would cause?

Or will I always have an Atlas-shaped hole in my heart unless I allow him to fill it?

He's expecting me to text him, but I think I need more time to process this. I don't even know what to say to him. I don't know what to do.

I'll let you know if I figure it out.

Lily

Chapter Three
Atlas

"'We finally reached the *shore*'?" Theo says. "You actually *said* that to her? Out loud?"

I shift uncomfortably on the couch. "We bonded over *Finding Nemo* when we were younger."

"You quoted a *cartoon*." Theo's head roll is dramatic. "And it didn't work. It's been over eight hours since you ran into her, and she still hasn't texted you."

"Maybe she got busy."

"Or maybe you came on too strong," Theo says, leaning forward. He clasps his hands between his knees and refocuses. "Okay, so what happened after you said all the cheesy lines?"

He's brutal. "Nothing. We both had to get to work. I asked if she still had my number, and she said she had it memorized, and then we said good—"

"Hold up," Theo interrupts. "She has your number *memorized*?"

"Apparently so."

"Okay." He looks hopeful. "This means something. No one memorizes numbers anymore."

I was thinking the same thing, but I also wondered if she memorized my number for other reasons. Back when I wrote it down and put it in her phone case, it was for an emergency. Maybe part of her feared the day she'd need it, so she memorized it for reasons that had nothing to do with me.

"So, what do I do? Text her? Call her? Wait until she reaches out to me?"

"It's been eight hours, Atlas. Calm down."

His advice is giving me whiplash. "Two minutes ago, you acted like eight hours without a text was too long. Now you're telling me to calm down?"

Theo shrugs and then kicks my desk to make his chair spin. "I'm twelve. I don't even have a phone yet, and you want my opinion on texting etiquette?"

It surprises me that he doesn't have a phone yet. Brad doesn't seem like he would be a strict father. "Why don't you have a phone?"

"Dad says I can have one when I turn thirteen. Two more months," he says wistfully.

Theo has been coming to the restaurant a couple of days a week after school since Brad's promotion six months ago. Theo told me he wanted to be a therapist when he grows up, so I let him practice on me. At first, the talks we would have were intended for his benefit. But lately, I feel like I'm the one benefiting.

Brad peeks his head into my office in search of his son. "Let's go. Atlas has work to do." He motions for Theo to stand up, but Theo just keeps spinning in my desk chair.

"Atlas is the one who called me in here. He needed advice."

"I'll never understand whatever this is," Brad says, pointing between me and Theo. "What advice do you get from my son? How to avoid your chores and win at *Minecraft*?"

Theo stands up and stretches his arms over his head. "Girls, actually. And winning isn't the point of *Minecraft*, Dad. It's more of a sandbox game." Theo looks over his shoulder at me as he's leaving my office. "Just text her." He says that like it's the obvious solution. Maybe it is.

Brad yanks him away from the door.

I settle back into my desk chair and stare at my blank phone screen. *Maybe she memorized the wrong number.*

I open her contact and hesitate. Theo could be right. I could have come on too strong this morning. We didn't say much when we ran into each other, but what we did say had meaning and intent. Maybe that scared her.

Or . . . maybe I'm right and she memorized the wrong number.

My fingers hover over my phone's keyboard. I want to text her, but I don't want to pressure her. However, she and I both know our lives would have turned out so different if I hadn't made so many missteps with her in the past.

I spent years making excuses for why my life wasn't good enough for her to be a part of it, but Lily always fit. She was a perfect fit. I refuse to let her walk away this time without a little more effort on my part. I'll start with making sure she has my correct number.

It was good seeing you today, Lily.

I wait to see if she's going to text me back. When I see the three dots pop up, I hold my breath in anticipation.

You too.

I stare at her response for way too long, hoping it'll be accompanied by another text. But it isn't. That's all I'm getting.

It's only two words, but I can read between the lines.

I sigh in defeat and drop my phone onto my desk.

Chapter Four
Lily

Mine and Ryle's situation has been an unconventional one since Emerson was born. I don't think many couples file divorce papers at the same time they sign their newborn's birth certificate.

As much as I was disappointed in Ryle for being the thing that forced me to have to make the decision to end our marriage, I didn't want to prevent him from bonding with our daughter. I cooperate with him as much as I can since his schedule is so hectic. I sometimes even take her to his work to visit him on his lunch break.

He's also had a key to my place since before Emerson was born. I only gave it to him because I lived alone and was afraid I'd go into labor and he'd need access to the apartment. But he never gave the key back after her birth, even though I've been meaning to ask him for it. He sometimes uses it on the rare occasions he has a late surgery and has extra time to spend with Emmy in the mornings after I head to work. That's why I haven't asked for it back. But lately, he's been using the key to bring Emmy home.

He texted me just before I closed the shop earlier and told me Emmy was tired, so he was taking her to my place to put her to bed. The frequency he's been using the key lately is making me wonder if Emmy is the only one he's trying to spend more time with.

My front door is unlocked when I finally make it to my apartment. Ryle is in the kitchen. He glances up at me when he hears the front door shut.

"I grabbed dinner," he says, holding up a bag from my favorite Thai place. "You haven't eaten, have you?"

I don't like this. He's been making himself more and more comfortable here. But I'm emotionally drained from the day already, so I shake my head and decide to confront the issue at a different time. "I haven't. Thank you." I set my purse on the table and pass the kitchen, heading for Emmy's room.

"I just laid her down," he warns.

I pause right outside her door and press my ear to it. It's quiet, so I back away from the door and head into the kitchen without waking her.

I feel awful about my short response to Atlas earlier, but this interaction with Ryle is confirming all my concerns. How am I supposed to start something with someone new when my ex still brings me dinner and has a key to my apartment?

I need to set firm boundaries with Ryle before I can even begin to entertain the idea of Atlas.

Ryle chooses a bottle of red wine from my tabletop wine rack. "Mind if I open this?"

I shrug as I spoon pad thai onto my plate. "Go ahead, but I don't want any."

Ryle puts the bottle back and opts for a glass of tea. I grab a water out of the fridge, and we both take a seat at the table.

"How was she today?" I ask him.

"A little cranky, but I had a lot of errands to run. I think she just got tired of going in and out of the car seat. She was better when we went over to Allysa's."

"When's your next day off?" I ask him.

"Not sure. I'll let you know." He reaches forward and uses his thumb to wipe something off my cheek. I flinch a little, but he doesn't notice. Or maybe he pretends not to. I'm not sure if he realizes the reaction I have anytime his hand comes near me is a negative one. Knowing Ryle, he probably thinks I flinched because I felt a spark.

After Emmy was born, there were moments here and there when I *would* feel a spark between us. He'd do or say something sweet, or he'd be holding Emmy while he sang to her, and I would feel that familiar desire for him bubbling up inside of me. But I somehow found it within me to pull myself out of the moment every time. It only takes one bad memory to immediately dull any fleeting feelings I have in his presence.

It's been a long, bumpy road, but those feelings are finally nonexistent.

I attribute that to the list I wrote of all the reasons why I chose to divorce him. Sometimes, after he leaves, I go to my bedroom and read it to reiterate that this arrangement is the best one for all of us.

Well. Maybe not this *exact* arrangement. I'd still like my key returned to me.

I'm about to take another bite of noodles when I hear a muffled ping come from my purse across the table. I drop my fork and quickly reach for my phone before Ryle does.

Not that he would read my texts, but the last thing I want right now is for him to even try to be polite by handing me my phone. He might see that the text is from Atlas, and I'm not prepared for the storm that would bring.

The text isn't from Atlas, though. It's from my mother. She's sending pics of Emmy she took earlier this week. I set the phone down and pick up my fork, but Ryle is staring at me.

"It was my mother," I say. I don't know why I even say that. I don't owe him an explanation, but I don't like the way he's staring at me.

"Who were you *hoping* it would be? You practically lunged across the table for your phone."

"No one." I take a drink. He's still staring. I have no idea how well Ryle can read me, but it looks like he knows I'm lying.

He spins his fork in his noodles and looks down at his plate with a hardened jaw. "Are you seeing someone?" There's an edge to his voice now.

"Not that it's any of your business, but no."

"Not saying it is my business. Just having a casual conversation."

I don't respond to that because it's a lie. Any recently divorced husband asking his ex-wife if she's seeing someone is making anything but casual conversation.

"I do think we need to have a more serious conversation at some point about dating," he says. "Before either of us brings other people around Emerson. Maybe lay some ground rules."

I nod. "I think we need to lay ground rules for a lot more than just that."

His eyes narrow. "Like what?"

"Your access to my apartment." I swallow. "I'd like my key back."

Ryle stares stoically before he responds. Then he wipes his mouth and says, "I can't put my daughter to bed?"

"That's not what I'm saying at all."

"You know my schedule is crazy, Lily. I hardly get to see her as it is."

"I'm not saying I want you to see her any less. I just want my key back. I value my privacy."

Ryle's expression is tight. He's upset with me. I knew he would be, but he's making this into more than it is. It has nothing to do with how much I want him to see Emmy. I just don't want him having easy access to my apartment. I moved out and divorced him for a reason.

It's not going to be a huge change, but it's one that needs to happen, or we'll be stuck in this unhealthy routine forever.

"I'll just start keeping her overnight, then." He says it with such conviction while eyeing me for a reaction. I know he can feel the discomfort I'm suddenly drowning in.

I keep my voice calm. "I don't think I'm ready for that."

Ryle drops his fork on his plate with a thud. "Maybe we need to modify the custody arrangement."

Those words infuriate me, but I somehow prevent my rage from boiling over. I stand and pick up my plate. "Really, Ryle? I ask for the key to *my* apartment back and you threaten me with court?"

We agreed to this arrangement, but he's acting like that was for *my* benefit rather than his. He knows I could have taken him to court for sole custody after everything he put me through. Hell, I never even had him arrested. He should be grateful I've been as generous as I have.

When I get to the kitchen, I set down my plate and grip the edges of the counter, allowing my head to drop between my shoulders. *Calm down, Lily. He's just reacting.*

I hear Ryle sigh regretfully, and then he follows me into the kitchen. He leans against the counter while I rinse my plate. "Can you at least give me a timeline?" His voice is lower when he speaks. "When will I get overnights with her?"

I press my hip against the counter and face him. "When she can talk."

"Why then?"

I hate that he even needs me to say this out loud. "So she can tell me if something happens, Ryle."

When the full meaning of what I've just said sinks in, he chews on his bottom lip with a small nod. I can see the frustration in the veins that rise in his neck. He pulls his keys out of his pocket and removes my apartment key. He tosses it on the counter and walks away.

When he grabs his jacket and disappears out the front door, I feel that familiar twinge of guilt creeping into my chest. The guilt is always followed by doubts like, *Am I being too hard on him?* and *What if he really has changed?*

I know the answers to these questions, but sometimes it feels good to read the reminders. I go to my room and pull the list out of my jewelry box.

1) He slapped you because you laughed.
2) He pushed you down a flight of stairs.
3) He bit you.

4) He tried to force himself on you.

5) You had to get stitches because of him.

6) Your husband physically hurt you more than once.

    It would have happened again and again.

7) You did this for your daughter.

I run my finger over the tattoo on my shoulder, feeling the small scars he left there with his teeth. If Ryle did these things to me at the highest points of our relationship, what would he be capable of at the lowest?

I fold the list and put it back in my jewelry box for the next time I might need a reminder.

Chapter Five
Atlas

"It was definitely targeted," Brad says, staring at the graffiti.

Whoever vandalized Bib's two nights ago decided to hit up my newest restaurant last night. Corrigan's has two damaged windows, and there's another message spray painted across the back door.

Fuck u Atlass.

They added an *s* and underlined *ass* in my name. I catch myself wanting to laugh at the cleverness, but my mood isn't making space for humor this morning.

Yesterday, the vandalism barely fazed me. I don't know if it was because I had just run into Lily and was still riding that high, but this morning I woke up stuck on her apparent avoidance of me. Because of that, the damage to my newest restaurant feels like it's cutting a little deeper.

"I'll check the security footage." I'm hoping it reveals something useful. I still don't know if I want to go to the police. Maybe if it's someone I know, I can at least confront them before I'm forced to resort to that.

Brad follows me into my office. I power on the computer and open the security app. I think Brad can feel my frustration, because he doesn't speak while I search the footage for several minutes.

"There," Brad says, pointing to the lower left-hand corner of the screen. I slow down the footage until we see a figure.

When I hit play, we both stare in confusion. Someone is curled up on the back steps, unmoving. We watch the screen for about half a minute, until I hit rewind again. According to the time stamp on the footage, the person remains on the steps for over two hours. Without a blanket, in a Boston October.

"They *slept* here?" Brad says. "They weren't too worried about getting caught, were they?"

I rewind the footage even more until it shows the person walking into the frame for the first time, a little after one in the morning. Because it's dark, it's hard to make out facial features, but they seem young. More like a teenager than an adult.

They snoop around for a few minutes—dig through the dumpster. Check the lock on the back door. Pull out the spray paint and leave their clever message.

Then they use the can of spray paint to attempt to break the windows, but Corrigan's windows are triple-paned, so the person eventually gets bored, or grows tired of trying to make a big enough hole to fit through like they did at Bib's. That's when they proceed to lie down on the back steps, where they fall asleep.

Just before the sun rises, they wake up, look around, and then casually walk away like the entire night never happened.

"Do you recognize him?" Brad asks.

"No. You?"

"Nope."

I pause the footage on what may be the clearest visual we can get of the person, but it's grainy. They're wearing jeans and a black hoodie with the hood pulled tight so that their hair isn't visible.

There's no way we would be able to recognize whoever this is if we saw them in person. It isn't a clear enough picture, and they never looked straight at the camera. The police wouldn't even find this footage useful.

I send the file to my email anyway. Right when I hit send, a phone pings. I glance at mine, but it's Brad who received a text.

"Darin says Bib's is fine." He pockets his phone and heads toward my office door. "I'll start cleaning up."

I wait for the file to finish sending to my email, then I start the footage over again, feeling more pity than irritation. It just reminds me of the cold nights I spent in that abandoned house before Lily offered me the shelter of her bedroom. I can practically feel the chill in my bones just thinking about it.

I have no idea who this could be. It's unnerving that they wrote my name on the door, and even more unnerving that they felt comfortable enough to hang out and take a two-hour nap. It's like they're daring me to confront them.

My phone begins to vibrate on my desk. I reach for it, but it's a number I don't recognize. I normally don't answer those, but Lily is still in the back of my mind. She could be calling me from a work phone.

God, I sound pathetic.

I raise the phone to my ear. "Hello?"

There's a sigh on the other end. A female. She sounds relieved that I answered. "Atlas?"

I sigh, too, but not from relief. I sigh because it isn't Lily's voice. I'm not sure whose it is, but anyone other than Lily is disappointing, apparently.

I lean back in my office chair. "Can I help you?"

"It's me."

I have no idea who "me" is. I think back to any exes that could be calling me, but none of them sound like this person. And none of them would assume I would know who they were if they simply said, *It's me.*

"Who's speaking?"

"*Me*," she says again, emphasizing it like it'll make a difference. "Sutton. Your *mother*."

I immediately pull the phone away from my ear and look at the number again. This has to be some kind of prank. How would my mother get my phone number? Why would she *want* it? It's been years since she made it clear she never wanted to see me again.

I say nothing. *I have nothing to say.* I stretch my spine and lean forward, waiting for her to spit out the reason she finally put forth the effort to contact me.

"I . . . um." She pauses. I can hear a television on in the background. It sounds like *The Price Is Right.* I can almost picture her sitting on the couch, a beer in one hand and a cigarette in the other at ten in the morning. She mostly worked nights when I was growing up, so she'd eat dinner and then stay up to watch *The Price Is Right* before going to sleep.

It was my least-favorite time of day.

"What do you want?" My voice is clipped.

She makes a noise in the back of her throat, and even though it's been years, I can tell she's annoyed. I can tell in that one release of breath that she didn't *want* to call me. She's doing it because she *has* to. She's not reaching out to apologize; she's reaching out because she's desperate.

"Are you dying?" I ask. It's the only thing that would prevent me from ending this call.

"Am I *dying*?" She repeats my question with laughter as if I'm absurd and unreasonable and an *ass . . . whole*. "No, I'm not *dying*. I'm perfectly fine."

"Do you need money?"

"Who doesn't?"

Every ounce of anxiety she used to fill me with returns in just these few seconds on the phone with her. I immediately end the call. I have nothing to say to her. I block her number, regretful that I gave her as long as I did to speak. I should have ended the call as soon as she told me who she was.

I lean forward over my desk and cradle my head in my hands. My stomach is churning from the unexpectedness of the last couple of minutes.

I'm surprised by my reaction, honestly. I thought this might happen one day, but I imagined myself not caring. I assumed I'd feel as indifferent toward her returning to my life as I did when she forced me to leave hers. But back then, I was indifferent to a lot of things.

Now I actually *like* my life. I'm proud of what I've accomplished. I have absolutely no desire to allow anyone from my past to come in and threaten that.

I run my hands over my face, forcing down the last few

minutes, then I push back from my desk. I walk outside to help Brad with the repairs and do my best to move beyond this moment. It's hard, though. It's like my past is crashing into me from all directions, and I have absolutely no one to discuss this with.

After a few minutes of both of us working in silence, I say to Brad, "You need to get Theo a phone; he's almost thirteen."

Brad laughs. "You need to get a therapist who's closer to your age."

Chapter Six
Lily

"Have you decided what you're doing for Emerson's birthday?" Allysa asks.

Allysa and Marshall threw a first birthday party for their daughter, Rylee, that was so big, it was worthy of a Sweet Sixteen. "I'm sure I'll just let her have a smash cake and give her a couple of presents. I don't have room for a big party."

"We could do something at our place," Allysa offers.

"Who would I invite? She'll be one; she has no friends. She can't even talk."

Allysa rolls her eyes. "We don't throw kids' parties for our *babies*. We throw them to impress our friends."

"You're my only friend, and I don't need to impress you." I hand Allysa an order from the printer. "Are we doing dinner tonight?"

We get together for dinner at least twice a week at their place. Ryle occasionally pops by, but I purposefully plan my visits on nights he's on call. I don't know if Allysa has ever noticed. If she has, she probably doesn't blame me. She says it's painful watching Ryle when I'm around because she also suspects he still has hope for us. She prefers to spend time with him when I'm not present.

"Marshall's parents are coming into town today, remember?"

"Oh yeah. Good luck with that." Allysa likes Marshall's parents, but I don't think anyone truly looks forward to hosting their in-laws for an entire week.

The front door chimes, and Allysa and I both look up at the same time. I doubt her world starts to spin like mine does, though.

Atlas is walking toward us.

"Is that . . ."

"Oh, God," I mutter under my breath.

"Yes, he *is* a god," Allysa whispers.

What is he doing here?

And why *does* he look like a god? It makes the decision I've been weighing that much more difficult. I can't even find my voice long enough to say hello to him. I just smile and wait for him to reach us, but the walk from the door to the front counter seems like it's expanded by a mile.

He doesn't take his eyes off me as he makes his way over. When he reaches us, he finally acknowledges Allysa with a smile. Then he looks back at me as he sets a plastic bowl with a lid on the counter. "I brought you lunch," he says casually, as if he brings me lunch every day and I should have been expecting it.

Ah, that voice. I forgot how far it reaches.

I grab the bowl, but I don't know what to say with Allysa hovering next to me, watching us interact. I glance at her and give her the look. She pretends not to notice, but when I don't stop staring at her, she eventually yields.

"Fine. I'll go flower the . . . *flowers*." She walks away, giving us privacy.

I turn my attention back to the lunch Atlas brought. "Thank you. What is it?"

"Our weekend special," Atlas says. "It's called *why are you avoiding me* pasta."

I laugh. Then I cringe. "I'm not avoid . . ." I shake my head with a quick sigh, knowing I can't lie to him. "I *am* avoiding you." I lean my elbows onto the counter and cover my face with my hands. "I'm sorry."

Atlas is quiet, so I eventually look up at him. He seems sincere when he says, "Do you want me to leave?"

I shake my head, and as soon as I do, his eyes crinkle a little at the corners. It's barely a smile, but it causes a warmth to tumble down my chest.

Yesterday morning when I ran into him, I said so much. Now I'm too confused to speak. I don't know how I'm supposed to have a full-on conversation with him about everything that's been going through my mind over the last twenty-four hours when I feel so tongue-tied around him.

He had the same impact on me when I was younger, but I was more naïve back then. I didn't know how rare men like Atlas were, so I didn't know how lucky I was to have him in my life.

I know now, which is why it terrifies me that I might screw this up. Or that *Ryle* might screw this up.

I lift the bowl of pasta he brought. "It smells really good."

"It *is* good. I made it."

I should laugh at that, or smile, but my reaction doesn't fit the conversation. I set the bowl aside. When I look at him again, he can see the war in my expression. He counters with a reassuring look. Not much is said between us, but the nonverbal cues we're trading are saying enough. My eyes are apologizing for my silence over the last twenty-four hours, he's silently telling me it's okay, and we're both wondering what comes next.

Atlas slides his hand slowly across the counter, closer to mine. He lifts his index finger and skims it down the length of my pinkie. It's the smallest, most tender move, but it makes my heart flip.

He pulls his hand back and clenches his fist as if he might have felt the same thing I did. He clears his throat. "Can I call you tonight?"

I'm about to nod when Allysa suddenly bursts through the door to the back, wide-eyed. She leans in and whispers, "Ryle is almost here."

My blood feels like it freezes in my veins. "*What?*" I don't say that so she'll repeat it. I say it because I'm shocked, but she repeats herself anyway.

"Ryle is pulling in. He just texted." She waves a hand toward Atlas. "You have ten seconds to hide him."

I'm sure Atlas can see the absolute fear in my expression when I look at him, but he very calmly says, "Where do you want me?"

I point to my office and rush him in that direction. Once we're in the office, I second-guess myself. "He might come in here." I cover my mouth with a shaky hand while I think, and then point to my office supply closet. "Can you hide in there?"

Atlas looks at the closet and then looks at me. He points at the door. "In the closet?"

I hear the front door chime, and I'm filled with even more urgency. "Please?" I open the closet door. It isn't the most ideal place to hide an actual human, but it's a walk-in closet. He'll fit just fine.

I can't even look him in the eye when he moves past me and into the closet. I could die right now. This is so mortifying. All I can do is murmur, "I'm so sorry," as I close the door.

I do my best to compose myself. Allysa is chatting with Ryle when I exit my office. He greets me with a nod, but his attention is back on Allysa. She's digging through her purse for something.

"They were in here earlier," she says.

Ryle is tapping his fingers impatiently.

"What are you looking for?" I ask her.

"Keys. I accidentally brought them with me, and Marshall needs the SUV to get his parents from the airport."

Ryle looks irritated. "Are you sure you didn't set them aside when I told you I was coming to get them?"

I tilt my head, focusing on Allysa. "You knew he was coming?" How could she forget to tell me he was on his way here when Atlas showed up?

She reddens a little. "I got sidetracked by . . . unexpected events." She holds up her hand in victory. "Found them!" She drops them in Ryle's palm. "Okay, bye, you can leave now."

Ryle makes a move like he's about to go, but then he turns and sniffs the air. "What smells so good?"

His and Allysa's eyes meet the bowl at the same time. Allysa pulls it to her, cradling it. "I cooked lunch for me and Lily," she lies.

Ryle raises an eyebrow. "*You* cooked?" He reaches for the bowl. "I have to see this. What is it?"

Allysa hesitates before handing him the bowl. "Yeah, it's chicken . . . baraba doula . . . meat." She looks at me and her eyes are wide. *She is such a horrible liar.*

"Chicken *what?*" Ryle opens the bowl and inspects it. "It looks like shrimp pasta."

Allysa clears her throat. "Yeah, I cooked the shrimp in . . . chicken stock. That's why it's called chicken baraba-doulameat."

Ryle puts the lid back on and looks at me with concern as he slides the bowl across the counter back to Allysa. "I'd order pizza if I were you."

I force a laugh, but so does Allysa. Both of us laughing makes our reaction seem way too compulsory for a joke that wasn't even funny.

Ryle's expression narrows. He takes a couple of steps back, a suspicious look in his eye. He must be used to the two of us having inside jokes that he isn't a part of, because he doesn't even question us. He spins and walks out of the flower shop in a rush to get the keys to Marshall. Allysa and I both stand as still as statues until we're sure he's left the building and is way out of earshot. Then I look at her incredulously.

"Chicken barba*what?* Did you just completely make up a new language?"

"I had to say *something*," she says defensively. "You stood there like a lump! You're welcome."

I wait a couple of minutes to make sure Ryle has had time to leave. I walk out front to ensure Ryle's car is gone.

Then I regretfully walk into my office and head to the supply closet to inform Atlas he's in the clear. I exhale before opening the door.

Atlas is waiting patiently, his arms crossed as he leans against a shelf, as if being hidden in a closet doesn't bother him in the least.

"I'm so sorry." I don't know how many apologies it will take to make up for what I just asked Atlas to do, but I'm prepared to say it a thousand more times.

"Is he gone?"

I nod, but rather than exit the closet, Atlas grabs my hand, pulls me in and closes the door.

Now we're both in the closet.

The *dark* closet. But not so dark that I can't see the flicker in his eyes that indicates he's holding back a smile. *Maybe he doesn't absolutely hate me for this.*

He releases my hand, but it's so cramped in here for the two of us, parts of him are grazing parts of me. My stomach knots, so I press my back into the shelf behind me in an attempt not to press into him, but it feels like he's draped over me like a warm blanket. He's so close, I can smell his shampoo. I very calmly try to breathe through my nerves.

"Well? Can I?" he asks, his voice a whisper.

I have no idea what he's asking me, but I want to answer with a confident *yes*. Rather than blurt out my consent to a question I don't even know, I silently count to three. Then I say, "Can you what?"

"Call you tonight."

Oh. He jumped right back into the conversation we were having out front, as if Ryle never even interrupted us.

I pull in my bottom lip and bite down on it. I want to say *okay* because I want Atlas to call me, but I also want Atlas to know that me hiding him from Ryle inside of this closet is probably on par with how the rest of our interactions will go since Ryle is always going to be in the picture, considering we share a child.

"Atlas . . ." I say his name like something awful is about to follow it up, but he interrupts me.

"Lily." He says my name with a smile, like nothing I could possibly add to his name would be awful.

"My life is complicated." I don't intend for it to come out like a warning, but it does.

"I want to help you uncomplicate it."

"I'm scared your presence is going to complicate it even more."

He raises an eyebrow. "I'll complicate *your* life or *Ryle's* life?"

"His complications become *my* complications. He's the father of my child."

Atlas dips his head ever so slightly. "Exactly. He's her father. He's not your husband, so you shouldn't allow your concern for his feelings to persuade you to give up what could be the second-best thing to ever happen to you."

He says that with such conviction, my heart feels like it's tumbling down my rib cage like a Plinko chip. *The second-best thing to ever happen to me?* I wish his confidence in us were contagious. "What's the *first*-best thing to ever happen to me?"

He looks at me pointedly. "Emerson."

Hearing him call my daughter the best thing to ever happen to me makes me damn near melt. I hug myself and hold back my smile. "You're going to make this difficult for me, huh?"

Atlas slowly shakes his head. "Difficult is the last thing I want to be for you, Lily." He moves and the door begins to open, spilling light into the closet. He faces me with one hand on the door and the other on the wall. "When's a good time to call you tonight?" He seems so at ease with this conversation, it makes me want to pull him back into the closet and kiss him so that maybe some of his assurance and patience will seep into me.

My mouth feels like cotton when I say, "Whenever."

His eyes settle on my lips for a beat, and I feel the look all the way to my toes. But then Atlas closes the door, shutting me alone inside the closet.

I deserved that.

A mixture of embarrassment, nervousness, and maybe even a little bit of desire is flooding my cheeks. I remain unmoving until I hear the faint chime of the front door being opened.

I'm fanning myself when Allysa opens the closet door moments later. I quickly drop my hands to my hips to hide what Atlas's presence does to me.

Allysa folds her arms across her chest. "You hid him in the closet?"

My shoulders fall with my shame. "I know."

"*Lily.*" She sounds disappointed in me, but what would she rather I have done? Reintroduced them to one another? "I mean, I'm glad you did it, because I'm not sure how that would have turned out, but . . . you hid him in the *closet*. You just shoved him in here like an old coat."

Her rehashing the moment isn't helping me recover from it. I move toward the front of the store with Allysa on my heels. "I had no choice. Atlas is the one guy on this earth Ryle would never approve of me dating."

"I hate to break it to you, but there's only one guy on this earth Ryle would approve of you dating, and that's Ryle."

I don't respond to that because I'm terrified that she's right.

"Wait," Allysa says. "Are you and Atlas *dating*?"

"No."

"But you just said he's the one guy Ryle would never approve of you dating."

"I said that because if Ryle had seen him here, that's what he would have assumed."

Allysa folds her arms over the counter and looks crestfallen. "I'm feeling very left out right now. There's a huge gap you need to fill in."

"Gap? What do you mean?" I try to look busy by pulling a vase toward me and moving some of the flowers around. Allysa takes the vase from me.

"He brought you lunch. Why did he bring you lunch if the two of you aren't actively talking? And if you're actively talking, why didn't you tell *me* about it?"

I pull the vase back from her. "We ran into each other yesterday. It was nothing. I haven't even spoken to him since before Emmy was born."

Allysa grabs the vase again. "I run into old friends every day. They don't bring me lunch." She slides the vase back to me. We're using it like a conch shell, as if we need it for permission to speak.

"Your friends probably aren't chefs. That's what chefs do: They cook people lunch." I slide the vase back to her, but she says nothing. She's concentrating so hard, it's like she's attempting to read my mind to get past all the lies she thinks I'm spewing. I pull the vase back from her. "It's honestly nothing. *Yet*. You'll be the first to know if anything changes."

She looks momentarily satisfied by that response, but there's a flicker of something in her face before she looks away. I can't tell if it's concern or sadness. I don't ask her, because I know this is hard for her. I imagine the idea of *any* man bringing me lunch who isn't Ryle probably makes her a little sad.

In Allysa's idea of a perfect world, she would have a brother who never hurt me, and I would still be her sister-in-law.

Chapter Seven
Atlas

"When you're working with flounder, always hold your knife like this." I demonstrate how to start with the dull end at the tail, but Theo looks away as soon as I begin to scale the fish.

"Gross," he mutters, covering his mouth. "I can't." Theo moves to the other side of the counter, putting space between himself and the cooking lesson.

"I'm only scaling it. I haven't even cut it open yet."

Theo makes a gagging sound. "I have no interest in working with food. I'll stick to being your therapist." Theo pushes himself onto the counter. "Speaking of, did you ever text Lily?"

"I did."

"She text you back?"

"Sort of. It was a short text, so I decided to take her lunch today to see where her head is at."

"That was a bold move."

"I've spent my life not making bold moves when it comes to her. I wanted to make sure she knew where I stood this time."

"Oh no," Theo says. "What cheesy thing did you say to her about fish and beaches and shores?"

I never should have told him what I said to Lily about

finally reaching the shore. I'm not going to hear the end of it. "Shut up. You've probably never even spoken to a girl; you're twelve."

Theo laughs, but then I notice an awkwardness settle over him when he thinks I'm not looking. He grows quiet, despite the ruckus going on around us. There are at least five other people in the kitchen right now, but everyone is so focused on their work, no one is paying attention to the conversation I'm having with Theo.

"You like someone?" I ask him.

He shrugs. "Kinda."

The discussions I have with Theo are usually one-sided. As much as he likes to ask questions, he doesn't answer very many, so I tread carefully. "Oh yeah?" I try to act casual with my response so he'll expand. "Who is she?"

Theo is looking down at his hands. He's picking at his thumbnail, but I can see his shoulders sink a little after my question, like I did something wrong.

Or *said* something wrong.

"Or *he*," I clarify. I whisper it to be sure he's the only one who hears it.

Theo's eyes dart up to mine.

He doesn't have to confirm or deny anything. I can see the truth written in the fear that's resting behind his eyes. I give my attention back to the fish I'm preparing, and as nonchalantly as possible, I say, "Do you go to school with him?"

Theo doesn't immediately answer. I'm not sure if I'm the first person he's admitted this part of himself to, so I want to make sure to treat that with the care it deserves. I want him to know he has an ally in me, but I also hope he's aware he has an ally in his father, too.

Theo looks around to make sure no one is hovering long enough to follow along with our conversation. "He's been in math club with me all year." His words are quick and concise, like he wants to release them and never say them again.

"Does your dad know?"

Theo shakes his head. I watch as he swallows what look like nervous thoughts.

I put down my knife when I'm done scaling the fish and move to the sink closest to Theo to wash my hands. "I've known your dad for a long time. He's one of my best friends for a reason. I don't surround myself with people who aren't good." I can see the reassurance settle in him when I say that, but I can also tell he's uncomfortable and probably wants to change the subject. "I would say you should text this person you like, but you're probably the only twelve-year-old left on earth without a cell phone. You'll never date anyone at this rate. You'll probably be single and phoneless forever."

Theo is relieved I'm ribbing him. "I'm so glad you decided to be a chef and not a therapist. You suck at advice."

"I take offense to that. I give good advice."

"Okay, Atlas. Whatever you say." He seems to loosen up. He follows me as I head back to my station. "Did you ask Lily out on a date when you went to her work?"

"No. I will tonight. I'm calling her when I get home." I walk by Theo and ruffle his hair on my way to the freezer.

"Hey, Atlas?"

I pause. His eyes are filled with concern, but one of the waiters pushes through the doors and walks between us, preventing Theo from saying whatever it was he was about to say. He doesn't have to say it, though.

"Not saying a word, Theo. Client confidentiality goes both ways."

That seems to reassure him. "Good, because if you said something to my dad, I would tell him how cheesy you are with your pickup lines." Theo mockingly presses his palms to his cheeks. "We finally reached the beach, my little whale."

I glare at him. "That's not at all how it went."

Theo points across the kitchen. "Look! It's sand—we've reached land!"

"Stop."

"Lily, what the heck, our boat is wrecked!"

He's still following me around the kitchen making fun of me when his dad's shift ends. I've never been happier to see him leave.

Chapter Eight
Lily

It's almost 9:30 at night, and I have no missed calls. Emerson has been asleep for an hour and a half, and she's usually awake by six in the morning. I go to bed around ten because if I don't get at least eight hours of sleep, I function at the capacity of a zombie. But if Atlas doesn't call before ten, I'm not sure I'll be able to sleep at all. I'll wonder if I should have apologized seventy more times for hiding him in a closet today.

I walk to the bathroom sink to start my nightly skin-care routine, and I take my phone with me. I've carried it with me every step since he showed up at lunchtime today and told me he'd call me tonight. I should have clarified what *tonight* meant.

To Atlas, *tonight* could mean eleven.

To me, it could mean eight.

We probably have two completely different definitions for what morning and night even mean. He's a successful chef who gets home to unwind after midnight, and I'm in my pajamas by seven in the evening.

My phone makes a noise, but it isn't a ringtone. It's making a noise like someone is trying to FaceTime me.

Please don't be Atlas.

I am not prepared for a video chat; I just put face scrub on. I look at the phone and sure enough, it's him.

I answer it and quickly flip the phone around so that he can't see me. I leave it on my sink while I speed up the cleansing process. "You asked if you could *call* me. This is a video chat."

I hear him laugh. "I can't see you."

"Yeah, because I'm washing my face and getting ready for bed. You don't need to see me."

"Yes, I do, Lily."

His voice makes my skin feel tingly. I flip the camera around and hold it up with an *I told you so* expression. My wet hair is still wrapped in a towel, I'm wearing a nightgown my grandmother probably used to own, and my face is still covered in green foam.

His smile is fluid and sexy. He's sitting up in bed, wearing a white T-shirt, leaning against a black wooden headboard. The one time I went to his house, I never went into his bedroom. His wall is blue, like denim.

"This was definitely worth the decision to video-chat," he says.

I set the phone back down, facing me this time, and finish rinsing. "Thanks for lunch today." I don't want to give him too much praise, but it was the best pasta I've ever had. And it was two hours old before I even had a chance to take a lunch break and eat it.

"You liked the *why are you avoiding me* pasta?"

"You know it was great." I walk to my bed once I'm finished in the bathroom. I prop my phone on a pillow and lie on my side. "How was your day?"

"It was good," he says, but he's not very convincing with the way his voice drops on the word *good.*

I make a face to let him know I don't believe him.

He looks away from the screen for a second, like he's processing a thought. "It's just one of those weeks, Lily. It's better now, though." His mouth curls into a slight grin, and it makes me smile, too.

I don't even have to make small talk. I'd be happy just staring at him in complete silence for an hour.

"What's your new restaurant called?" I already know it's his last name, but I don't want him to know I googled him.

"Corrigan's."

"Is it the same kind of food as Bib's?"

"Sort of. It's fine dining, but with an Italian-inspired menu." He rolls onto his side, propping his phone on something so that he's mirroring my position. It feels like old times when we'd stay up late chatting on my bed. "I don't want to talk about me. How are you? How's the floral business? What's your daughter like?"

"That's a lot of questions."

"I have a lot more, but let's start with those."

"Okay. Well. I'm good. Exhausted most of the time, but I guess that's what I get for being a business owner and a single mother."

"You don't look exhausted."

I laugh. "Good lighting."

"When does Emerson turn one?"

"On the eleventh. I'm going to cry; this first year went so fast."

"I can't get over how much she looks like you."

"You think so?"

He nods, and then says, "But the flower shop is good? You're happy there?"

I move my head from side to side and make a face. "It's okay."

"Why just okay?"

"I don't know. I think I'm tired of it. Or tired in general. It's a lot, and it's tedious work for not very much financial return. I mean, I'm proud that it's been successful and that I did it, but sometimes I daydream about working in a factory assembly line."

"I can relate," he says. "The idea of being able to go home and not think about your job is tempting."

"Do you ever get bored of being a chef?"

"Every now and then. It's why I opened Corrigan's, honestly. I decided to take more of an ownership role and less of a chef role. I still cook several nights a week, but a lot of my time goes to keeping them both running on the business side."

"Do you work crazy hours?"

"I do. But nothing I can't work a date night around."

That makes me smile. I fidget with my comforter, avoiding eye contact because I know I'm blushing. "Are you asking me out?"

"I am. Are you saying yes?"

"I can free up a night."

We're both smiling now. But then Atlas clears his throat, like he's preparing for a caveat. "Can I ask you a difficult question?"

"Okay." I try to hide my nerves over what he's about to ask.

"Earlier today you mentioned your life was complicated. If this . . . *us* . . . becomes something, is it really going to be an issue for Ryle?"

I don't even hesitate. "Yes."

"Why?"

"He doesn't like you."

"Me specifically or any guy you might potentially date?"

I scrunch up my nose. "You. Specifically you."

"Because of the fight at my restaurant?"

"Because of a lot of things," I admit. I roll onto my back and move my phone with me. "He blames most of our fights on you." Atlas is clearly confused, so I elaborate without making things too uncomfortable. "Remember when we were teenagers and I used to write in my journal?"

"I do. Even though you never let me read anything."

"Well, Ryle found the journals. And he read them. And he didn't like what he read."

Atlas sighs. "Lily, we were kids."

"Jealousy doesn't have an expiration date, apparently."

Atlas presses his lips into a thin line for a moment, like he's attempting to push down his frustration. "I really hate that you're stressing over his potential reaction to things that haven't even happened yet. But I get it. It's the unfortunate position you're in." He looks at me reassuringly. "We'll take it one step at a time, okay?"

"One very *slow* step at a time," I suggest.

"Deal. Slow steps." Atlas adjusts the pillow beneath his head. "I used to see you writing in those journals. I always wondered what you wrote about me. *If* you wrote about me."

"Almost everything was about you."

"Do you still have them?"

"Yeah, they're in a box in my closet."

Atlas sits up. "Read me something."

"No. *God*, no."

"Lily."

He looks so hopeful and excited at the possibility, but I can't read my teenage thoughts out loud to him over Face-Time. I'm growing red just thinking about it.

"Please?"

I cover my face with a hand. "No, don't beg." I'll give in to those blue puppy-dog eyes if he doesn't stop looking at me like he is.

He can see he's wearing me down. "Lily, I have ached since I was a teenager to know what you thought of me. One paragraph. Just give me that much."

How can I say no to that? I groan and toss the phone on the bed in defeat. "Give me two minutes." I walk to my closet and pull down the box. I carry it over to my bed and begin flipping through the journals to find something that won't embarrass me too much. "What do you want me to read? My retelling of our first kiss?"

"No, we're going slow, remember?" He says that teasingly. "Start with something from the beginning."

That's much easier. I grab the first journal and flip through it until I find something that looks short and not too humiliating. "Do you remember the night I came to you crying because my parents were fighting?"

"I remember," he says. He settles into his pillow and puts one arm behind his head.

I roll my eyes. "Get comfy while I mortify myself," I mutter.

"It's me, Lily. It's *us*. There's nothing to be embarrassed about."

His voice still has that same calming effect it's always had. I sit cross-legged and hold the phone with one hand and my journal in the other, and I begin to read.

A few seconds later the back door opened and he looked behind me, then to the left and right of me. It wasn't until he looked at my face that he saw I was crying.

"You okay?" he asked, stepping outside. I used my shirt to wipe away my tears, and noticed he came outside instead of inviting me in. I sat down on the porch step and he sat down next to me.

"I'm fine," I said. "I'm just mad. Sometimes I cry when I get mad."

He reached over and tucked my hair behind my ear. I liked it when he did that and I suddenly wasn't nearly as mad anymore. Then he put his arm around me and pulled me to him so that my head was resting on his shoulder. I don't know how he calmed me down without even talking, but he did. Some people just have a calming presence about them and he's one of those people. Completely opposite of my father.

We sat like that for a while, until I saw my bedroom light turn on.

"You should go," he whispered. We could both see my mom standing in my bedroom looking for me. It wasn't until that moment that I realized what a perfect view he has of my bedroom.

As I walked back home, I tried to think about the entire

time Atlas has been in that house. I tried to recall if I'd walked around after dark with the light on at night, because all I normally wear in my room at night is a T-shirt.

Here's what's crazy about that, Ellen: I was kind of hoping I had.

—Lily

Atlas isn't smiling when I finish reading. He's staring at me with a lot of feeling, and the heaviness in his eyes is making my chest tight.

"We were so young," he says. His voice carries a little bit of ache in it.

"I know. Too young to deal with the stuff we dealt with. Especially you."

Atlas isn't looking at his phone anymore, but he's moving his head in agreement. The mood has shifted, and I can tell he's thinking about something else entirely. It brings me back to what he tried to brush off earlier when he said it's been *one of those weeks.*

"What's bothering you?"

His eyes return to his phone. He seems like he might brush it off again, but then he just sighs and readjusts himself so that he's sitting higher up against his headboard. "Someone vandalized the restaurants."

"Both of them?"

He nods. "Yeah, it started a few days ago."

"You think it's someone you know?"

"It's not anyone I recognize, but the security footage wasn't very clear. I haven't reported it to the police yet."

"Why haven't you?"

His eyebrows furrow. "Whoever it is seems younger—maybe in their teens. I guess I'm worried they might be in a similar situation to the one I was in back then. Destitute." The tension in his eyes eases a bit. "And what if they don't have a Lily to save them?"

It takes a few seconds for what he says to register. When it does, I don't smile. I swallow the lump in my throat, hoping he can't see my internal reaction to that. It's not the first time he's mentioned I saved him back then, but every time he says it, I want to argue with him. I didn't save him. All I did was fall in love with him.

I can see *why* I fell in love with him. What owner is more concerned about the situation of the person vandalizing their business than they are with the actual damage being done? "Considerate Atlas," I whisper.

"What was that?" he says.

I didn't mean to say that out loud. I slide a hand over the heat moving across my neck. "Nothing."

Atlas clears his throat, leaning forward. A subtle smile materializes. "Back to your journal," he says. "I wondered if you knew I could see into your bedroom window back then, because after that night, you left that light on a hell of a lot."

I laugh, glad he's lightening the mood. "You didn't have a television. I wanted to give you something to watch."

He groans. "Lily, you *have* to let me read the rest."

"No."

"You locked me in a closet today. Letting me read your journals would be a good way to apologize for that."

"I thought you weren't offended."

"Maybe it's a delayed offense." He begins to nod slowly. "Yeah . . . starting to feel it now. I'm *really* offended."

I'm laughing when Emmy begins to work up a cry across the hall. I sigh because I don't want to hang up, but I'm also not the mom who can let her child cry it out. "Emmy's waking up. I have to go. But you owe me a date."

"Name the time," he says.

"I'm off on Sundays, so a Saturday night might be good."

"Tomorrow is Saturday," he says. "But we're going slow."

"I mean . . . that's pretty slow if we're counting from the first day we met. That puts a lot of years between meeting you and going on a first date with you."

"Six o'clock?"

I smile. "Six is perfect."

As soon as I say that, Atlas squeezes his eyes shut for two seconds. "Wait. I can't tomorrow. *Shit.* We're hosting an event; they need me at the restaurant. Sunday?"

"I have Emmy Sunday. I'd rather wait before bringing her around you."

"I get that," Atlas says. "Next Saturday?"

"That'll give me time to line up someone to watch her."

Atlas grins. "It's a date, then." He stands up and begins walking through his bedroom. "You're off on Sundays, right? Can I call you this Sunday?"

"When you say 'call,' do you mean video chat? I want to be prepared this time."

"You couldn't be unprepared if you tried," he says. "And yes, it'll be a FaceTime. Why would I waste time with a phone call when I can look at you?"

I like this flirty side of Atlas. I have to bite my bottom lip for two seconds in order to hold back my grin. "Goodnight, Atlas."

"'Night, Lily."

Even the way he makes such intense eye contact while saying goodbye makes my stomach flip. I end the call and press my face into my pillow. I squeal like I'm sixteen again.

Chapter Nine
Atlas

"Let me see a picture," Theo says. He's sitting on the back steps watching me pick up shattered glass and several bags of trash from the third incident, which occurred last night. Brad called this morning to let me know Bib's was hit again. He and Theo met me here to clean it up, even though I told him not to worry about coming. I hate when my employees have to show up for anything on the only day of the week we're closed.

"I don't have a picture of her," I say to Theo.

"So she's ugly?"

I toss the box of glass into the dumpster. "She's gorgeous and way out of my league."

"Ugly would still be out of your league," he deadpans. "She doesn't have social media?"

"She does, but it's set to private."

"You aren't her friend on anything? Facebook? Instagram? Do you even have a Snapchat?"

"What do you know about Snapchat? You don't even have a phone."

"I have my ways," he says.

His dad comes back outside with a trash bag. He holds it open, and we start throwing some of the scattered garbage in it while Theo remains on the steps. "I would help, but I just took a shower," he says.

"You showered yesterday," Brad says.

"Yeah, and I'm still clean." Theo focuses on me again. "Do you have social media?"

"No, I don't have time for that."

"Then how do you know her stuff is set to private?"

I've occasionally attempted to look her up online, and as much as I don't want to admit that, I'm not sure there's a person on this planet who hasn't done a few Google searches on people from their past. "I've looked her up before. You have to have a profile and follow her to see her stuff."

"So make a profile and follow her," Theo says. "I swear, sometimes you make things harder than they need to be."

"It's complicated. She has an ex-husband who doesn't like me, and if he saw that we were friends online it might become an issue for her."

"Why doesn't he like you?" Theo asks.

"We got into a fight. Here at the restaurant, actually," I say, nudging my head toward the building.

Theo's eyebrows lift slightly. "Seriously? Like a real fight?"

Brad straightens up. "Wait. That guy was Lily's *husband*?"

"I thought you knew that," I say.

"None of us knew who he was, or why you were fighting him. That was the only time we've ever seen you kick someone out of the restaurant, though. Makes so much sense now."

I guess this is the first time I've talked about it since it happened. I remember I left for the night right after that fight with Ryle, so no one had a chance to ask me about it. When I came back to work the following Monday, people could probably read my mood and see that I still didn't want to talk about it.

"What did you get into a fight about?" Theo asks.

I glance at Brad, because he's aware of what Lily went through. Lily told him and Darin at my house. But Brad looks like he's leaving it up to me whether or not I'm honest with Theo. I usually am about almost anything, but it's not my place to share Lily's business.

"I don't even remember," I mutter.

I do think this could be a good teaching moment with Theo about how never to treat a partner, but it's a part of Lily's life I don't feel comfortable talking about without her present. It's also a part of her life I shouldn't have interfered with, even though I wouldn't take it back if given the chance. As immature as my reaction might have been that night when I hit Ryle, I was holding back. I wanted to do more than just punch him. I had never been that angry at another human—not even my mother or stepfather. Not even Lily's father.

It's one thing to dislike someone for how they treat me, but it's an entirely different kind of anger when the person I admire the most in this world is mistreated.

My phone begins to buzz in my pocket. I quickly pull it out and see that Lily is attempting to return my FaceTime from an hour ago. She was driving and said she would call me when she got home.

We've exchanged several texts since our chat on Friday, but I've been anxious to talk to her face-to-face again.

"Is that her?" Theo asks, perking up.

I nod and try to pass him on the steps, but he stands up and follows me into the restaurant.

"Seriously?" I ask, facing him.

"I want to see what she looks like."

I have to answer it before I miss the call, so I slide my finger across the screen while trying to shut Theo outside. "I'll screenshot it for you. Go help your dad." The video connects, and Theo is still trying to push his way inside. "Hey," I say, smiling at Lily on the screen.

"Hey," Lily says.

"Let me see," Theo whispers, snaking his arm around the door in an attempt to snatch my phone.

"Give me a second, Lily." I hold the phone to my chest so that she can't see anything, and then I open the back door far enough to press my palm against Theo's face. I guide him back down the top step. "Brad, get your child."

"Theo, come here," Brad says. "Help me with this."

Theo's shoulders slump, but he finally relents and turns toward his father. "But I'm *clean*," he mumbles.

I close the door and pull the phone away from my chest. Lily is laughing. "What was that?"

"Nothing." I walk to my office and close and lock the door for privacy. "How's your day?" I take a seat on the couch.

"Good. We just got back from lunch with my mother and her boyfriend. Went to a little sandwich shop on Borden; it was cute."

"How is your mother?" We haven't talked about her parents at all, other than her mentioning her father passed away.

"She's really good," Lily says. "She's been dating a guy

named Rob. He makes her happy, although it's a little weird seeing her giddy over a man. I like him, though."

"She lives in Boston now?"

"Yeah, she moved here after my father died to be closer to me."

"That's good. I'm glad you have family here."

"What about you? Does your uncle still live in Boston?"

My uncle?

Oh. I did tell her that. I squeeze the back of my neck and wince. "My uncle." I can't remember the exact lie I told her back then—it's been so long. "My uncle died when I was nine, Lily."

Her eyebrows wrinkle in confusion. "No, you moved in with an uncle when you were eighteen. It's why you left."

I sigh, wishing I could go back and redo most of our time together back then, and the things I told her or failed to tell her in order to spare her feelings. But wouldn't we all go back if we could redo our teenage years? "I lied to you. I didn't have an uncle in Boston at that point."

"What?" She's still shaking her head, trying to make it make sense. She doesn't seem angry, though. More confused than anything. "Then who did you go live with?"

"No one. I couldn't keep sneaking into your bedroom forever. I knew it wouldn't end well, and other than you, there was nothing in that town that could help me better my situation. Boston had shelters and resources. I told you my uncle was still alive so you wouldn't worry about me."

Lily's head falls back against her headboard and she closes her eyes for a bit. "Atlas." She says my name with sympathy. When she opens her eyes again, it looks like she's attempting not to tear up. "I don't know what to say. I thought you had family."

"I'm sorry I lied. I wasn't trying to be malicious, I just wanted to spare—"

"Don't apologize," she says, interrupting me. "You did the right thing. Winter was about to hit, and you might not have survived it in that house." She wipes at a tear. "I can't imagine how hard that was. Moving to Boston at that age with nothing. No one."

"It worked out," I say, flashing a grin. "It all worked out." I'm attempting to pull her out of the mood I just sunk her in. "Don't think about where we used to be; just think about where we are."

She smiles. "Where are you right now? Is that your office?"

"It is." I spin the phone around so she can get a glimpse of it. "It's small. Just a couch and a computer, but I'm rarely in here. I spend most of my time in the kitchen."

"Are you at Bib's?"

"Yeah. Both restaurants are closed on Sundays—I'm just here cleaning up."

"I can't wait to visit Corrigan's. Is that where we're going on our date next Saturday?"

I laugh. "No way am I bringing you to either of my restaurants on a date. The people I work with are too curious about my personal life."

She grins. "Funny, because I'm curious about your personal life, too."

"I'm an open book for you. What do you want to know?"

She contemplates that for several seconds, and then

comes back with, "I want to know who the people in your life are. You didn't really have anyone when we were teenagers, but you're an adult now, with businesses and friends and a whole life I know very little about. Who are your people, Atlas Corrigan?"

I don't know how to respond to that with anything but laughter.

She doesn't smile in return, though, which makes me think she's asking the question more out of concern for me than curiosity. I look at her gently, hoping to ease some of that worry. "I have friends," I say. "Some of them you met a while back at my house. I don't have family, but it's not a void I feel. I like my career, and my life." I pause, and then say something completely honest. "I'm happy, if that's what you're wondering."

I see the corner of her mouth lift. "Good. I was always curious about where you ended up. I tried to find you on social media, but I didn't have any luck."

That makes me laugh, considering Theo and I just had this conversation. "I don't use social media much." If I told her I'd use it every day if her pages weren't private, Theo might say that confession would scare her off. "I have profiles for the restaurants, but two of my employees manage them." I let my head fall back against the couch. "I'm too busy for it. I downloaded TikTok a few months ago, but that was a mistake. Sucked me in for hours one night, and I missed a meeting the next morning. I deleted the app later that day."

Lily laughs. "I would do just about anything to watch you make TikTok videos."

"Never gonna happen."

Lily's attention is stolen away for a moment, and then she starts to lift up on her bed, but pauses. "Hold on a second. I need to set my phone down." She drops the phone, but I don't think she realizes it catches on something and flips so that it's at an angle. The camera is on her, and I see her adjust Emerson from one breast to another. It's only a few seconds, almost too quick for me to realize what's happening before it's over. I don't think she meant for the camera to be pointed at her.

When she notices the phone, her eyes go wide for a second, and then the screen goes black as soon as her hand meets it. When it's pointed at her face again, she's covering her eyes with splayed fingers. "I am so sorry."

"For what?"

"I think I just flashed you."

"You did, but it's not something you should apologize for. I should thank you."

She laughs, appearing to appreciate that comment. "Nothing you haven't seen before," she says with an adorably embarrassed shrug. She adjusts a pillow under the arm she's using to hold Emerson while she breastfeeds. "I'm trying to wean her, since she's about to turn one. We were down to once a day, but Sundays are hard because I'm with her all day." She scrunches up her nose. "I'm sorry. I doubt you want to know breastfeeding details."

"I can't think of a single subject you could discuss that would bore me."

"Oh, I bet I can think of one before our date," she says, treating my comment like it's a challenge. She glances away from her phone screen. I can't see Emerson, but I can tell

Lily's looking down at her because she gets this smile on her face that I only see when she's talking about or looking at her daughter. It's a smile born from pride, and one of my favorite expressions to see flash across Lily's face.

"She's falling asleep," Lily whispers. "I should go."

"Yeah, I should probably go, too." I don't want to leave Brad and Theo to clean up the majority of the damage outside without me.

"I might call you later tonight, if that's okay," Lily says.

"Of course it is." I remember what Theo said about wanting to see a picture of Lily, so before she ends the call, I take a quick screenshot. It makes an obvious screenshot noise, and Lily tilts her head curiously.

"Did you just take a—"

"I wanted a picture of you," I say quickly. "Bye, Lily." I end the call before I let myself be too embarrassed by that. I had no idea it would make that noise and that she would be able to hear it. Theo better appreciate this.

I open my office door and find Brad sweeping the kitchen. I'm confused, because the kitchen is cleaned after closing, and the damage done to the restaurant overnight was contained to the outside. "Did they not clean the floors last night?"

"Kitchen's fine—I'm just pretending to sweep," he says. Brad clocks the confusion on my face, so he elaborates. "I wanted Theo to have to clean up most of the mess outside since he hates doing it so much. It's a dad thing."

"Oh. Makes sense." It makes *no* sense, but I leave Brad to fake-sweep and head back outside.

Theo is grimacing as he uses his thumb and index finger

to barely lift a piece of trash. "This is so gross," he mutters, dropping it into the bag. "You need to hire a private security guard or something; this is getting out of hand."

That's not a bad idea.

I hold my phone in front of Theo's face so he can see the picture of Lily I just screenshotted.

He pulls his neck back, surprised. "That's Lily?"

"That's Lily." I slide my phone into my pocket and take the trash bag from Theo.

"That explains it." He drops down onto the top step.

"Explains what?"

"Why you get so tongue-tied around her and say the stupid stuff you say."

I disagree with his belief that the things I say to her are stupid, but he's right about one thing. She's so beautiful, I do sometimes feel tongue-tied around her. "I can't wait until you start dating," I say. "I'm going to give you so much shit."

Chapter Ten
Lily

"Mom, it's fine. Really." I'm holding the phone between my cheek and my neck. "I'm already at Allysa's; it's not an inconvenience at all."

"Are you sure? Rob said he could watch her."

"No, Rob needs to take care of you."

"Okay. Tell Emmy her nannie is sorry."

"Nannie? Is that what you're going by now?"

"I'm trying it out," she says. "I didn't like *grandma*."

She's referred to herself as a grandmother in four different ways since Emmy was born, but none of them have stuck yet. "Love you, Mom. Hope you feel better."

"Love you, too."

I end the call and then grab Emmy out of her car seat. I'm relieved to see Ryle's car isn't in his assigned spot. I wasn't planning on coming to the building where he and Allysa both have apartments, but my mother and Emmy came down with the same illness this week.

When I picked her up from my mother's yesterday, Emmy had a slight fever. It peaked around two in the morning, and nothing I did helped. It was gone by the time I had to get ready for work today, though. But then it hit my mother this afternoon with a vengeance, and I had to go pick up Emmy in the middle of the workday. I had a little bit of a panic moment because tonight is my date with Atlas. I thought I was going to have to cancel, but Allysa saved the day.

I didn't tell her why I needed a sitter. I texted her and asked if she could watch Emmy for a few hours this afternoon and into tonight, and she responded with one word. **Gimme.**

I warned her that Emmy had a fever last night, but Emmy and Rylee spend so much time together, we stopped worrying about one getting the other sick months ago, since it happens every other week. Emmy probably got the fever from Rylee to begin with.

I knock on Allysa's door, and when she opens it, she's immediately grabbing for Emerson. "Come here," she says. She pulls Emerson to her and squeezes her. "She smells so good. Rylee doesn't smell like a baby anymore. Makes me sad." She pushes the door open to invite me in, and when I walk inside holding the diaper bag, Allysa finally registers my outfit. "Hold up," she says. She points a finger up and down my body. "What's this? Why am I babysitting?"

I really don't want to tell her where I'm going, but it's Allysa. She reads me better than anyone. She can see the hesitation on my face and takes it for exactly what it is. "Is this a *date* outfit?" She whispers it and then closes the front door. "Is it the Greek god?"

"Atlas. Yes. Please don't tell your brother."

Right when I say that, I notice Marshall standing close by in the living room. He immediately covers his ears and says, "I heard nothing. I see nothing. Lalalalalala." He walks through the foyer and disappears into the kitchen.

Allysa brushes his presence off with a wave. "He's so good at being neutral; don't worry about him." She motions for me to follow her into the living room. Rylee is in a playpen, so Allysa walks Emmy over to her. "Rylee, look who's here!"

Rylee smiles when she sees Emmy. The girls are starting to show excitement in each other's presence. I love that they're not too far apart in age. The six-month gap feels smaller and smaller the older Emmy gets.

"Where is he taking you?"

I smooth my hands down my outfit, and then flick off a piece of lint. "To dinner, but I've never been to this place. I hope I'm not overdressed."

"Is this your first date with him? You seem nervous."

"It is our first date, and I *am* nervous. But it's a different kind of nervous. A good nervous. I know him so well already, so I don't feel like I'm about to have to spend an evening with a stranger."

Allysa studies me for a moment with gentle eyes. "You seem excited. I've missed this side of you."

"Yeah. Me too." I bend to give both Emmy and Rylee kisses. "I won't be out too late. I have to get back to the shop and close up for Lucy, so he's picking me up there. I should be back around nine thirty, so try to keep her up until then if you don't mind."

"Why are you coming back so early? That's lame."

"I didn't sleep last night. I'm exhausted. But I don't want to cancel the date, so I'm going to power through."

"Ugh. Motherhood," Allysa says, rolling her eyes. "I'll keep her awake—go have fun. Drink a coffee or a five-hour or something."

I've lost count of the number of coffees I've had today. "Love you. Thanks for saving the day," I say on my way out the door.

"That's what I'm here for," she singsongs.

Chapter Eleven
Atlas

I wanted the day to go by faster, so I decided to help out in the kitchen at Bib's even though I prepared for the night with a full staff. Now I smell like garlic. This is the third time I've tried scrubbing the smell off, to no avail. But if I don't leave now, I'll be late meeting her.

We're taking it slow, so I'm picking her up at her work rather than her apartment. I have no idea where she lives now, or if she still lives in the apartment building I showed up at almost two years ago when she needed help. For whatever reason, where we live is something that hasn't come up in our conversations. She probably doesn't even know I sold my house and moved into the city earlier this year. I'm curious how far apart we live from each other now.

"I smell cologne," Darin says after he passes me. He stops walking toward the freezer and turns to give me a once-over. "Why are you wearing cologne? Why are you dressed up?"

I sniff my hands. "I don't smell like garlic?"

"No, you smell like you're going out. Are you leaving?"

"I *am* leaving. I'll be back around closing time, though. I think I might stay the night here and see if I can catch whoever is vandalizing the restaurants." There were several days of a quiet stretch between incidents, but we got hit for a fourth time last night. It wasn't too costly, though. This time they just scattered the trash everywhere again. That's a lot easier to clean up than repainting has been. That may be because Brad keeps bringing Theo to help. I should probably give Theo a heads-up that the more he complains about a chore, the more likely he's going to be made to do that chore.

I plan to confront whoever is doing the damage tonight and see if I can't figure out their motive and talk them down before I get the police involved. I'm confident most things can be handled with a simple, honest conversation rather than a dramatic intervention, but I have no idea who I'm dealing with.

Darin leans in and quietly says, "Who you going out with? Lily?"

I dry my hands on a towel and nod once.

Darin smiles and walks away. I like that my friends like Lily. They brought her up a couple of times after our poker night, but I think they could tell it bothered me. I didn't like discussing Lily when she wasn't a part of my life.

But now it looks like there's a possibility she's back in the picture. Maybe. This might be why I'm so nervous: because I know what a huge risk Lily is taking by going out with me tonight. If things progress with us, that could impact her life in negative ways. Which might be why I started to feel the immense pressure two hours ago of making sure this date is worth it for her.

But I smell like I'm terrified of vampires, so it's already not going my way.

•   •   •

I pull into the parking lot at five minutes to six. Lily must have been waiting for me, because she exits her store and locks the door behind her before I'm even out of my car.

As soon as I lay eyes on her, I get even more nervous. She looks incredible. She's wearing a black jumpsuit and heels. She pulls on her jacket and meets me in the middle of the parking lot.

I lean in and greet her with a quick kiss on her cheek. "You look stunning." I swear she reddens a little after I say that.

"Do I? I didn't sleep last night. I feel like I look ninety."

"Why didn't you sleep?"

"Emmy ran a fever all night. She's better now, but . . ." Lily yawns. "I'm sorry. I just drank coffee. It'll hit in a minute."

"It's okay. I'm not tired, but I do smell like garlic."

"I like garlic."

"Good thing."

Lily leans back on her heels and looks down at her outfit. "I wasn't sure what to wear since I've never been to this restaurant."

"I've never been there, either, so I have no idea. But I have a feeling you'll be fine." I chose a new restaurant I've been wanting to try. It's about a forty-five-minute drive, but I figured that would give us time to catch up on the way over.

"I have a present for you," she says. "It's in my car. Let me grab it."

I follow her to her car and watch her retrieve something from the console. When she hands it to me, I can't hold back a smile. "Is this your journal?" She read another quick passage to me last night, but she was so embarrassed reading it out loud, she refused to give me more.

"That's one of them. We'll see how tonight goes before I give you the other one."

"No pressure or anything." I walk her to my car and open the passenger door for her. She starts to yawn again as I'm closing her door.

I feel bad, like maybe she's too exhausted for this date. I have no idea what it's like to raise a child. I feel kind of selfish that I'm not offering to reschedule, so before I back out of the parking lot, I speak up. "If you'd rather go home and sleep, we can do this next weekend."

"There's nothing else I'd rather do than this, Atlas. I'll sleep when I'm dead." She clicks her seat belt. "You actually do smell like garlic."

I think she's kidding. Lily used to joke all the time when we were younger. It's one of the things I loved most about her—that she always seemed to be in a good mood despite all the bad things surrounding her. It's that same strength I admired in her in the days I was with her after she found out she was pregnant in the emergency room. I know that was one of the lowest points of her life, but she was able to smile through it all, and even spent an entire evening impressing my friends with her humor during a poker night.

Everyone handles stress differently, and none of those ways is necessarily wrong, but Lily handles it with grace. And grace just happens to be the quality I find the most attractive in people.

"How'd you manage to get away on a Saturday night?" Lily asks.

I hate that I'm driving because I want to look at her while I respond. I've never seen her look this . . . womanly?

Is that a compliment? I don't even know. I probably shouldn't say it out loud in case it isn't, but when Lily and I fell in love, neither of us were what we would now consider adults. But it's different tonight. We're grown-ups with careers, and she's a mother and a boss and independent. *It's sexy as hell.*

The only other time I've spent with her as adults was when she was technically still with Ryle, so it felt wrong thinking of her the way I am now. *Like I want her.*

I keep my focus on the road and try not to create a lull in our conversation, but I think I might be a little flustered. That surprises me.

"How did I manage getting away?" I say, pretending like I'm mulling over the question rather than obsessing about how much I want to stare at her. "I hire dependable people."

Lily smiles at that. "Do you always work on weekends?"

I nod. "I usually only take off Sundays, when we're closed. The occasional Monday."

"What do you enjoy the most about your job?"

She's full of questions tonight. I give her a sidelong glance and smile. "Reading the reviews."

She makes a noise like she's shocked. "I'm sorry," she says. "Did you say *reviews*? You read your restaurant reviews?"

"Every single one."

"*What?* Oh my God, you must not have a single insecurity. I make Serena run our social media so I can *avoid* reviews."

"Your reviews are great."

She practically turns her entire body toward me in the seat. "You read *my* reviews?"

"I read reviews for anyone I know who owns a business. Is that weird?"

"It's not *not* weird."

I flip on my blinker. "I like reading reviews. I feel like business reviews are a reflection of the owner, and I want to know what people think of my restaurants. The constructive criticism helps. I haven't had the kitchen experience a lot of chefs have, and critics are some of the best teachers."

"What do you get out of reading reviews about *other* people's businesses?"

"Nothing, really. I just find it entertaining."

"Do I have any bad ones?" Lily looks away from me, half turning so that she's facing forward again. "Never mind, don't answer that. I'm just going to pretend they're all good and that everyone loves my flowers."

"Everyone *does* love your flowers."

She presses her lips together in an attempt to suppress her smile. "What's your *least*-favorite part of your job?"

I love that she's asking me such random questions. It reminds me of all the nights we would stay up late, and she would pepper me with questions about myself. "Up until last week, it was health inspections," I admit. "They're extremely stressful."

"Why up until last week? What changed?"

"The vandalism."

"Did it happen again?"

"Yeah, twice this week."

"And you still have no idea who it is?"

I shake my head. "No clue."

"Do you have any angry ex-girlfriends?"

"Nah, I doubt it. They don't seem the type."

Lily kicks off her heels and pulls one of her legs into her seat, making herself more comfortable. "How many serious relationships have you had?"

She's going there. Okay. "Define 'serious.'"

"I don't know. More than two months?"

"One," I say.

"How long were you together?"

"A little more than a year. I met her while I was in the military."

"Why'd you break up?"

"We moved in together."

"That's why you broke up?"

"I think living together escalated the realization that we were incompatible. Or maybe we were just at different points in our lives. I was focused on my career, and her focus was on which outfits to wear to the clubs I was too tired to go to with her. When I got out of the military and moved back to Boston, she stayed behind and moved into a loft with two of her friends."

Lily laughs. "I cannot picture you in a club."

"Yeah. That's why I'm single, I guess." My phone rings with an incoming call from Corrigan's, interrupting us before I'm able to throw her own question back at her. "I have to take this," I say.

"Go ahead."

I answer the call over Bluetooth. It ends up being a freezer issue that requires me to make two more phone calls before I've got it sorted out and a repair technician on the way there. When I'm finally able to give my attention back to

Lily, I glance over at her and find her asleep, her head limp against her shoulder. I hear a dainty snore coming from her.

The coffee never kicked in, I guess.

I let her sleep all the way to the restaurant. We pull in about ten minutes to seven. It's dark, and the restaurant looks crowded, but we have a few minutes before I have to check in for our reservation, so I let her rest.

Her snore is as endearing as she is. It's delicate, almost too light to hear. I take a quick video I can use to tease her with later, and then I reach into the backseat and grab her journal. I know she said not to read it in front of her, but technically I'm not. She's asleep.

I open it to the first page and begin reading.

I read the first entry, completely captivated. I feel like I'm breaking a rule reading this, but she's the one who brought it.

I read the second entry. Then the third. Then I log into my reservation app and cancel our reservation because unless I wake her up this very second, we're going to be late. I'd rather our table go to someone else, because Lily looks like she's been needing this sleep for a while.

And I want to read another entry. I'll take her somewhere else for dinner once she wakes up.

Every word she wrote is taking me right back to when we were teenagers. There are so many times I want to laugh at the things she says and how she says them, but I stifle my laughter so that I don't startle her.

I eventually read a passage that I'm almost positive is leading up to our first kiss. I look at the clock and we've already been sitting here for half an hour, but Lily is still sound asleep, and I can't stop in the middle of this entry. I keep reading, hoping she stays asleep long enough for me to get to the end of this one.

"I need to tell you something," he said.

I held my breath, not knowing what he was going to say.

"I got in touch with my uncle today. My mom and I used to live with him in Boston. He told me once he gets back from his work trip I can stay with him."

I should have been so happy for him in that moment. I should have smiled and told him congratulations. But I felt all of the immaturity of my age when I closed my eyes and felt sorry for myself.

"Are you going?" I asked.

He shrugged. "I don't know. I wanted to talk to you about it first."

He was so close to me on the bed, I could feel the warmth of his breath. I also noticed he smelled like mint, and it made me wonder if he uses bottled water to brush his teeth before he comes over here. I always send him home every day with lots of water.

I brought my hand up to the pillow and started pulling at a feather sticking out of it. When I got it all the way out, I twisted it between my fingers. "I don't know what to say, Atlas. I'm happy you have a place to stay. But what about school?"

"I could finish down there," he said.

I nodded. It sounded like he had already made up his mind. "When are you leaving?"

I wondered how far away Boston is. It's probably a few hours, but that's a whole world away when you don't own a car.

"I don't know for sure that I am."

I dropped the feather back onto the pillow and brought my hand to my side. "What's stopping you? Your uncle is offering you a place to stay. That's good, right?"

He tightened his lips together and nodded. Then he picked up the feather I'd been playing with and he started twisting it between his fingers. He laid it back down on the pillow and then he did something I wasn't expecting. He moved his fingers to my lips and he touched them.

God, Ellen. I thought I was gonna die right then and there. It was the most I'd ever felt inside my body at one time. He kept his fingers there for a few seconds, and he said, "Thank you, Lily. For everything." He moved his fingers up and through my hair, and then he leaned forward and planted a kiss on my forehead. I was breathing so hard, I had to open my mouth to catch more air. I could see his chest moving just as hard as mine was. He looked down at me and I watched as his eyes went right to my mouth. "Have you ever been kissed, Lily?"

I shook my head no and tilted my face up to his because I needed him to change that right then and there or I wasn't gonna be able to breathe.

Then—almost as if I were made of eggshells—he lowered his mouth to mine and just rested it there. I didn't know what to do next, but I didn't care. I didn't care if we just stayed like that all night and never even moved our mouths, it was everything.

His lips closed over mine and I could kind of feel his hand shaking. I did what he was doing and started to move my lips like he was. I felt the tip of his tongue brush across my lips once and I thought my eyes were about to roll back in my head. He did it again, and then a third time, so I finally did it, too. When our tongues touched for the first time, I kind of smiled a little, because I'd thought about my first kiss a lot. Where it would be, who it would be with. Never in a million years did I imagine it would feel like this.

He pushed me on my back and pressed his hand against my cheek and kept kissing me. It just got better and better as I grew more comfortable. My favorite moment was when he pulled back for a second and looked down at me, then came back even harder.

I don't know how long we kissed. A long time. So long, my mouth started to hurt and my eyes couldn't stay open. When we fell asleep, I'm pretty sure his mouth was still touching mine.

We didn't talk about Boston again.
I still don't know if he's leaving.

—*Lily*

Wow.

Wow.

I close the journal and look over at Lily. She wrote our first kiss with so much detail, it makes me feel inferior to my teenage self.

Did it actually happen that way?

I remember that night, but I was a hell of a lot more

nervous than Lily described me to be. It's funny how, when you're a teenager, you think you're the only inexperienced, nervous human on the planet. You think almost every other teenager has life figured out way better than you do, but it isn't that way at all. We were both scared. And infatuated. And in love.

I had fallen in love with her long before our first kiss, though. I loved her more than I had ever loved anyone before that moment. I think I loved her more than I've ever loved anyone *after* that moment.

I think I still might.

There's so much Lily doesn't know about that part of my life. So much I want to tell her now that I've read her version of some of our time together. It's obvious she has no clue how instrumental she was in my life back then. At a time when everyone was turning their backs to me, Lily was the only one who stepped up.

She's still sound asleep, so I pull out my phone and open a blank note. I start typing, detailing what my life was like before she entered it. I don't mean to write as much as I do, but I guess I have a lot I want to say to her.

It's another twenty minutes before I finally finish typing everything, and another five minutes before Lily finally begins to rouse.

I set my phone in the cupholder, unsure if I'm going to allow her to read what I just wrote. I might wait a few days. A few weeks. She wants to take things slow, and I'm not sure what I said toward the end of that letter matches her idea of "slow."

Her hand goes up, and she scratches her head. She's facing the window, so I don't see her face when her eyes open, but I can tell when she's awake because she sits straight up. She stares out her window for a beat, then swings her head in my direction. A few strands of hair are stuck to her cheek.

I'm leaning against my door, watching her casually, as if this is completely normal first-date behavior.

"Atlas." She says my name like it's an apology and a question at the same time.

"It's okay. You were tired."

She grabs her phone and looks at the time. "Oh my *God*." She leans forward, pressing her elbows into her thighs and her face into her palms. "I can't believe this."

"Lily, it's fine. Really." I hold up the journal. "You kept me company."

She eyes the journal and then groans. "This is *mortifying*."

I toss the journal into the backseat. "I personally found it enlightening."

Lily hits me playfully on my shoulder. "Stop laughing. I feel too bad for it to be funny."

"Don't feel bad, you're exhausted. And probably hungry. We could grab a burger on the drive back."

Lily falls dramatically against her seat. "Let the fancy chef take the girl for fast food since she slept through her date. Why not?" She flips the visor down and notices the hair stuck to her cheek. "Wow, I am such a *mom*. Is this our last date? It is. Did I ruin this already? I wouldn't blame you."

I put the car in reverse. "Not even close after everything I just read. Not sure anything could top this date."

"You have very low standards, Atlas."

I find her self-deprecation adorably attractive. "I have a question about your journal."

"What?" She's wiping away a smear of mascara. Everything about her seems so defeated now that she thinks she ruined our date. I can't stop smiling, though.

"The night of our first kiss . . . did you put the blankets in the washer on purpose? Was that a trick to get me to sleep in your bed?"

She scrunches up her nose. "You read that far?"

"You were asleep for a long time."

She contemplates my question, and then nods an admission. "I wanted you to be my first kiss back then, and that wouldn't have happened if you kept sleeping on the floor."

She's probably right about that. And it worked.

It's *still* working, because reading her description of our first kiss brought back every feeling she pulled out of me that night. She could sleep the entire way back home, and I'd still think this was the best date I've ever been on.

Chapter Twelve
Lily

"I can't believe you let me sleep for that long." It's been ten minutes, and my stomach is still rolling from embarrassment. "Did you finish reading the whole journal?"

"I stopped after I read about our first kiss."

That's good. That's not too embarrassing. But if he would have read about the first time we had sex while I was sleeping in the seat next to him, I'm not sure I could have recovered.

"This is so not fair," I mutter. "You have to do something mortifying so the scales even out, because right now I feel like I've completely ruined our night."

Atlas laughs. "You think me doing something to mortify myself will make you feel better about tonight?"

I nod. "Yes, that's the law of the universe. Eye for an eye, humiliation for humiliation."

Atlas taps his thumb on his steering wheel as he massages his jaw with his free hand. Then he nudges his head toward his phone, which is sitting in the cupholder. "Open the Notes app on my phone. Read the first one."

Oh, wow. I was kidding, but I snatch up his phone so fast. "What's your password?"

"Nine five nine five."

I enter the numbers and then glance over his home screen while I have it open. Every app is tucked neatly into a folder. He has zero unread texts and one unread email. "You're a neat freak. Who has *one* unread email?"

"I don't like clutter," he says. "Side effect of the military. How many unread emails do you have?"

"Thousands." I open the Notes app and click on the most recent one. As soon as I see the two words at the top, I drop the phone, pressing it facedown on my thigh. *"Atlas."*

"Lily."

I can feel my embarrassment being swallowed up by a warm wave of anticipation falling over me. "You wrote me a *Dear Lily* letter?"

He nods slowly. "You were asleep for quite a while." When he glances at me, his smile falters, like he's worried about whatever it is he wrote. He faces forward again, and I can see the roll of his throat.

I lean my head against the passenger window and begin to read silently.

Dear Lily,

You're going to be mortified when you wake up and realize you fell asleep on our first date. I'm a little too excited for your reaction. But you seemed so tired when I picked you up, it actually makes me happy to see you getting some rest.

This past week has been surreal, hasn't it? I was beginning to think I may never be a part of your life in any significant way, and then poof, you show up.

I could go on and on about what that run-in meant to me, but I promised my therapist I'd stop saying cheesy shit to you. Don't worry, I plan on breaking that promise many times, but you asked if we could take things slow, so I'll give it a few more dates.

Instead, I think I'm going to steal a page from your playbook and talk about our past. It's only fair. You let me read some of your most intimate thoughts at such a vulnerable point in your life, I figure it's the least I can do to give you some insight into my life at that time.

My version is a little grittier, though. I'll try to spare you the worst of the details, but I'm not sure you can fully know what your friendship meant to me without knowing what I went through before you came along.

I told you some of it—about how I ended up in the position I was in, living in that abandoned house. But I had felt homeless a lot longer than that. My whole life, really, even though I had a house and a mother and, occasionally, a stepfather.

I don't remember what things were like when I was young. I have this fantasy that maybe she was a good mother once upon a time. I do remember a day trip we took to Cape Cod where we tried coconut shrimp for the first time, but if she was a decent mother outside of that one day, that one meal, that part of her never became a core memory for me.

My core memories were stretches of time spent alone, or just trying to stay out of her way. She was quick to anger and quick to respond. For the first ten or so years of my life, she was stronger and faster than me, so I spent the better part of a decade hiding from her hand, from her cigarettes, from the lash of her tongue.

I know she was stressed. She was a single mother working nights to try and provide for me, but as many excuses as I made for her back then, I've seen my fair share of single mothers navigate life just fine without resorting to the things my mother did.

You've seen my scars. I won't go into the details, but as bad as it was, it got even worse when she was on her third marriage. I was twelve when they met.

Little did I know, the age of twelve would be my only peaceful year. She was always gone because she was with him, and when she was home, she was actually in a decent mood because she was falling in love. Funny how love for a partner can make or break how some people treat their own children.

But twelve turned into thirteen turned into Tim moving in with us, and the next four years of my life were hell on earth. When I wasn't making my mother angry, I was making Tim angry. When I was home, I was being yelled at. When I was at school, the house was being destroyed by their fights, and I'd be expected to clean up after them when I got home.

Life with them was a nightmare, and by the time I was finally strong enough to take up for myself, that's when Tim decided he didn't want to live with me anymore.

My mother chose him. I was forced to leave. They didn't have to ask twice; I was more than ready to go, but that's because I had somewhere to go.

Until I didn't. I was gone three months before the

friend I was staying with moved with his family to Colorado.

At that point, I had no one and nowhere else to go, and no money to get there if I did, so I was forced to go back to my mother and ask if I could come back home.

I still remember the day I showed back up to that house. I had barely been gone three months, and the place was already falling apart. The yard hadn't been mowed since the last time I'd done it before being kicked out. All the window screens were missing, and there was a gaping hole where the doorknob used to be. By the looks of the place, you would think I'd been gone for years.

My mother's car was in the driveway, but Tim's wasn't. It looked like her car had been there for a while. The hood was propped open, and there were tools scattered near it, along with at least thirty beer cans someone had shaped in the form of a pyramid against the garage door.

Even the newspapers had piled up on the cracked concrete walkway. I remember picking them up and setting them on one of the old iron chairs to dry out before I knocked on the door.

It felt weird knocking on the door of a house I had lived in for years, but on the off chance Tim was home, I wasn't about to open the door without permission. I had a house key still, but Tim had made it very clear that he'd turn me in for trespassing if I ever tried to use it.

I couldn't have used it even if I wanted to. There was no doorknob.

I could hear someone making their way across the living room. The curtain on the small window at the top half of the front door moved, and I saw my mother peek outside. She stared for a few seconds, unmoving.

She eventually opened the door a few inches. Far enough that I could see that, at two o'clock in the afternoon, she was still in her pajamas, which were an oversized Weezer T-shirt one of her exes had left behind. I hated that shirt because I liked that band. Every time she wore it, she ruined them a little more for me.

She asked what I was doing there, and I didn't immediately want to give her my reasons. Instead, I asked her if Tim was home.

She opened the door a bit more and folded her arms so tightly together, it made one of the band members on her shirt look decapitated. She told me Tim was at work and asked what I wanted.

I asked her if I could come inside. She contemplated my question and then looked over my shoulder, her eyes scanning the street. I don't know what she was checking for. Maybe she was afraid a neighbor would witness her allowing her own son to visit.

She left the door open for me while she went to her bedroom to change. The house was eerily dark, I remember. All the curtains were drawn, creating a sense of confusion on what time of day it was. It didn't help that the clock on the stove was blinking, and the time was off by over eight hours. If I still lived there, that's something else I would have fixed.

If I still lived there, the curtains would have been open. The kitchen counters wouldn't have been covered with dirty dishes. There wouldn't have been a missing doorknob, or an unkempt yard, or days' worth of soggy newspapers pil-

ing up. I realized in that moment that I was the one who had been keeping that house together all the years I was growing up.

It gave me hope. Hope that maybe they realized I was an asset rather than an inconvenience, and they would allow me to return home until I finished high school.

I saw a doorknob kit on the kitchen table, so I picked it up and inspected it. The receipt was beneath it. I looked at the date on the receipt, and it was purchased over two weeks prior.

The doorknob was the right fit for the front door. I didn't know why Tim hadn't installed it if he'd had it for two weeks, so I found the tools in a kitchen drawer and opened the package. It was several minutes before my mother came out of her room, but by the time she did, I already had the new doorknob in place on the front door.

She asked what I was doing, so I twisted the knob and opened the door a little to show her it worked.

I'll never forget her reaction. She sighed and said, "Why do you do shit like this? It's like you want him to hate you." She snatched the screwdriver out of my hand and said, "Maybe you should go before he realizes you were here."

Part of the reason I could never get along with anyone in that house was because their reactions always seemed misplaced. When I would help out around the house without being asked, Tim would say it was because I was antagonizing him. When I wouldn't help with something, he'd say it was because I was lazy and ungrateful.

"I'm not trying to upset Tim," I said. "I fixed your doorknob. I was just trying to help."

"He was going to do it as soon as he had the time."

Part of Tim's problem was that he always had the time. He never kept a job more than six months and spent more time gambling than he did with my mother.

"Did he get a job?" I remember asking her.

"He's looking."

"Is that where he is right now?"

I could see in her expression that Tim wasn't out job hunting. Wherever he was, I was sure it was putting my mother even more in debt than she already was. Her debt was probably the straw that broke the camel's back and got me kicked out in the first place. When I found a stash of maxed-out, past-due credit card bills in her name, I confronted Tim about them.

He didn't like being confronted. He preferred the preteen version of me he met to the near adult I grew into. He liked the version of me he could push around without being pushed back. The version of me he could manipulate without me calling him out.

That version of me left between the ages of fifteen and sixteen. Once Tim realized he couldn't threaten me physically anymore, he tried ruining my life in other ways. One of those ways was leaving me without a place to live.

I eventually swallowed my pride and came right out with it. I told my mother I had nowhere to go.

My mother's expression wasn't just void of empathy, it was full of annoyance. "I hope you aren't asking to move back in after everything you did."

"Everything I did? You mean when I called him out because his gambling addiction put you in debt?"

That's when she called me an asshole. Or ass whole, *rather. She always said that word wrong.*

I attempted to plead with her, but she quickly resorted to the person I was used to. She hurled the screwdriver at me. It was so sudden and unexpected because we weren't even arguing at that point, so I wasn't able to duck in time. It hit me right above my left eye, in the center of my eyebrow.

I rubbed my fingers across the cut, and they came away smeared with blood.

All I did was ask to move home. I didn't disrespect her. I didn't curse at her. I simply showed up and fixed her front door and tried to reason with her, and I ended up with a bloody gash.

I remember staring at my fingers, thinking, "Tim didn't do this. My mother did this."

For so long, I had blamed Tim for everything that went wrong in that household, but everything wrong with that household started with her. Tim simply amplified what was already an awful environment.

I remember thinking that I would rather be dead than back with her. Up until that moment, there was a part of me that still held something for her. I don't know if it was a sliver of respect, but I was somehow able to appreciate that she had kept me alive when I was younger. But isn't that the most basic thing a parent should do when they decide to bring a child into the world?

I realized at that point I had been giving her too much credit. I always blamed our lack of a bond on her being a single mother, but there were a lot of busy single mothers out there who somehow still bonded with their children. Mothers who took up for their children when they were being mistreated. Mothers who wouldn't look the other way when their thirteen-year-old came away from a punishment with a black eye and a busted lip. Mothers who didn't allow their husbands to force their school-aged child into homelessness. Mothers who didn't throw screwdrivers at their children's heads.

Despite realizing what an uncaring human she truly was, I made one last attempt to pull humanity out of her. "Can I at least get some of my stuff before I leave?"

"You don't have anything," she said. "We needed the space."

I couldn't look at her after that. It was as if she wanted nothing more than to erase me from her life, so I vowed in that moment to help her do just that.

The blood was dripping into my eye when I was walking away from the house.

I can't tell you what the rest of that day was like. To feel so incredibly unwanted, unloved, alone. I had no one. Nothing. No money, no belongings, no family.

Just a wound.

We're impressionable when we're younger, and when you're told you are nothing for years on end by everyone you should mean something to, you start to believe it. And you slowly start to become nothing.

But then I met you, Lily. And even though I was nothing, when you looked at me, you somehow saw something. Something I couldn't see. You were the first person in my life to show an interest in who I was as a human. No one *had ever asked me questions about myself the way you did. After those few months I spent getting to know you, I stopped feeling like I was nothing. You made me feel interesting and unique. Your friendship gave me worth.*

Thank you for that. Even if this date leads nowhere and we never speak again, I will always be grateful to you for somehow seeing something in me that my own mother was blind to.

You're my favorite person, Lily. And now you know why.

Atlas

My throat is so thick with burgeoning tears, I can't even verbally respond to what I just read. I set the phone on my leg and wipe at my eyes. I hate that he's driving right now, because if we were parked, I'd throw my arms around him and hug him tighter than he's ever been hugged. I'd probably kiss him, too, and pull him into the backseat, because no one has ever said such heartbreakingly sad things in such a sweet way to me before.

Atlas reaches across the seat and grabs his phone. He drops it back into the cupholder, but then he reaches for my hand. He threads his fingers through mine and squeezes my hand while staring straight ahead. That move causes a commotion in my chest. I wrap my other hand over the top of his, and holding hands like this reminds me of all the bus rides when we'd just sit in silence, sad and cold, holding on to each other.

I stare out the window, and he stares straight ahead, and neither of us says a word on our drive back to the city.

We stop and grab to-go burgers just two miles from my flower shop. Atlas knows I don't want Emerson to be up too far past her bedtime, so we eat in the parking lot of Lily Bloom's. Our conversation since getting back into the city and ordering burgers has been much lighter. It isn't lost on me that I'm not mortified anymore. Him being vulnerable with me seemed to be the reset button I needed for our date to get back on track.

We've been discussing all the places we've traveled. He has me beat by a long shot, considering the time he spent in the Marines. He's been to five different countries, and the only place I've been outside of the country is Canada.

"You've never even been to Mexico?" Atlas asks.

I wipe my mouth with a napkin. "Never."

"Did you and Ryle not have a honeymoon?"

Ugh. I hate the sound of his name in the middle of this date. "No, we eloped in Vegas. Didn't have time for a honeymoon."

Atlas takes a sip of his drink. When he looks at me, his eyes are piercing, like he's hoping to unpack the thoughts I'm not saying. "Did you want a wedding?"

I shrug. "I don't know. I knew Ryle never wanted to get married, so when he said we should go to Vegas and get married, I saw it as a window of opportunity that might close. I guess I felt like eloping was better than not marrying him at all."

"What if you get married again? You think you'll do it differently?"

I laugh at that question, and nod immediately. "Absolutely. I want it all. Flowers and bridesmaids and shit." I pop a fry into my mouth. "And romantic vows, and an even more romantic honeymoon."

"Where would you go?"

"Paris. Rome. London. I have no desire to sit on a hot beach somewhere. I want to see all the romantic places in Europe and make love in every city and take pictures kissing in front of the Eiffel Tower. I want to eat croissants and hold hands on trains." I drop my empty container of fries into the sack. "What about you?"

Atlas reaches for my free hand, and he holds it. He doesn't answer me. He just smiles at me and squeezes my hand, like what he wants is a secret that's too soon to spill.

Holding his hand feels like such a natural thing. Maybe because we used to do this so much as teenagers, but sitting in this car with him and *not* holding his hand feels more out of place than holding hands does.

Even with the hitch I put into our date by falling asleep, the entire night has felt easy and comfortable. Being near him is second nature. I trace a finger over the top of his wrist. "I need to go."

"I know," he says, rubbing his thumb over mine. Atlas's phone pings, so he reaches for it with his free hand and reads the incoming text. He sighs quietly, and the way he drops his phone back into the cupholder makes me think he's irritated with whoever just texted him.

"Everything okay?"

Atlas forces a smile, but it's a pathetic attempt. I see right through it, and he knows it. He breaks eye contact and looks down at our hands. He flips mine over until it's faceup, and he begins to trace the lines in my palm. His finger feels like a lightning rod, zapping electricity from my hand throughout the rest of my body. "My mother called me last week."

That confession takes me aback. "What did she want?"

"I don't know, I ended the call before she could tell me, but I'm pretty sure she needs money."

I thread our hands together again. I don't know what to say to him. That has to be hard, not hearing from your mother for almost fifteen years, and then she finally reaches out when she needs something. It makes me so grateful that my mother is a huge part of my life.

"I didn't mean to drop that on you when you're in a hurry. We should save some conversation for our second date." He smiles at me, and it instantly flips the mood. It's remarkable how his smile can dictate the feelings occurring inside my own chest. "Come on, I'll walk you to your car."

I laugh because my car is literally two feet away. But Atlas rushes around the front of his car and opens my door, then helps me out. And then, with one step each, we're at my car.

"Fun walk," I tease.

He flashes a brief smile, and I don't know if he means for it to be seductive, but I'm suddenly warm all over, despite the cold weather. Atlas peeks over my shoulder, nudging his head toward my car. "Do you have more journals in there?"

"Just had the one on me."

"Shame," he says. He leans a shoulder against my car, so I do the same, facing him.

I have no idea if we're about to kiss. I wouldn't object,

but I also just ate onions after sleeping for over an hour, so I doubt my mouth is at its most appealing right now.

"Do I get a redo?" I ask.

"A redo of what?"

"This date. I'd like to be awake for the next one."

Atlas laughs, but then his laugh dissipates. He stares at me for a beat. "I forgot how fun it is being around you."

His words confuse me because *fun* is not what I would call our time together back then. It was sad, at best. "You think those times were fun?"

He lifts a shoulder in a half shrug. "I mean, it was the lowest point of my life, sure. But my memories with you from back then are still some of my favorites."

His compliment makes me blush. I'm glad it's dark.

But he's right. It was a low point in both of our lives, but being with him was still somehow the highlight of my teenage years. I guess *fun* is the perfect way to describe what we made of it. And if we somehow had fun together at such a low point in both of our lives, it makes me wonder what we could be like at our highest.

It's the exact opposite of the thoughts I had about Ryle last week. I've experienced the lowest of lows with Atlas, and he has never been anything but incredible and respectful to me. Yet, the man I chose to be my husband somehow disrespected me in ways no one deserves . . . all while we were at such a high point in our lives.

I'm grateful for Atlas because I know he's the standard I now hold people to. He's the standard I should have held Ryle to from the very beginning.

There's a convenient gust of cold air that sweeps between

us. It would be the perfect excuse for Atlas to pull me to him, but he doesn't. Instead, the quietness builds between us until there's only one thing left to do. Either kiss or say goodnight.

Atlas brushes a strand of my hair from my forehead. "I'm not going to kiss you yet."

I hope my disappointment isn't obvious, but I know it is. I practically deflate in front of him. "Is it my punishment for falling asleep?"

"Of course not. I'm just feeling inferior after reading about our first kiss."

I sputter laughter. "Inferior to *who*? Yourself?"

He nods. "Teenage Atlas through your eyes was quite the charmer."

"So is adult Atlas."

He groans a little, like he already wants to change his mind about the kiss. The groan makes things feel a little more serious. He moves fluidly away from the car until he's standing right in front of me. I press my back against my car door and look up at him, hoping he's about to kiss the hell out of me.

"Also, you asked me to take things slow, so . . ."

Dammit. I did do that. I said *very* slow, if I remember correctly. *I hate myself.*

Atlas leans forward, and I close my eyes. I feel his breath scattering across my cheek right before he presses a quick kiss against the side of my head. "Goodnight, Lily."

"Okay."

Okay? Why did I say "okay"? I'm so flustered.

Atlas laughs softly. When I open my eyes, he's backing away from me, heading to the driver's side of his car. Before he leaves, he rests his arm on the roof of the car and says, "I hope you get some sleep tonight."

I nod, but I don't know if that's going to be possible. I feel like every bit of caffeine I've consumed today has just kicked in all at once. I won't be able to sleep after this date. I'm going to be thinking about the letter he let me read. And when I'm not thinking about that, I'm going to be replaying our first kiss in my head all night long, wondering what part two is going to feel like.

• • •

"Just keep swimming, swimming, swimming . . ."

The familiar sounds of *Finding Nemo* are coming from Allysa and Marshall's living room when I open the door to their apartment.

When I pass by the kitchen, Marshall is standing in front of the refrigerator with both doors wide open. He nods a greeting, and I wave, but I don't make small talk with him because I'm aching to hug Emerson.

When I enter the living room, I'm shocked to find Ryle on the sofa. He didn't mention he would be off work tonight. Emerson is asleep on his chest, and Allysa is nowhere around.

"Hey."

Ryle doesn't look up to greet me, but he doesn't have to look up for me to know something is bothering him. I can see the firm set of his jaw—a dead giveaway that he's angry. I want to pick up Emerson, but she looks peaceful, so I leave her on Ryle's chest. "How long has she been asleep?"

Ryle is still staring at the television, one of his hands

protectively on Emmy's back, the other behind his head. "Since this movie started."

I recognize the scene, which lets me know it's been about an hour.

Allysa finally walks into the room, breathing life into it. "Hey, Lily. I'm sorry she's asleep; we tried so hard to keep her awake." We give each other a two-second glance. She silently apologizes that Ryle is here. I silently tell her it's okay. They're siblings—I can't expect him not to show up when he knows she's babysitting his daughter.

Ryle motions for Allysa. "Can you put Emerson on her pallet? I need to talk to Lily."

The curtness in his voice alarms both me and Allysa. We give each other another look as she pries Emerson off Ryle's chest. The ache to hold her only grows wider as Allysa lays her on the pallet.

Ryle stands up, and for the first time since I walked in, he makes eye contact with me. He gives me a once-over, noticing the outfit and the heels I'm wearing. I can see the slow roll of his throat. He nudges his head upward, indicating he wants to speak to me on the rooftop balcony.

Whatever conversation this is, he wants complete privacy.

He exits the apartment to head to the roof, and I look toward Allysa for guidance. Once Ryle is out of earshot, she says, "I told him you had an event tonight."

"Thanks." Allysa swore she wouldn't tell Ryle about my date, but I can't figure out why he's so angry if he doesn't know where I've been. "Why is he upset?"

Allysa shrugs. "No idea. He seemed fine when he showed up an hour ago."

I know better than anyone how Ryle can seem fine one second and absolutely the opposite of fine the next. But I usually know what's setting him off.

Did he find out I went on a date? *Did he find out it was with Atlas?*

Once I'm on the roof, I locate Ryle leaning over the ledge, looking down. My stomach is already in knots. My heels click against the floor as I make my way over to him.

Ryle glances at me briefly. "You look . . . *nice.*" He says it in a way that makes it seem like an insult rather than a compliment. Or maybe that's just my guilt.

"Thank you." I lean against the ledge, waiting for him to speak up about whatever is bothering him.

"Did you just get back from a date?"

"I had an event." I go along with Allysa's lie. There's no point in being honest with him, because it's too soon to know if this thing with Atlas is going anywhere yet, and the truth would only upset Ryle more. I press my back against the ledge and fold my arms over my chest. "What is it, Ryle?"

He waits a beat before he finally speaks. "I've never seen that cartoon before tonight."

Is he just trying to make small talk or is he angry about something? I'm confused by this whole conversation.

Until I'm not.

I swear, I can be such an idiot sometimes. *Of course he's upset.* He once read all my journal entries. He knows how much that movie means to me after having read everything I wrote about it, but I guess now that he's finally seen it, he's connected the dots. And by the looks of it, he's added some dots of his own.

He turns now, facing me with an expression full of betrayal. "You named our daughter *Dory*?" He takes a step closer. "You chose my daughter's middle name because of your connection with *that man*?"

I feel an immediate pulsing in my temples. *That man.* I break eye contact with him while I think of how to properly communicate this. When I chose the name Dory as Emerson's middle name, I didn't do it for Atlas. That movie meant something to me long before Atlas came into the picture, but I probably should have thought twice about it before going through with naming her that.

I clear my throat, making room for the truth. "I chose that name because the character inspired me when I was younger. It had nothing to do with anyone else."

Ryle releases an exasperated, disappointed laugh. "You're a real piece of work, Lily."

I want to argue with him, to further prove my point, but I'm getting nervous. His demeanor is bringing back every fear of him I've ever held. I try to defuse the situation by escaping it.

"I'm going home now." I start to head toward the stairs, but he's faster than me. He moves past me, and then he's in between me and the door to the stairwell. I take a nervous step back. I slip my hand in my pocket in search of my phone in case I need to use it.

"We're changing her middle name," he says.

I keep my voice firm and steady when I respond. "We named her Emerson after your brother. That's your connection to her name. Her middle name is *my* connection. It's only fair. You're reading too much into it."

I try to sidestep around him, but he moves with me.

I glance over my shoulder to measure the distance between myself and the ledge. Not that I feel like he'd throw me over it, but I also didn't think he'd be capable of shoving me down a flight of stairs.

"Does he know?" Ryle asks.

He doesn't have to say Atlas's name for me to know exactly who he's talking about. I feel the guilt swallowing me, and I'm worried Ryle can sense it.

Atlas does know Emerson's middle name is Dory, because I made it a point to tell him. But I honestly didn't name my daughter for Atlas. I named her for *me*. Dory was my favorite character before I even knew Atlas Corrigan existed. I admired her strength, and I only named her that because strength is the one trait I hope my daughter has more than anything else.

But Ryle's reaction is making me want to apologize, because *Finding Nemo* does mean something to both Atlas and me, and I knew it when I ran after Atlas on the street to tell him about her middle name.

Maybe Ryle deserves to be angry.

Therein lies our issue, though. Ryle can be angry, but that doesn't mean I deserve everything that accompanies his anger. I'm falling back into that same trap of forgetting that nothing I could do would warrant his extreme past reactions.

I may not be perfect, but I don't deserve to fear for my life every time I make a mistake. And this may have been a mistake that deserves more discussion, but I don't feel comfortable having a conversation about it with Ryle on a rooftop without witnesses.

"You're making me nervous. Can we please go back downstairs?"

Ryle's entire demeanor changes as soon as I say that. It's like he punctures against the sharp insult. "Lily, *come on*." He moves away from the door and walks all the way to the other side of the balcony. "We're arguing. People argue. *Christ*." He spins away from me, giving me his back now.

Here comes the gaslighting. He's attempting to make me feel crazy for being scared, even though my fear is more than warranted. I stare at him for a moment, wondering if the argument is over or if he has more to say. I want it to be over, so I open the door to the stairwell.

"Lily, wait."

I pause because his voice is much calmer, which leads me to believe he might be capable of a verbal disagreement rather than an explosive fight tonight. He walks back over to me with a pained expression. "I'm sorry. You know how I feel about anything related to him."

I do know, which is precisely why I've had such conflicting feelings about Atlas potentially being a part of my life again. The simple idea of having to confront Ryle with that information makes me want to vomit. Especially now.

"It upset me to find out that our daughter's middle name might have been something you chose to deliberately hurt me. You can't expect something like that not to affect me."

I lean against the wall and fold my arms over my chest. "It had nothing to do with you or Atlas and everything to do with me. I swear." Just mentioning Atlas's name out loud seems to get it stuck in the air between us, like it's a tangible thing Ryle can reach out and punch.

Ryle nods once with a tight expression, but it appears that he accepts that answer. I honestly don't know if he should. Maybe I did do it subconsciously to hurt him. I don't even know at this point. His anger is making me question my intentions.

This all feels so grossly familiar.

We're both quiet for a while. I just want to go to Emerson, but Ryle seems to have more to say, because he moves closer, placing a hand on the wall beside my head. I'm relieved that he doesn't look angry anymore, but I'm not sure I like the look in his eye that has replaced the anger. It's not the first time he's looked at me this way since our separation.

I feel my entire body stiffen at his gradual change in demeanor. He moves a couple of inches closer, *too* close, and dips his head.

"Lily," he says, his voice a scratchy whisper. "What are we *doing*?"

I don't respond to him because I'm not sure why he's asking that. We're having a conversation. One he started.

He lifts a hand, fingering the collar of my jumpsuit, which is peeking out beneath my coat. When he sighs, his breath moves through my hair. "Everything would be so much easier if we could just . . ." Ryle pauses, maybe to think about the words he's about to say. The words I don't want to hear.

"Stop," I whisper, preventing him from finishing.

He doesn't complete his thought, but he also doesn't back away. If anything, it feels like he moves even closer. I've done nothing in the past that would make him think it's okay to move in on me like this. I do nothing that gives him hope for us other than foster a civil coparenting relationship. He's the one always trying to push my boundaries and straddle the line of what I'm okay with, and I'm honestly tired of it.

"What if I've changed?" he asks. "*Really* changed?" His eyes are full of a mixture of sincerity and sorrow.

It does nothing for me. *Absolutely nothing.* "I don't care if you've changed, Ryle. I hope you *have*. But it's not my responsibility to test that theory."

Those words hit him hard. I see it when he has to take a moment to swallow whatever unkind response he knows he shouldn't give me right now. He stops talking, stops looking at me, stops hovering.

He huffs, frustrated, and then backs away and makes his way toward the stairs, hopefully to his own apartment. He slams the door shut behind him.

I don't immediately follow, for obvious reasons. I need space. I need to process.

This isn't the first time he's asked me what we're doing—like our divorce is some long game I'm playing. Sometimes he'll say it in passing, sometimes in a text. Sometimes he makes it a joke. But every time he suggests how senseless our divorce is, I recognize it for what it is. A manipulation tactic. He thinks if he treats our divorce like we're being silly, I'll eventually agree with him and take him back.

His life would be easier if I took him back. Allysa's and Marshall's lives might even be made easier by it, because they wouldn't have to dance around our divorce and their relationship with him.

But *my* life wouldn't be easier. There's nothing easy about fearing for your safety any time you make a misstep.

Emerson's life wouldn't be easier. I've lived her life. There's nothing easy about living in that kind of household.

I wait for my anger to dissipate before heading back downstairs, but it doesn't. It just builds and builds with every step I descend. I feel like the reaction I'm having is too big for what just happened, or maybe that's just how I've conditioned myself to feel when I'm around Ryle. Maybe it's a combination of that and my lack of sleep. Maybe it's the date with Atlas that I almost ruined. Whatever it is that's making me react so intensely catches up with me right outside of Allysa's apartment door.

I need a moment to collect my emotions before being near my daughter, so I sit on the floor of the hallway to cry it out. I like to shed tears in private. Happens quite regularly, unfortunately, but I've been finding myself getting overwhelmed a lot. Divorce is overwhelming; being a single mother is overwhelming; running a business is overwhelming; dealing with an ex-husband who still scares you is overwhelming.

And then there's that splinter of fear that creeps into my conscience when Ryle says something to suggest our divorce was a mistake. Because sometimes I do wonder if my life wouldn't be so overwhelming if I still had a husband who shared some of the burdens of raising his child. And sometimes I wonder if I'm overreacting by not allowing my daughter to have overnights with her own father. Relationships and custody agreements don't come with a blueprint, unfortunately.

I don't know if every move I make is the right one, but I'm doing my best. I don't need his manipulation and gaslighting on top of that.

I wish I were at home; I would walk straight to my jewelry box and pull out the list of reminders. I should take a picture of it so I always have it on my phone in the future. I definitely underestimate how difficult and confusing interactions with Ryle can be.

How do people leave these cycles when they don't have the resources I had or the support from their friends and family? How do they possibly stay strong enough every second of the day? I feel like all it takes is one weak, insecure moment in the presence of your ex to convince yourself you made the wrong decision.

Anyone who has ever left a manipulative, abusive spouse and somehow stayed that course deserves a medal. A statue. A freaking *superhero* movie.

Society has obviously been worshipping the wrong heroes this whole time because I'm convinced it takes less strength to pick up a building than it does to permanently leave an abusive situation.

I'm still crying a few minutes later when I hear Allysa's door open. I look up to find Marshall exiting the apartment carrying two bags of trash. He pauses when he sees me sitting on the floor.

"Oh." His eyes dart around, as if he's hoping someone else will help me. Not that I need help. I just needed a moment of respite.

Marshall sets the bags on the floor and walks over. He takes a seat across from me and stretches out his legs. He scratches uncomfortably at his knee. "I'm not sure what to say. I'm not good at this."

His discomfort makes me laugh through my tears. I toss

up a frustrated hand. "I'm fine. I just need to cry sometimes when Ryle and I fight."

Marshall pulls up a leg like he's about to stand up and go after Ryle. "Did he hurt you?"

"No. No, he was fairly calm."

Marshall relaxes back to the floor, and I don't know why, maybe it's because he's the unlucky one in front of me right now, but I unload all my thoughts on him.

"I think that's the problem—that he actually had a *right* to be mad at me this time, and he was relatively calm about it. Sometimes we can argue, and it doesn't lead to anything more than a disagreement. And when that happens, I start to question whether I overreacted by asking for a divorce. I mean, I know I didn't overreact. I *know* I didn't. But he has this way of planting seeds of doubt in me, like maybe things could have gotten better if I just gave him more time to work on himself." I feel bad that I'm laying all this on Marshall. It's not fair to him because Ryle is his best friend. "I'm sorry. This isn't your issue."

"Allysa cheated on me."

Marshall's words stun me silent for a good five seconds. "Wh-what?"

"It was a long time ago. We worked through it, but dammit, it hurt like hell. She broke my heart."

I'm shaking my head in an attempt to process this information. He keeps talking, though, so I try to keep up.

"We weren't in a good place. We were going to different colleges and trying to make long distance work, and we were young. And it wasn't even anything big. She had a drunk make-out with some guy at a party before she remembered how amazing I am. But when she told me . . . I've never been so angry in my life. Nothing had ever cut me like that did. I wanted to retaliate: I wanted to cheat on her, so she'd know how it felt; I wanted to slash her tires and max out her credit cards and burn all her clothes. But no matter how mad I was, when she was standing right in front of me, I never, not for one second, thought about physically hurting her. If anything, I just wanted to hug her and cry on her shoulder."

Marshall looks at me with sincerity. "When I think about Ryle hitting you . . . I get absurdly angry. Because I love him. I do. He's been my best friend since we were kids. But I also hate him for not being better. Nothing you have done and nothing you could do would excuse any man's hands on you out of anger. Remember that, Lily. You made the right choice by leaving that situation. You should never feel guilty for that. Pride is the only thing you should feel."

I had no idea how heavily any of this was weighing on me, but Marshall's words lift so much weight off me, I feel like I could float.

I'm not sure those words could mean more coming from anyone else. There's something about getting validation from someone who loves Ryle like a brother that's reaffirming. Empowering.

"You're wrong, Marshall. You're pretty damn good at this."

Marshall smiles and then helps me to my feet. He picks up his trash bags and I head back inside their apartment to find my daughter and hug her so tight.

Chapter Thirteen
Atlas

It's amazing how a night can go from being something I've been hoping would happen for years, to something I've been dreading would happen for years.

If I hadn't received that text just as I was dropping off Lily, I absolutely would have kissed her. But I want our first kiss as adults to be free from distraction.

The text was from Darin, informing me that my mother is at Bib's. I didn't tell Lily about the text because I hadn't yet told her my mother was attempting to work her way back into my life. And then as soon as I told her about my mother calling me, I regretted it. The date was going so well, and I was risking that by ending it on such a somber note.

I didn't text Darin back because I didn't want to interrupt my time with Lily. But even after the date ended and we drove away in separate cars, I still didn't text Darin back. I drove around for half an hour trying to figure out what to do.

I'm hoping my mother got tired of waiting for me. I took my time arriving back to the restaurant, but I'm here now, and I guess I need to confront this. She seems adamant about speaking with me.

I park in the alley behind Bib's so that I can go through the back door in case she's waiting in the restaurant lobby, or at a table. I'm not sure she would recognize me if she saw me, but I'd rather have the advantage by approaching her on my terms.

Darin notices me enter through the back door and immediately makes his way over.

"You get my text?"

I nod and remove my coat. "I did. Is she still here?"

"Yeah, she insisted on waiting. I sat her at table eight."

"Thanks."

Darin looks at me cautiously. "Maybe I'm overstepping, but . . . I swear you said your mother was dead."

That almost makes me laugh. "I never said *dead*. I said she was gone. There's a difference."

"I can tell her you aren't coming in tonight." He must sense the storm brewing.

"It's okay. I have a feeling she isn't going away until I talk to her."

Darin nods and then spins to head back to his station in the kitchen.

I'm glad he's not asking too many questions, since I have no idea why she's here, or who she even is now. She probably wants money. Hell, I'd give it to her if it means I don't have to deal with her calling or showing up again.

I should prepare for that outcome. I go to my office and grab a handful of cash out of the safe and then I make my way through the kitchen doors, out into the restaurant. I hesitate before glancing at table eight.

When I do, I'm relieved to see her back is to me.

I calm myself with a deep breath and then I make my way over to her. I don't want to have to hug her or fake niceties, so I let no time lag between us making eye contact and me taking a seat directly across from her.

She has the same unaffected expression she's always had when she looks across the table at me. There's a small frown playing at the corner of her mouth, but it's always there. She's constantly, albeit inadvertently, frowning.

She looks worn. It's only been about thirteen or so years since I've seen her last, but there are decades' worth of new lines that have formed around her eyes and mouth.

She takes me in for a moment. I know I look vastly different from the last time she saw me, but she makes no indication that she's surprised by that. She's completely stoic, as if I'm the one who should speak first. I don't.

"Is this all yours?" she finally asks, waving a hand around the restaurant.

I nod.

"Wow."

To anyone else watching us, they might think she's impressed. But they don't know her like I know her. That one word was meant as a putdown, as if she's saying, *Wow, Atlas. You're not smart enough for something like this.*

"How much do you need?"

She rolls her eyes. "I'm not here for money."

"What is it, then? You need a kidney? A *heart*?"

She leans back against her seat, resting her hands in her lap. "I forgot how hard it is to have a conversation with you."

"Then why do you keep trying?"

My mother's eyes narrow. She's only ever known the version of me that was intimidated by her. I'm no longer intimidated. Just angry and disappointed.

She huffs, and then brings her arms back up to the table, folding them together. She looks at me pointedly. "I can't find Josh. I was hoping you've talked to him."

I know it's been a long time since I've seen my mother, but I can't for the life of me place anyone named Josh. *Who the hell is Josh? A new boyfriend she thinks I should know about? Is she still using drugs?*

"He does this all the time but never for this long. They're threatening to file truancy charges on me if he doesn't show back up to school."

I am so lost. "Who is Josh?"

Her head falls back as if she's irritated that I'm not following along. "*Josh.* Your little brother. He ran away again."

My . . . *brother?*

Brother.

"Did you know parents can go to jail for truancy violations? I'm looking at *jailtime*, Atlas."

"I have a *brother?*"

"You knew I was pregnant when you ran away."

I absolutely didn't know . . . "I didn't run away—you kicked me out." I don't know why I clarify that; she's fully aware of that fact. She's just trying to deflect blame. But her kicking me out when she did makes so much more sense now. They had a baby on the way, and I no longer fit into the picture.

I bring both arms up and clasp my hands behind my head, frustrated. Shocked. Then I drop them to the table again and lean forward for clarity. "I have a *brother?* How old is he? Who's his . . . Is he Tim's son?"

"He's eleven. And yes, Tim is his father, but he left years ago. I don't even know where he lives now."

I wait for this to fully hit. I was expecting anything and everything *but* this. I have so many questions, but the most important thing right now is to figure out where this kid is. "When was the last time you saw him?"

"About two weeks ago," she says.

"And you reported it to the police?"

She makes a face. "No. Of course not. He's not missing, he's just trying to piss me off."

I have to squeeze my temples to refrain from raising my voice. I still don't understand how she found me or why she thinks an eleven-year-old kid is trying to teach her a lesson, but I'm laser focused on finding him now. "Did you move back to Boston? Did he go missing here?"

My mother makes a confused face. "Move back?"

It's like we're speaking two different languages. "Did you move back here or do you still live in Maine?"

"Oh, God," she mutters, attempting to remember. "I came back, like, ten years ago? Josh was just a baby."

She's lived here for ten years?

"They're going to arrest me, Atlas."

Her child has been missing for two weeks, and she's more worried about being arrested than she is about him. *Some people never change.* "What do you need me to do?"

"I don't know. I was hoping he reached out to you and that maybe you knew where he was. But if you didn't even know he existed—"

"Why would he reach out to me? Does he know about me? What does he know?"

"Other than your name? Nothing; you were never around."

My adrenaline is rushing through me so fast, I'm shocked I'm still sitting across from her. My whole body is tense when I lean forward. "Let me get this straight. I have a little brother I never knew about, and he thinks I didn't care that he *existed*?"

"I don't think he actively thinks about you, Atlas. You've been absent his whole life."

I ignore her dig because she's wrong. Any kid that age would think about the brother they believed abandoned them. I'm sure he hates the idea of me. Hell, he's probably the one who has been—*Shit. Of course.*

This explains so much. I would bet both of my restaurants that he's the one who has been vandalizing them. And why the misspelling reminded me of my mother. The kid is eleven; I'm sure he's capable of googling my information.

"Where do you live?" I ask her.

She practically squirms in her seat. "We're in between houses, so we've been staying at the Risemore Inn for the past couple of months."

"Go back there in case he shows up," I suggest.

"I can't afford to stay there anymore. I'm in between jobs, so I'm staying with a friend for a couple of days."

I stand up and pull the money out of my pocket. I drop it on the table in front of her. "The number you called me on the other day—is that your cell?"

She nods, sliding the money off the table and into her hand.

"I'll call you if I find out anything. Go back to the hotel and try to get the same room. He needs you to be there if he comes back."

My mother nods, and for the first time, she looks some-what ashamed. I leave her to sit in that feeling without saying goodbye. I'm hoping she's feeling at least a fraction of what she made me feel for years. What she's likely making my little brother feel right now.

I can't believe this. She went and made a whole human and didn't think to tell me?

I walk straight through the kitchen and out the back door. No one is in the alley right now, so I take a moment to pull myself together. I'm not sure I've ever been this stunned.

Her child is out there running the streets of Boston all alone and she waits two goddamn weeks before doing any-thing about it? I don't know why it surprises me. This is who she is. It's who she's always been.

My phone begins to ring. I'm so on edge, I want to throw it at the dumpster, but when I see it's Lily attempting to Face-Time me, I steady myself.

I slide my finger across the screen, prepared to tell her it isn't a good time, but when her face pops up, it feels like the perfect time. I'm relieved to hear from her, even though it's only been an hour since I last saw her. I'd give anything to reach through the phone and hug her.

"Hey." I try to keep my voice stable, but there's a sharp-ness to it that cuts through. She can tell because her expres-sion grows concerned.

"Are you okay?"

I nod. "Things sort of went south after I went back to work. I'm fine, though."

She smiles, but it's kind of sad. "Yeah, my night went south, too."

I didn't notice at first, but it looks like she's been crying. Her eyes are glassy and a little puffy. "Are *you* okay?"

She forces another smile. "I will be. I just wanted to say thank you for tonight before I went to sleep."

I hate that she's not standing in front of me right now. I don't like seeing her sad; it reminds me too much of all the times I saw her sad when we were younger. At least back then I was close enough to hug her. *Maybe I still can.*

"Would a hug make you feel better?"

"Obviously. I'll be fine after I get some sleep, though. Talk tomorrow?"

I have no idea what happened between our date and this phone call, but she looks completely defeated. She looks very similar to how I feel.

"Hugs take two seconds, and you'll sleep so much better. I'll be back here before they even know I've left. What's your address?"

A small grin peeks through her gloom. "You're going to drive five miles just to give me a hug?"

"I'd *run* five miles just to give you a hug."

That makes her smile even bigger. "I'll text you my address. But don't knock too loud; I just put Emmy down."

"See you soon."

Chapter Fourteen
Lily

I've been out of the dating loop for a while, so if *hug* is code for something else, I have no idea.

Surely a hug still just means a hug.

I can barely work social media, much less keep up with slang. I swear, I'm the most out-of-touch millennial I know. It's as if I skipped right over Gen X and into Boomer territory. I'm a Boomer millennial. A *boollennial*. Hell, my mother is a Boomer and probably knows more about these things than I do. She's the one with a new boyfriend. I should call her and ask for pointers.

I brush my teeth, just in case a hug is a *kiss*. And then I change clothes twice, until I end up back in the pajamas I had on when I FaceTimed him. I'm trying way too hard to look like I'm not trying too hard. Sometimes being a woman is so dumb.

I'm pacing my apartment, anxious for his knock. I don't know why I'm so nervous; I just spent three hours with him.

Well, one and a half if I don't count the nap I took in the middle of our date.

Several dozen paces later, there's a light tap on my apartment door. I know it's Atlas, but I glance through the peephole anyway.

He even looks good all distorted through a peephole. I smile when I noticed he changed, too. Just his jacket, but still. He was wearing a thick black coat when we went out earlier, but now he's wearing a simple gray hoodie.

Dear God. I like it so much.

I open the door, and Atlas leaves zero seconds between our first moment of eye contact and when his arms sweep me in for a hug.

He holds me so tight, it makes me want to ask him what was so bad about the last hour, but I don't. I just quietly hug him back. I settle my cheek against his shoulder and revel in the comfort of him.

Atlas didn't even step inside my apartment. We're just standing in the doorway, as if a hug still just means a hug. His cologne is nice. It reminds me of summer, like he's defying the cold. He seemed so concerned about smelling like garlic earlier, but all I could smell was this same cologne.

He lifts a hand to the back of my head and rests it there gently. "You okay?"

"I am now." My response is muffled against him. "You?"

He sighs, but he doesn't say he's okay. He just leaves his answer hanging in his exhale, until he slowly releases me. He lifts a hand and runs his fingers down a piece of my hair. "I hope you get some sleep tonight."

"You too," I say.

"I'm not going home, I'm staying at the restaurant tonight." He shakes that sentence off like he shouldn't have said anything. "It's a long story, and I need to get back. I'll catch you up on everything tomorrow."

I want to invite him in and make him give me all the details right now, but I feel like he'd offer them up if he were in the mood. I'm certainly not in the mood to talk about what happened with Ryle, so I'm not going to force him to talk about whatever put a damper on *his* night. I just wish there was a way I could make it better.

I perk up when I think of something that might do the trick. "Do you need more reading material?"

His eyes glint with a twinge of excitement. "I do, actually."

"Wait here." I head to my bedroom and look in my box of things, searching for the next journal. When I find it, I take it back to him. "This one is a little more graphic," I tease.

Atlas takes the journal with one hand and then slides his other arm around my lower back and tugs me against him. Then, quickly, he steals a peck. It's so soft and fast, it doesn't even fully register that he kissed me until it's over.

"Goodnight, Lily."

"Goodnight, Atlas."

Neither of us moves. It feels like it might hurt if we separate. Atlas pulls me even tighter against him and then he lowers his lips to the spot near my collarbone where my tattoo is hidden beneath my shirt. The tattoo he doesn't even know is there. He kisses it unknowingly, and then, sadly, he leaves.

I close the door and press my forehead against it. I feel all the familiar feelings of a crush, but this time those feelings are accompanied by worry and hesitation, even though it's Atlas, and Atlas is one of the good ones.

I blame Ryle for that. He took what little trust I had left in men thanks to my father, and he stripped me of it.

But I think this crush is a sign that Atlas might be able to give back what my father and Ryle took from me. My stomach moves from the flutters Atlas left me with to what feels like a six-foot drop on that thought, because I know how that would make Ryle feel.

The more joy I get from my interactions with Atlas, the more dread I feel about having to break the news to Ryle.

Chapter Fifteen
Atlas

When I was in the military, I was stationed with a friend who had family from Boston. His aunt and uncle were getting ready to retire and wanted to sell their restaurant. It was called Milla's, and when I visited it on leave one year, I absolutely fell in love with the place. I can say it was the food, or the fact that it was located in Boston, but the truth is, I fell in love with it because of the preserved tree growing in the center of the main dining room.

The tree reminded me of Lily.

If anything is going to remind someone of their first love, trees are probably the last thing you want as a reminder. They're everywhere. Which is probably why I've thought about Lily every day since I was eighteen, but that could also be because I still, to this day, feel like I owe her my life.

I'm not sure if it was the tree, or the fact that the restaurant came almost fully stocked and staffed, but I felt a pull to buy it when it became available. It wasn't my goal to own a restaurant right out of the military. I had planned to work as a chef to gain experience, but when this opportunity presented itself, I couldn't walk away from the prospect. I used the money I saved up from my time as a Marine, and I secured a business loan, bought the restaurant, changed the name, and created a whole new menu.

Sometimes I feel guilty for the success Bib's has had—like I haven't paid my dues. I didn't just inherit the staff, who already knew what they were doing, but I inherited customers as well. I didn't build it from the ground up, which is why I feel a heavy amount of imposter syndrome when people congratulate me on the success of Bib's.

That's why I opened Corrigan's. I don't know that I was trying to prove anything to anyone other than myself, but I wanted to know that I could do it. I wanted the challenge of creating something from nothing and watching it flourish and grow. Like what Lily wrote in her journal about why she liked growing things in her garden when we were teenagers.

Maybe that's why I feel more protective of Corrigan's than I do over Bib's, because I created it from nothing. That might also be the reason I put more effort into protecting it. Corrigan's has a working security system and is a hell of a lot harder to break into than Bib's.

Which is why I chose to spend tonight at Bib's, even though Corrigan's is due to be broken into if we're going by the rotating schedule this kid has developed. The first night was Bib's, the second night was Corrigan's, he took a few days off, and then the third and fourth incidents were at Bib's. I may be wrong, but I have a feeling he'll show up here again before going back to Corrigan's, simply because he's had more success getting into the less secure of the two places. I just hope tonight isn't one of the nights he decides not to show up.

He'll definitely show up here if he's hungry. Bib's is his

better bet for food, which is why I'm hiding on the far side of the dumpster, waiting. I pulled over one of the tattered chairs the smokers use on their breaks, and I've been passing time by reading. Lily's words have kept me company. A little too well, because there have been several times I've been so engrossed in this journal, I forget that I'm supposed to be on alert.

I don't know for certain if the kid who has been vandalizing my restaurants is the same kid who shares a mother with me, but the timing makes sense. And the targeted insults that he's been spray painting make sense if they're coming from a kid who despises me. I can't think of anyone else who would have a good reason to be angry with me more than a little boy who feels abandoned by his older brother.

It's almost two in the morning. I check the security app on my phone for Corrigan's, but there's nothing new happening over there, either.

I go back to reading the journal, even though the last couple of entries have been painful to read. I didn't realize how much my leaving for Boston impacted Lily when she was younger. In my mind at that age, I felt like an inconvenience in her life. I had no idea how much she felt I *brought* to her life. Reading the letters she wrote back then has been a lot more difficult than I expected it to be. I thought it would be fun to read her thoughts, but when I started reading them, I remembered how cruel our childhoods were to us. I don't think about it much anymore because I'm so far removed from the life I lived back then, but I'm being thrown back into those moments from every angle this week, it seems. The information in the journal entries, my mother, finding out I have a brother—it all feels like everything I've tried running from has formed a slow leak that's threatening to sink me.

But then there's Lily and her impeccable timing being back in my life. She always seems to show up when I need a lifeline.

I flip through the rest of the journal and see that I'm already halfway through the last entry she made. I have very little recollection of that night because of the dreadful way it ended. Part of me doesn't even want to experience it from her point of view, but I can't not know how I left her feeling for all those years.

I open the last entry and pick up where I left off.

He took my hands in his and told me he was leaving sooner than he planned for the military, but that he couldn't leave without telling me thank you. He told me he'd be gone for four years and that the last thing he wanted for me was to be a sixteen-year-old girl not living my life because of a boyfriend I never got to see or hear from.

The next thing he said made his blue eyes tear up until they looked clear. He said, "Lily. Life is a funny thing. We only get so many years to live it, so we have to do everything we can to make sure those years are as full as they can be. We shouldn't waste time on things that might happen some-day, or maybe even never."

I knew what he was saying. That he was leaving for the military and he didn't want me to hold on to him while he was gone. He wasn't really breaking up with me be-cause we weren't ever really together. We'd just been two people who helped each other when we needed it and got our hearts fused together along the way.

It was hard, being let go by someone who had never really grabbed hold of me completely in the first place. In all the time we've spent together, I think we both sort of knew this wasn't a forever thing. I'm not sure why, because I could easily love him that way. I think maybe under normal circumstances, if we were together like typical teenagers and he had an average life with a home, we could be that kind of couple. The kind who comes together so easily and never experiences a life where cruelty sometimes intercepts.

I didn't even try to get him to change his mind that night. I feel like we have the kind of connection that even the fires of hell couldn't sever. I feel like he could go spend his time in the military and I'll spend my years being a teenager and then it will all fall back into place when the timing is right.

"I'm going to make a promise to you," he said. "When my life is good enough for you to be a part of it, I'll come find you. But I don't want you to wait around for me, because that might never happen."

I didn't like that promise, because it meant one of two things. Either he thought he might never make it out of the military alive, or he didn't think his life would ever be good enough for me.

His life was already good enough for me, but I nodded my head and forced a smile. "If you don't come back for me, I'll come for you. And it won't be pretty, Atlas Corrigan."

He laughed at my threat. "Well, it won't be too hard to find me. You know exactly where I'll be."

I smiled. "Where everything is better."

He smiled back. "In Boston."

And then he kissed me.

Ellen, I know you're an adult and know all about what comes next, but I still don't feel comfortable telling you what happened over those next couple of hours. Let's just say we both kissed a lot. We both laughed a lot. We both loved a lot. We both breathed a lot. A lot. And we both had to cover our mouths and be as quiet and still as we could so we wouldn't get caught.

When we were finished, he held me against him, skin to skin, hand to heart. He kissed me and looked straight in my eyes.

"I love you, Lily. Everything you are. I love you."

I know those words get thrown around a lot, especially by teenagers. A lot of times prematurely and without much merit. But when he said them to me, I knew he wasn't saying it like he was in love with me. It wasn't that kind of "I love you."

Imagine all the people you meet in your life. There are so many. They come in like waves, trickling in and out with the tide. Some waves are much bigger and make more of an impact than others. Sometimes the waves bring with them things from deep in the bottom of the sea and they leave those things tossed onto the shore. Imprints against the grains of sand that prove the waves had once been there, long after the tide recedes.

That was what Atlas was telling me when he said "I

love you." He was letting me know that I was the biggest wave he'd ever come across. And I brought so much with me that my impressions would always be there, even when the tide rolled out.

After he said he loved me, he told me he had a birthday present for me. He pulled out a small brown bag. "It isn't much, but it's all I could afford."

I opened the bag and pulled out the best present I'd ever received. It was a magnet that said "Boston" on the top. At the bottom in tiny letters, it said, "Where everything is better." I told him I would keep it forever, and every time I look at it I'll think of him.

When I started out this letter, I said my sixteenth birthday was one of the best days of my life. Because up until that second, it was.

It was the next few minutes that weren't.

Before Atlas had shown up that night, I wasn't expecting him, so I didn't think to lock my bedroom door. My father heard me in there talking to someone, and when he threw open my door and saw Atlas in bed with me, he was angrier than I'd ever seen him. And Atlas was at a disadvantage by not being prepared for what came next.

I'll never forget that moment for as long as I live. Being completely helpless as my father came down on him with a baseball bat. The sound of bones snapping was the only thing piercing through my screams.

I still don't know who called the police. I'm sure it was my mother, but it's been six months and we still haven't talked about that night. By the time the police got to my bedroom and pulled my father off of him, I didn't even recognize Atlas, he was covered in so much blood.

I was hysterical.

Hysterical.

Not only did they have to take Atlas away in an ambulance, they also had to call an ambulance for me because I couldn't breathe. It was the first and only panic attack I've ever had.

No one would tell me where he was or if he was even okay. My father wasn't even arrested for what he'd done. Word got out that Atlas had been staying in that old house and that he had been homeless. My father became revered for his heroic act—saving his little girl from the homeless boy who manipulated her into having sex with him.

My father said I'd shamed our whole family by giving the town something to gossip about. And let me tell you, they still gossip about it. I heard Katie on the bus today telling someone she tried to warn me about Atlas. She said she knew he was bad news from the moment she laid eyes on him. Which is crap. If Atlas had been on the bus with me, I probably would have kept my mouth shut and been mature about it like he tried to teach me to be. Instead, I was so angry, I turned around and told Katie she could go to hell. I told her Atlas was a better human than she'd ever be and if I ever heard her say one more bad thing about him, she'd regret it.

She just rolled her eyes and said, "Jesus, Lily. Did he brainwash you? He was a dirty, thieving homeless kid who was probably on drugs. He used you for food and sex and now you're defending him?"

She's lucky the bus stopped at my house right then. I grabbed my backpack and walked off the bus, then went inside and cried in my room for three hours straight. Now my head hurts, but I knew the only thing that would make me feel better is if I finally got it all out on paper. I've been avoiding writing this letter for six months now.

No offense, Ellen, but my head still hurts. So does my heart. Maybe even more right now than it did yesterday. This letter didn't help one damn bit.

I think I'm going to take a break from writing to you for a while. Writing to you reminds me of him, and it just all hurts too much. Until he comes back for me, I'm just going to keep pretending to be okay. I'll keep pretending to swim, when really all I'm doing is floating. Barely keeping my head above water.

—Lily

I close the journal after reading the last page.

I don't know what to feel because I feel everything. Rage, love, sadness, happiness.

I've always hated that I couldn't remember most of that night no matter how hard I tried to think back on every word that was said between us. The fact that Lily wrote it all down is a gift—albeit a sad one.

There were so many things about that time in my life that I was afraid she was too fragile to hear. I only wanted to protect her from the negative stuff going on in my life, but reading her words has shown me that she didn't need protecting from it. If anything, she could have helped me through it.

It makes me want to write her another letter, but even more, it makes me want to be in her presence, talking about these things face-to-face. I know we're taking things slow, but the more I'm around her, the more impatient I am to be around her again.

I stand up to take the journal inside and to grab something to drink for the wait, but I pause as soon as I come to a stand. There's a streetlight at the other end of the alley creating a spotlight on the building, and there's a shadow moving across the light. The shadow travels across the building in the other direction, as if whatever is casting the shadow is coming my way. I back up a step so that I can remain hidden.

Someone eventually comes into view. A kid closes in on the back door.

I don't know if this kid is my brother, but it's definitely the same person I saw on the security footage at Corrigan's. The same clothes, the same hoodie tightened around their face.

I remain hidden and watch them, becoming more and more convinced by the second that it's exactly who I think it is. He's built like me. He even moves like me. I'm filled with anxious energy because I want to meet him. I want to tell him that I'm not angry and that I know what he's going through.

I'm not sure I was even angry at whoever was doing this before I knew it could potentially be my brother. It's hard to be angry at a kid, but it's especially hard to be angry at one who was raised by the same woman who attempted to raise me. I know what it's like to have to do what you can to survive. I also know what it's like when you'd do anything to get someone's attention. *Anyone's.* There were times in my child-hood I just wanted to be noticed, and I have a feeling that's exactly what's going on here.

He's hoping to be caught. This is more a cry for attention than anything.

He walks right up to the back door of the restaurant without an ounce of hesitation. This place has become famil-iar to him. He checks the back door to see if it's locked. When it doesn't open, he pulls a new can of spray paint out of his hoodie. I wait for him to lift it, and that's when I decide to make my presence known.

"You're holding it wrong." My voice startles him. When he spins around and looks up at me and I see how young he really is, my heartstrings stretch so tight, it feels like they're about to pop. I try to imagine Theo out here alone in the middle of the night like this.

There's still a youthfulness to the fear in his eyes. When I start walking toward him, he backs up a step, looking around for a quick escape. But he doesn't attempt to run.

I'm sure he's curious about what's going to happen. Isn't this why he's been showing up here night after night?

I hold out my hand for the can of spray paint. He hesi-tates, but then hands it to me. I demonstrate how to hold it the proper way. "If you do it like this, it won't drip. You hold it too close."

Every emotion is running across his face as he studies me, from anger to fascination to betrayal. The two of us are quiet as we take in just how much we look alike. We both took after our mother. Same jawline, same light eyes, same mouths, down to the unintentional frown. It's a lot for me to take in. I've been resigned to the idea that I had no family, yet here he is in the flesh. It makes me wonder what he's feeling while he looks back at me. Anger, obviously. Disappointment.

I lean a shoulder against the building, looking down at him with complete transparency. "I didn't know you existed, Josh. Not until a few hours ago."

The kid shoves his hands into the pockets of his hoodie and looks at his feet. "Bullshit," he mutters.

The hardness in him at such a young age makes me sad. I ignore the anger in his response and pull my keys out to unlock the back door to the restaurant. "You hungry?" I hold the door open for him.

He looks like he wants to run, but after a moment of indecision, he ducks his head and walks inside.

I flip on the lights and make my way into the kitchen. I grab the ingredients to make him a grilled cheese and I start cooking while he walks around slowly, taking everything in. He touches things, opens drawers, cabinets. Maybe he's taking inventory for the next time he decides to break in. Or maybe his curiosity is a cover for his fear.

I'm plating his food when he finally speaks up. "How do you know who I am if you didn't know I existed?"

This feels like it could lead to a lengthy conversation, and I'd rather have it while he's more comfortable. There isn't a table back here with seating, so I motion toward the doors that lead into the dining room. There's enough light from the exit signs that I don't have to power up the dining room lights.

"Sit here." I point to table eight and he takes a seat in the exact spot our mother sat in earlier tonight. He starts eating as soon as I set his food down. "What do you want to drink?"

He swallows, and then shrugs. "Whatever."

I go back to the kitchen and pour him a glass of ice water and then slide into the booth across from him. He drinks half of it in one gulp.

"Your mother showed up here tonight," I say. "She's looking for you."

He makes a face that indicates he doesn't care, and then he continues eating.

"Where have you been staying?"

"Places," he says with a mouthful.

"Are you in school?"

"Not lately."

I let him get in a few more bites before I continue. The last thing I want to do is run him off with too many questions. "Why did you run away?" I ask. "Because of her?"

"Sutton?"

I nod. I wonder what kind of relationship they have if he doesn't even call her "Mom."

"Yeah, we got in a fight. We always fight over the stupidest shit." He eats his last bite, then downs the rest of his water.

"And your dad? Tim?"

"He left when I was little." His eyes roam around the room, landing on the tree. When he looks back at me, he tilts his head. "Are you rich?"

"If I was, I wouldn't tell you. You've tried to rob me several times now."

I can see a smirk playing across his lips, but he refuses to release it. He relaxes into the booth more, pulling his hoodie away from his face. Strands of greasy brown hair fall forward, and he pushes them back. His hair holds the shape of a cut that's long overdue, with sides that have grown out too long and uneven to be intentional.

"She told me you left because of me. She said you didn't want a brother."

I have to hold back my irritation. I pull his empty plate of food and his glass toward me, and I stand up. "I didn't know about you until today, Josh. I swear. I would have been around if I had."

He eyes me from his seat, studying me. Wondering if he can trust me. "You know about me now." He says that like it's a challenge to do better. To prove his low expectations of the world wrong.

I nudge my head toward the doors to the kitchen. "You're right. Let's go."

He doesn't immediately get out of the booth. "Where to?"

"My house. I have a room for you as long as you stop cussing so much."

He raises an eyebrow. "What are you, some kind of religious nutjob?"

I motion for him to stand up. "An eleven-year-old muttering cuss words all the time seems desperate. It's not cool until you're at least fourteen."

"I'm not eleven, I'm twelve."

"Oh. She said you were eleven. *Still*. Too young to be cool."

Josh stands up and starts to follow me through the kitchen.

I spin and face him as I push back through the doors.

"And for future reference, you spelled *asshole* wrong. There's no *w*."

He looks surprised. "I thought that looked funny after I wrote it."

I put his dishes in the sink, but it's almost three in the morning and I'm not in the mood to wash them. I flip out the lights and have Josh lead the way out the back door. When I'm locking it, he says, "Are you going to tell Sutton where I am?"

"I don't know what I'm going to do yet," I admit. I start walking down the alley, and he rushes to catch up with me.

"I'm thinking of going to Chicago, anyway," he says. "I probably won't stay more than one night at your place."

I laugh at the idea that this kid thinks I'm going to allow him to run off to another city now that I know he exists. *What am I getting myself into?* I have a feeling my day-to-day responsibilities have just doubled. "Do we have any other siblings I don't know about?" I ask him.

"Just the twins, but they're only eight."

I stop in my tracks and look at him.

He grins. "I'm kidding. It's just the two of us."

I shake my head and grab the back of his hoodie, pulling it down over his head. "You're something."

He's smiling when we make it to my car. I'm smiling, too, until I feel a sharp stab of worry in the center of my gut.

I've known him for half an hour. I've known *of* him for a fraction of a day. Yet I suddenly feel like I'll be protective of him for a lifetime.

Chapter Sixteen
Lily

You lose your mornings after having children.

I used to open my eyes and lie in bed for several minutes before grabbing my phone and catching up on everything I might have missed while I slept. I'd have a cup of coffee, and then mentally map out my day while I showered.

But now that I have Emmy, her early morning cry rips me out of bed, and I become her gopher before I even have time to pee. I rush to change her, rush to clothe her, rush to feed her. By the time I'm finished with morning mother duties, I'm late for work and barely have time to do those things for myself.

It's why I cherish Sunday mornings. It feels like the only day of the week I get any sense of calm. When Emmy wakes up on Sundays, I always bring her back to bed with me. We lie together and I listen to her babble and there's absolutely no rush to get up or be somewhere.

Sometimes, like right now, she falls back to sleep, and I just stare at her for long stretches of time—marveling at the wonder that is motherhood.

I grab my phone and take a picture of her to text to Ryle, but I hesitate before hitting send. I don't miss Ryle at all, but it does make me sad in moments like this that Ryle doesn't get to do this with us, or that I don't get to share in the joys *they* have together. There's nothing better than adoring the child you made with the person you made them with, which is why I always try to text him pictures and videos. But I'm still upset about last night and don't really feel like reaching out yet. I save the picture for a more peaceful day.

Fucking Ryle.

Divorce is difficult. I knew it would be, but it's so much harder than I anticipated. And navigating divorce with a child in the mix is a million times trickier. You're stuck interacting with that person for the remainder of your life. You have to either figure out a way to plan birthday parties together or figure out a way to be okay with having separate celebrations. You have to plan on which holidays each of you get to spend with your child, which days of the week, down to which hours of the day sometimes.

You can't snap your fingers and be done with the person you married and divorced. You're stuck with them. Forever.

I'm stuck dealing with Ryle's feelings forever, and frankly, I'm growing tired of always feeling sorry for him, worried for him, fearful of him, *considerate* of his feelings.

How long am I supposed to wait before I start dating someone else without Ryle being justified in his jealousy? How long do I have to wait before I tell him I'm dating Atlas if Atlas and I become a thing? How long until I get to start making decisions about my own life without worrying about his feelings?

My phone vibrates. It's my mother calling. I slide softly out of the bed to walk to the living room before answering it.

"Hey."

"Can I have Emerson today?"

I laugh at her blatant disregard for her daughter now that she has a granddaughter. "I'm good, how are you?" My mother loves Emmy as much as I do—I'm convinced of that. When Emmy turned six weeks old, my mother started taking her for a few hours at a time while I worked. She actually stayed at her house overnight last month—it was Emmy's first night away from me since she'd been born. She had fallen asleep at my mother's, and neither of us wanted to wake her, so I went back for her the next morning.

"Rob and I are close by; we could come pick her up in twenty minutes. We're going to the botanical gardens; I thought it would be fun to get her out. I'm sure you could use the break."

"Yeah, sure. I'll get her dressed."

• • •

Half an hour later, there's a knock at my door. I open it and let my mother and Rob inside. My mother beelines across the living room, straight to Emmy, who is on a pallet on the floor.

"Hi, Mom." I say it teasingly.

"Look at this adorable outfit," my mother says, picking her up. "Did I buy her this?"

"No, it's a hand-me-down from Rylee, actually." It's nice that Rylee is six months older. We haven't had to buy Emmy many clothes because Allysa gives me more than enough of Rylee's. And they're always in great condition because I don't think Rylee ever wears an outfit twice.

Emmy is wearing the outfit Rylee wore at her first birthday party. I was hoping it would eventually be passed down to Emmy, because it's adorable. It's a pair of pink leggings with green whole watermelons on them, and a green long-sleeved top with a pink slice of watermelon in the center of it.

My mother has bought almost everything else Emmy wears, including the blue jacket I'm putting on her right now.

"That doesn't match her outfit," my mother says. "Where's the pink jacket I bought her?"

"It's too little, and it's a jacket, and she's one year old. It doesn't matter if she doesn't match."

My mother huffs, and I can tell by that look on her face that Emmy is going to come home in a brand-new jacket this afternoon. I kiss Emmy on the cheek, and my mother heads for the door.

I hand Rob the diaper bag, and he hoists it over his shoulder. "Want me to carry her?" he asks my mother.

She squeezes Emmy tighter. "I've got her." She addresses me over her shoulder. "We'll be back in a few hours."

"About what time?" I ask her. I don't usually clarify a time with her, but I'm thinking about asking Atlas what he's doing right now. We can maybe grab lunch since we're both off today and I'm kid-free.

"I'll text you. Why? Are you going somewhere?" she asks. "I figured you'd just catch up on sleep."

I don't dare tell her I might sneak away to meet a guy. She'd ask me questions well past the botanical garden closing hours. "Yeah, I'll probably just sleep. I'll keep my phone on, though. Have fun."

My mother is out the door and down the hallway, but Rob pauses and looks at me. "Make sure you park your car in the same spot. She'll notice if you move it, and she'll ask questions." He winks, a clear indication that he can read me better than she can.

"Thanks for the heads-up," I whisper.

I close the door and go find my phone. I've been rushing to get Emmy dressed and out the door, so I haven't looked at my phone since I hung up with my mother. I have a missed call from Atlas from twenty minutes ago.

My stomach flips with anticipation. I hope he's off today. I use my phone camera to check my appearance, and then I call him back over video chat.

I hated when he called me over video chat the first time, but now it feels like the natural thing to do. I always want to see his face. I like seeing what he's wearing and where he's at and the faces he makes when he says the things he says.

I'm already smiling when I hear the sound that indicates he's answered the call. He lifts the phone, and when I finally make out what I'm looking at, I can see he's standing in an unfamiliar kitchen. It's white and bright and different from the kitchen I remember when I visited his house almost two years ago.

"Morning," he says. He's smiling, but he looks tired, like he either just woke up or is about to fall asleep.

"Hey."

"Sleep well?" he asks.

"I did. Finally." I squint my eyes trying to see past him. "Did you remodel your kitchen?"

Atlas glances over his shoulder, and then looks back at me. "I moved."

"What? When?"

"Earlier this year. Sold my house and got a place closer to the restaurant."

"Oh. That's nice." Closer to the restaurant means closer to me. I wonder how far apart we live now. "Are you cooking?"

Atlas aims his phone at his countertop. There's a pan of eggs, a pile of bacon, pancakes, and . . . *two plates. Two* glasses of juice. My heart drops. "That's a lot of food," I say, attempting to hide the immense jealousy running through me.

"I'm not alone," he says, panning the screen back to his face.

My disappointment must be clearly written all over me, because he immediately shakes his head.

"No, Lily. That's not . . ." He laughs and seems flustered. His reaction is adorable but not entirely reassuring yet. He holds the phone up a little higher until I can see a person standing behind him. I'm not sure who's with him, but it isn't another woman.

It's a kid.

A kid who looks just like Atlas, and he's staring right at me with eyes that look identical to Atlas's eyes. *Does he have a child I don't know about?*

What is going on?

"She thinks I'm your son," the kid says. "You're freaking her out."

Atlas immediately aims the phone back at his own face. "He's not my son. He's my brother."

Brother?

Atlas moves the phone so that I'm looking at his brother again. "Say hi to Lily."

"No."

Atlas rolls his eyes and shoots me an apologetic look. "He's kind of a jerk." He says that right in front of his little brother.

"Atlas!" I whisper, shocked at every part of this conversation.

"It's okay, he knows he's a jerk."

I see the kid laugh behind him, so I know he knows Atlas is kidding. But I am so confused. "I had no idea you had a brother."

"I didn't know, either. Found out last night after our date."

I think back on last night and how it was obvious something was bothering him about the text he received, but I had no idea it was a family issue. I guess this explains why his mother was trying to contact him. "Sounds like you have a lot to work through today."

"Wait, don't hang up yet," he says. He walks out of the kitchen and into another room for privacy. He closes a door and sits down on his bed. "Biscuits still have about ten minutes, I can chat."

"Wow. Pancakes *and* biscuits. He's a lucky kid. I had black coffee for breakfast."

Atlas smiles, but his smile doesn't reach his eyes. He seemed like he was in a good mood in front of his brother, but now that I have him alone, I can see the stress in the way he's holding himself. "Where's Emmy?" he asks.

"My mother has her for a few hours."

When it registers that we're both off work and I don't have Emmy, he sighs like he's bummed. "You mean you actually have a free day?"

"It's okay, we're taking it slow, remember? Besides, it's not every day you find out you have a little brother."

He dives a hand through his hair and sighs. "He's the one who has been vandalizing the restaurants."

I startle at that comment. I need to hear more of this story.

"That's why my mother tried calling me last week, to see if I'd heard from him. I feel like a dick for blocking her number now."

"You didn't know." I'm standing in my living room, but I want to sit down for this conversation. I walk to the couch and set my phone on the arm of it, propping it up with the PopSocket. "Did he know about you?"

Atlas nods. "Yeah, and he thought I knew about him, which is why he was taking out his anger on my restaurants. Other than the thousands of dollars he cost me, he seems like a good kid. Or he at least seems like he has the potential to be a good kid. I don't know, he's gone through a lot of the shit I went through with my mother, so there's no telling what that's done to him."

"Is your mother there, too?"

Atlas shakes his head. "I haven't told her I found him yet. I spoke to a friend of mine who's a lawyer, and he said the sooner I tell her the better, so she can't use it against me."

Use it against him? "Are you wanting to get custody of him?"

Atlas nods without hesitation. "I don't know if that's what Josh wants, but there isn't another option I could live with. I know what kind of mother she is. He mentioned wanting to find his father, but Tim is even worse than my mother."

"What kind of rights do you have as his brother? Any?"

Atlas shakes his head. "Not unless my mother agrees to let him live with me. Not looking forward to that conversation. She'll say no just to spite me, but . . ." Atlas releases a heavy sigh. "If he stays with her, he won't have a chance in hell. He's already harder than I was at that age. Angrier. I'm afraid of what that anger might turn into if he doesn't gain some stability in his life. But who's to say I'm capable of something like this? What if I fuck him up more than my mother has?"

"You won't, Atlas. You know you won't."

He accepts my reassurance with a quick flash of a smile. "That's easy for you to say; you're a natural at this whole raising-kids thing."

"I just fake it well," I say. "I have no idea what I'm doing. No parent does. We're all full of imposter syndrome, winging it every minute of the day."

"Why is that both comforting and terrifying?" he asks.

"You just summed up parenthood with those two words."

He exhales. "I should probably get back in there and make sure he isn't robbing me. I'll call you later today, okay?"

"Okay. Good luck."

The way Atlas silently mouths the word *goodbye* in return is sexy as hell.

When I end the call, I fall onto my bed and sigh. I love the way I feel after I talk to him. He makes me giddy and energized and happy, even when the call is as shocking and chaotic as that one was.

I wish I knew where he lived. I'd go give him a drive-by hug like the one he gave me last night. I hate that he's dealing with this, but at the same time I'm happy for him. I can't imagine how alone he's felt since I met him, not having a single family member in his life.

And that poor kid. It's like Atlas all over again, as if one kid feeling that unloved by their mother wasn't enough.

My phone chimes, indicating I have a text. I smile when I see it's from him. I smile even bigger when I see how long the text is.

Thank you for being the most comforting part of my life right now. Thank you for always being the beacon I need every time I feel lost. Whether you mean to shine on me or not. I am grateful for you. I've missed you. I absolutely should have kissed you.

I'm covering my mouth with my hand when I finish reading it. I'm filled with so much emotion, I don't know where to put it.

Josh is lucky to have you in his life now.

Within seconds, Atlas hearts my text. Then I send another one.

And you're right. You absolutely should have kissed me.

Atlas hearts that text, too.

Chapter Seventeen
Atlas

Josh doesn't trust me, but I'll wear him down. I'm willing to bet he doesn't trust anyone, so I'm not taking it personally. If his childhood is anything like mine was, I'm sure he's been toughened at the age of twelve in a way that no kid should be familiar with.

As much as he glares at me with distrustful eyes, I can also sense that he's curious about me. He doesn't ask many questions, but he watches me in a way that makes it obvious he has a million questions on the tip of his tongue. For whatever reason, he keeps swallowing them down. He's probably wondering why I went so easy on him last night after finding out he's the one who damaged my restaurants. He's also probably wondering why I didn't know about him, and how I turned out so vastly different from my mother and Tim.

Whatever he's wondering, he's attempting to keep a tight lid on his expressions. I don't want to make him feel uncomfortable, so I've been doing most of the talking while he eats breakfast. It's not that hard; I have just as many questions for him as he does for me. It's one of the reasons I couldn't sleep last night when we finally made it to my house. I kept listening for the sound of him trying to sneak out of the house. I was honestly shocked he was still here this morning.

As much as my questions are probably annoying him, I can remember what it was like to be twelve. All I wanted was for someone to be interested in who I was, even if they were faking interest. If his life is anything like mine was, he's gone twelve years being ignored, and I refuse to allow him to feel that way under my roof. But I've only been asking him safe questions. I'll ease into the more difficult stuff.

Josh eats one thing at a time. A biscuit first, then bacon. He's cutting into the pancakes for the first time when I say, "What are you interested in? Any hobbies?"

He takes a bite, and one of his eyebrows raises a bit, but I don't know if it's because of the food or my question. "Why?"

"Why am I asking you what you're interested in?"

His neck is stiff when he nods.

"I've missed twelve years of your life. I want to know who you are."

Josh breaks eye contact and forks more pancakes into his mouth. "Manga," he mutters.

That surprises me. But thanks to Theo, I actually know what manga is. "What's your favorite series?"

"*One Piece.*" He shakes his head, erasing that answer. "No, *Chainsaw Man* is probably my favorite."

That's about as far into that conversation as I can go without sounding ignorant. "We can go to a bookstore later today if you want."

He nods. "These are good pancakes."

"Thanks."

I watch him take a drink of his juice, and when he sets the glass down, he says, "What are you interested in?" He nods toward the plate. "Other than cooking."

I don't know how to answer that. Most of my time is given to my restaurants. Whatever time I have left over is spent on house repairs, laundry, sleep. "I like the Cooking Channel."

Josh chuckles. "That's sad."

"Why?"

"I said besides cooking."

It's a harder question than I thought, now that it's being thrown back at me. "I like museums," I say. "And going to the movies. And traveling. I just don't do any of those things."

"Because you're always working?"

"Yeah."

"Like I said. Sad." He leans over his plate to catch another bite of pancake.

The get-to-know-you questions are backfiring, so I cut right to the chase. "What was your fight about?"

He shrugs. "Half the time I don't even know what the hell I do wrong. She just gets mad for no reason."

I can relate to that. I let him eat for a while before I pose another question. "Where have you been staying?"

Josh doesn't look at me. He scoots food around on his plate for a moment, and then says, "Your restaurant." His eyes slowly journey back over to mine. "You have a really comfortable couch in your office."

"You've been sleeping *inside* the restaurant? For how long?"

"Two weeks."

I'm in shock. "How have you been getting in?"

"You don't have an alarm at that one restaurant, and I finally figured out how to pick the lock after a few tries. Your other restaurant was too hard to get into, though."

"You know how to pick . . ." I can't help but laugh. Brad and Darin are going to love saying *I told you so.* "Why'd you go from sleeping there to vandalizing it?"

Josh looks at me reluctantly. "I don't know. I guess I was mad." He pushes his plate away and leans back in his chair. "What now? Do I have to go back to her?"

"What do you want to happen?"

"I want to live with my dad." He scratches at his elbow. "Can you help me find him?"

I want to find Tim about as much as I wanted to find my mother, which is not at all. "Do you know anything about him?"

"I think he lives in Vermont now. I just don't know where."

"When's the last time you saw him?"

"A few years ago. But he doesn't know where to find me anymore."

Josh looks every bit his age right now. A fragile kid, abandoned by his father but refusing to lose hope. I don't want to be the one to rip that from him, so I just nod. "Yeah, I'll see what I can do. But for now, I need to let your mother know you're okay. I have to call her."

"Why?"

"If I don't, this could be considered kidnapping."

"Not if I'm here willingly," he says.

"Even if you're here willingly. You aren't old enough to decide where you want to live, and right now, your mother has legal custody of you."

He grows visibly irritated. He stabs at his breakfast with a scowl, but doesn't take another bite.

I step away to call Sutton. I unblocked her number after she left my restaurant last night in case she needed to get in touch with me. I dial her number and put the phone to my ear. After a few rings, she finally answers with a very groggy hello.

"Hey. I found him."

"Who is this?"

I briefly close my eyes while I wait for her to wake up and remember her son is missing. After a few quiet seconds, she goes, "Atlas?"

"Yeah. I found Josh."

I can hear rustling from her end like she's hopping out of bed. "Where has he been?"

I really don't want to answer that. I know she's his mother, but I feel like it's none of her business where he's been, which is an unusual opinion to have. "I'm not sure where he's been, but he's with me now. Listen . . . I was wondering if he could stay here for a while? Maybe give you a break?"

"You want him to stay there with *you?*" The way she puts the emphasis on that last word makes me wince. This is going to be harder than I thought. She's the type of person who fights for the sake of fighting, no matter what outcome she really wants.

I could enroll him in school and make sure he attends," I offer up. "Take the truancy heat off you." It's quiet on her end, like maybe she's contemplating that.

"Such a *martyr,*" she mutters. "Bring him back. Now." She ends the call.

I attempt to call her back three times, but she sends the calls to voice mail.

"That didn't sound promising," Josh says. He's standing

in the doorway of the kitchen. I'm not sure how much he heard on my end, but at least he couldn't hear her end.

I slide my phone in my pocket. "She wants you back today. But I'll call a lawyer tomorrow. Hell, I'll call Child Protective Services if you want me to. There's just not much I can do on a Sunday."

Josh's shoulders drop when I say that. "Will you at least give me your phone number?" He asks that like he's scared I'm going to say no.

"Of course. I'm not going to abandon you now that I know you exist."

He picks at a hole in his sleeve, avoiding eye contact with me when he says, "I wouldn't blame you for being mad at me. I cost you a lot of money."

"You did do that," I say. "Those croutons were expensive."

Josh laughs for the first time this morning. "Dude, those croutons were fucking *delicious*."

I groan. "Don't use that word."

•   •   •

The Risemore Inn is clear on the other side of Boston. It takes us forty-five minutes with traffic to get there, and it's not even a weekday. When we pull into the parking lot, Josh doesn't immediately get out of the car. He just sits quietly in the passenger seat, staring at the building like it's the last place he wants to be.

I wish I didn't have to return him to his mother, but I put in another call to my lawyer friend this morning after talking with Sutton. He said if I want to go about this the right way without her having ammunition against me, the only thing I can do is return him. And then, if I want to take her to court, he said I need to get a lawyer and go through the process.

Anything done *outside* the process could be a mark against me.

Apparently, you can't just kidnap your sibling, even if you know they're in danger.

I wanted to explain all of this to Josh in more detail—to let him know I'm not just abandoning him with her—but he's so hell-bent that he's going to live with his dad, I'm not sure he even wants to live with me. And I'm not sure I'm prepared to raise a little brother, but as long as I'm alive, there's no way I can willingly leave him in this woman's permanent custody without at least trying.

Until I can figure out what to do next, I don't want him to find himself in a situation where he has no food to eat, or no money to extend their hotel stay. I pull out my wallet and hand him a credit card.

"Can I trust you with this?"

Josh looks at the credit card in my hand, and his eyes grow a little wide. "I don't know why you would. I've spent the last two weeks trying to destroy your businesses."

I push the credit card toward him. "Use it for basic ne-cessities. Food, minutes for your phone." We stopped on the way here and got him a prepaid phone so he could stay in touch with me. "Maybe some new clothes that fit."

Josh reluctantly takes the credit card out of my hand. "I don't even know how to use one of these."

"You just swipe it. But don't tell Sutton you have it." I

point at his phone. "Hide it between your case and your phone."

He pops the case off his phone and puts the credit card inside of it. Then he says, "Thank you." He puts his hand on the car door. "Are you coming to talk to her?"

I shake my head. "It's probably best if I don't. It'll probably just make her angrier."

Josh sighs, and then gets out of the car. We stare at each other for a few seconds before he finally closes the car door.

I feel like such a dick bringing him back here. But I have to do this the right way. If I don't return him, she could file charges on me. And knowing her, she probably would. It's best if I just leave him for today and then as soon as the week begins tomorrow, I can make phone calls and figure out what I can do to move him in with me.

I know if he stays here with her, he isn't going to have a chance in hell. I lucked out finding Lily. She saved my life. But I'm not sure there's enough luck in the world for *both* of us to be saved by a random stranger.

I'm all he has.

I remain in my car as Josh makes his way across the parking lot. He walks up the stairs and knocks on the second door from the end. He looks over his shoulder at me, so I wave right as the door swings open.

I can see the rage in Sutton's eyes all the way from my position in the parking lot. She immediately begins yelling at him. *And then she slaps him.*

My hand is on the door handle before Josh even has a chance to react to the slap. Sutton's hand is now gripping Josh's arm as she yanks him into the hotel room. I'm several feet away from my car when I see him trip over the threshold and disappear into the room.

I'm taking the stairs two at a time, my heart racing. I reach the door before she even closes it. Josh is still trying to scramble to his feet, but she's hovering over him, scolding him.

"I could have gone to *jail*, you little shit!"

She has no idea I'm behind her. I wrap my arm around her waist and pull her away from Josh by picking her up and dropping her onto the mattress behind me. It happens so fast, she's too shocked to react.

I help Josh to his feet. His phone is a few feet away on the floor, so I grab it and hand it to him, then urge him toward the door.

Sutton realizes what's happening, and she jumps off the bed. She's following us out the door. "Bring him back!" I feel her hands on me now. She's yanking at my shirt, trying to get me to stop or move aside so she can get to Josh.

I urge him forward. "Go to the car." He continues toward the stairs, and then I stop walking and spin around to face her. She sucks in a quick gasp after seeing the absolute fury in my eyes. Then she slaps her palms against my chest and shoves me.

"He's *my* son!" she yells. "I'll call the police!"

I release an exasperated laugh. I want to tell her to call the police. I want to scream at her. But most of all, I want to get Josh away from her. She's not going to ruin his life on my watch.

I don't even have the energy to say anything to her at all. This woman isn't worth my words. I just walk away, leaving her screaming at me like old times.

Josh is already sitting in the front seat of my car when I make it back. I slam my door and grip my steering wheel with both hands before starting the car. I need to calm myself down before I get back on the road.

Josh seems unusually calm for what just happened. It makes me wonder if that's an average interaction between them because he isn't even breathing heavily. He's not crying. He's not cussing. He's just watching me, and I realize how I react in this moment is quite possibly something he'll absorb for a lifetime.

I slide my hands down the steering wheel and calmly exhale.

Josh's cheek is red, and there's a small gash on his forehead that's bleeding. I retrieve a napkin from the glove box and hand it to him, then flip the visor down so he can see where to wipe.

"I saw her slap you, but where'd the cut come from?"

"I think I hit the TV stand."

Slow and steady, Atlas. I put my car in reverse and back out of the parking lot. "Maybe we should swing by the emergency room and have them check out your cut. Make sure you don't have a concussion."

"It's okay. I can usually tell when it's a concussion."

He can usually tell? I clench my jaw as soon as he says that. I realize I have absolutely no idea what kind of hell this kid has already been through, and I was about to send him right back into the fire. "Better to be safe," I say, but what I mean is, *Better to get this documented in case we need proof of her abuse at a later date.*

Chapter Eighteen
Lily

It's been five days since I've seen Atlas. I try not to stress over how busy we are because I know it'll get better once I'm comfortable enough to let him spend time around Emmy. But the responsible thing to do is to let Emmy's father know when I start seeing someone else before I bring anyone around her.

It's just frustrating that the responsible thing to do is also a terrifying thing to do. I plan to put it off for as long as possible. There's no shame in being patient.

The flower shop is understaffed this week with Lucy's upcoming wedding, and Atlas has been dealing with legal stuff regarding custody, running two businesses, and taking care of a kid. On top of all that, the fever my mother had last week turned into the full-fledged flu, so she hasn't been able to watch Emmy at all. I've brought her with me two out of the three days I've worked this week.

It's just been a week from hell. Too busy to even get a drive-by hug.

Ryle and Marshall took the girls to the zoo today. Emmy is more than likely too young to enjoy it, so it should make for an interesting day for Ryle.

The custody exchange was fine this morning, even though we haven't spoken since our conversation on the roof last week about her middle name. He was a little curt, but I prefer his curtness to the subtle passes he sometimes still makes at me.

Allysa is working with me today since she doesn't have Rylee. She just returned with coffee now that we're caught up on everything. We got all our orders out with the delivery truck an hour ago, so this is the first time we've actually had time to speak in private since my date with Atlas last week.

Allysa hands me my coffee and then taps the mouse on the computer to check for new online orders.

"What are you wearing to Lucy's wedding?" I ask her.

"We're not going."

"What?"

"We can't. It's my parents' fortieth wedding anniversary. Ryle and I are doing that surprise dinner."

She told me about that, but I had no idea it was the same day as Lucy's wedding.

"It's the only evening Ryle could get away," she says.

I deflate. I hate Ryle's schedule. I know it'll get better over time, when he's no longer one of the newest surgeons on staff, but even when his hours aren't making custody difficult, he's making my best friend choose between a wedding and her parents.

I know it's not Ryle's fault, but I like silently blaming stuff on him that he has no control over. It feels good.

"Does Lucy know you aren't going?"

Allysa nods. "She's fine with it. Two less mouths to feed." She takes a sip of her coffee. "Are you taking Atlas?"

"I didn't invite him. I thought you and Marshall were going, and I didn't want to ask you and Marshall to lie for me again." I felt bad that I asked Allysa to watch Emmy last week for my date because I knew she'd have to lie to Ryle if it came up. And she *did* end up having to lie to him.

"When are you planning to tell Ryle you're back on the dating scene?"

I groan. "Do I have to?"

"He'll find out eventually."

"I wish I could just pretend I was dating some guy named Greg. I don't know that he'd be as threatened by a Greg. Maybe I don't have to be specific about who I'm dating, and he won't be as angry. I'll ease him into the knowledge of it being Atlas after a decade or two."

Allysa laughs, but then she looks at me curiously. "Why does Ryle hate Atlas so much, anyway?"

"He didn't like that I kept mementos from back when Atlas and I dated."

Allysa is staring at me. Waiting. "What else?"

I shake my head. There's nothing else. "What do you mean?"

"Did you cheat on Ryle with Atlas?"

"*What?* No. *God,* no. I never would have done that to Ryle." I'm a little offended by her question, but then again I'm not. Ryle's reaction would naturally make anyone question what led to that kind of reaction.

Allysa's eyes are swimming in puzzlement. "I still don't get it. If you weren't actively cheating on him with the guy, why does Ryle hate him?"

I release an exaggerated sigh. "I've asked myself that a million times, Allysa."

She makes an annoyed face only siblings could reserve

for each other. "I never wanted to ask because I thought you were ashamed that you cheated on my brother and just didn't want to tell me."

"I haven't even kissed Atlas since I was sixteen. Ryle just couldn't handle that my past sometimes crept into my present, in an absolutely platonic way."

"Wait. You haven't kissed Atlas since you were sixteen?" She latched on to the absolute wrong point of this conversation. "Not even on your date last week?"

"We're taking it slow. And that's fine by me. The slower we take things, the more time it gives me before I have to break it to your brother."

"I think you should just rip off the Band-Aid." She points at my phone on the counter. "Text Ryle right now and tell him you're dating Atlas. He'll get over it; he doesn't have a choice."

"This is something I need to tell him in person."

"You're too considerate."

"You're too naïve. If you think Ryle is going to *get over it,* you don't know your brother very well."

"I've never claimed to." Allysa sighs and drops her chin into her hand. "Marshall told me he told you I cheated on him."

I am so glad she's changing the subject. "Yeah, that was a shock."

"Drunken mistake. I was nineteen; nothing counts before you turn twenty-one."

I laugh. "Is that right?"

"Yep." She hops on the counter and starts swinging her legs. "Tell me more about Atlas. Tell me like I'm your best friend and not your ex-husband's sister."

And we're back to this conversation. That was a quick break. "You sure this isn't awkward for you?"

"Why, because Ryle is my brother? No, not awkward at all. He should have been nicer to you, and then you wouldn't have to date Greek gods." She wiggles her eyebrows with a grin. "So, what's he like? He seems mysterious."

"He's not, really. Not to me." I can feel the smile wanting to spread across my face, so I let it. "He's so easy to talk to. And he's kind. He's *Marshall* kind, but not as outgoing. He's more reserved. He works a lot, and I have Emmy all the time, so it's been hard to make time for anything together. Plus, he just found out he has a little brother this week, so his life is kind of chaotic right now. Texts and phone calls are our primary source of communication, so that sucks."

"Is that why you keep checking your phone?"

I can feel my cheeks warm when she says that. I hate that she's noticed. I've tried my best to be inconspicuous with this. I don't want anyone to know how often Atlas and I text, or how often I *think* about texting him, or how often I think *about* him.

Maybe I'm scared to talk about it with Allysa because I don't want to allow myself to be happy about Atlas until I know Ryle isn't going to be furious over Atlas.

I receive a text right in the middle of that thought, and it takes everything in me to fight my smile when I look at my phone and read it.

"Is that him?" Allysa asks.

I nod.

"What's he saying?"

"He asked me if I want him to bring me lunch."

"*Yes*," Allysa says emphatically. "Tell him you're starving, and so is your friend."

I laugh and then reply to Atlas with, **Could you bring lunch for two today? My coworker gets jealous when you bring me food.**

He immediately replies with, **Be there in an hour.**

· · ·

When Atlas finally shows up, both Allysa and I are busy with customers. He's carrying a brown paper bag. I motion for him to wait by the counter, so he stands patiently while we finish up. Allysa is finished first, and for at least five minutes, she and Atlas are having a conversation I can't hear from this side of the shop. I'm trying to give my attention to the customer in front of me, but knowing Allysa is speaking freely to Atlas has me more than nervous. I never know what's going to come out of her mouth.

Atlas looks pleased, though. Whatever she's telling him, he's enjoying it.

It feels like a decade later when I'm finally free to join them. Atlas leans in and greets me with a kiss on the cheek when I reach him. His fingers graze my elbow for several seconds after our greeting before he pulls his hand away. That simple physical gesture sends a current through me, making it hard to focus without being too obvious that I get giddy around him.

Allysa smiles at me knowingly. "Adam Brody, huh?"

I have no idea what she's referring to until I look at Atlas and he's grinning. I had a poster of Adam Brody on my bedroom wall the first time Atlas came to my house.

I shove Atlas's arm. "I was fifteen!"

He laughs, and I love that Allysa is being nice to him. I know she has every right to give complete loyalty to her brother, but it's not in her to be rude to people simply because other people don't like them.

She's not a ride-or-die friend, nor is she a ride-or-die sister. That's what I love the most about her, because I'm not ride-or-die, either. If you do something stupid, I'm going to be the friend who tells you you're doing something stupid. I'm not going to join you in your stupidity.

I want my friends to treat me the same way. I prefer honesty over loyalty any day, because with honesty *comes* loyalty.

"Thank you for lunch," I say. "Did you get Josh's school situation settled?"

Atlas has been working to enroll him in a school more local to where he lives, rather than the school Josh was in all the way across town.

"I did. Fingers crossed they don't look too hard into the enrollment forms I had to fill out. I lied a little."

"I'm sure it'll be fine," I say. "I can't wait to meet him."

"How old is he?" Allysa asks.

"He just turned twelve," Atlas says.

"Whoa," Allysa says. "Worst age ever. But at least you don't have to pay for day care. Silver lining." Allysa snaps her fingers. "Speaking of children, Lily won't have Emerson next Saturday because she's going to a wedding. A night out all by herself as a single adult."

I roll my head and look at her. "I was about to invite him. I didn't need your help."

Atlas perks up. "A wedding, huh?" A sly smile plays on his lips. "You plan on sleeping through it?"

I immediately blush, and that makes Allysa curious. Atlas turns to her and says, "She didn't tell you she slept through our first date?"

I'm not even looking at Allysa, but I can feel her staring. "I was tired," I say, excusing the inexcusable. "It was an accident."

"Oh, I absolutely need more of this story," Allysa says.

"She fell asleep on our drive there. Slept in a parking lot for over an hour. We never even made it into the restaurant."

Allysa starts laughing, and I kind of want to crawl under the counter and hide now.

"Who's getting married?" Atlas asks me.

"My friend Lucy. She works here."

"What time?"

"It's at seven. Nighttime wedding if you can swing it."

"I can." Atlas does this thing with his eyes where he briefly looks like he wishes we were alone. It's sending tingles of warmth crawling down my spine. "I need to get back. Enjoy your lunch." He nods at Allysa. "It was nice officially meeting you."

"You too," she says.

He gets halfway to the exit when he starts whistling. He walks away in a cheerful mood, and it makes my heart swell to see him so happy. I have no idea if his good mood has anything to do with me, but the teenage girl in me who was worried about him all those years ago is extremely pleased to see him doing so well in life.

"What's wrong with him?"

When I glance at Allysa, she's staring curiously at the door Atlas just disappeared out of. "What do you mean?"

"Why isn't he married? Why doesn't he have a girl-friend?"

"Hopefully he'll have a girlfriend soon." I can't say it without smiling.

"He's probably bad in bed. Maybe that's why he's single."

"He is definitely not bad in bed."

Her jaw drops. "You said you haven't even kissed him yet; how would you know?"

"As *adults*," I say. "You forget I have a history with him. He was my first, and he was very, very good. And I'm sure he's gotten even better."

Allysa stares at me for a beat, then says, "I'm happy for you, Lily." But she's frowning. "Marshall is going to like him, too. He's so *likable*." She says that like it's the worst possible outcome.

"And that's a bad thing?"

"I don't know if it's a *good* thing," she says. "This whole thing is muddled; you know that. I don't need to explain it to you. But I can absolutely see why you're hesitant to tell Ryle. Knowing his ex-wife is sharing a bed with that block of perfection has to be extremely emasculating."

I raise a brow. "Not as emasculating as beating your wife should feel." I'm a little shocked when the words come out of my mouth, but I can't take them back. I don't think I need to, though, because luckily, my best friend isn't a ride-or-die sister.

Rather than be offended, Allysa agrees with a nod. "Touché, Lily. Touché."

Chapter Nineteen
Atlas

I have no idea if twelve is too young to take an Uber, but I didn't want to leave Josh at my place alone after school again, so I had one drop him off here at the restaurant. We discussed earlier this week that he should probably help out up here to pay off the damages he accrued.

I've been watching the Uber on a map, so I meet him out front. When he gets out of the car, he looks like a completely different kid from the one I met several days ago. He's wearing clothes that fit him, I took him for a haircut yesterday, and he's carrying a backpack full of books rather than cans of spray paint.

I doubt Sutton would even recognize him if she saw him.

"How was school?" Today was his second day at the new school. Yesterday he said it was okay but didn't expand.

"It was okay."

I guess that's as much as I'll get from a twelve-year-old. I open the door to my restaurant, and Josh pauses before walking in. He looks up at the building and assesses it. "Funny how I slept here for two weeks but this is the first time ever I'm walking through the entrance."

I laugh and follow him into the restaurant. I'm excited for him to meet Theo, even though I haven't had a chance to tell Theo about Josh yet. Theo arrived a few minutes ago and came through the back right as I was heading toward the front to fetch Josh.

Theo hasn't been to the restaurant since last week, and I haven't brought Josh around because I had to take some time off in order to attempt to get his life straightened out. When we walk through the double doors that lead to the busy kitchen, Josh pauses in wonder. He stares wide-eyed at the commotion. I'm sure the place is a lot different during the day than it was when he'd sleep here at night.

The door to my office is open, which means Theo must be in there doing his homework. I lead Josh in that direction, and he follows me as we make our way into the office. Theo is seated at my desk, reading. He looks up at me, then looks at Josh. He leans back in the desk chair and pulls in his chin. "What are you doing here?"

"What are *you* doing here?" Josh asks Theo.

They're asking each other this like they know each other. I didn't think they would since the schools here are so big, and there are so many. I wasn't even sure which school Theo attended. "Do you two know each other?"

Theo says to me, "Yeah, he's a new kid at my school." Then to Josh, he says, "But how do you know Atlas?"

Josh drops his backpack and nudges his head toward me as he plops onto the sofa. "He's my brother."

Theo looks at me and then at Josh. Then at me. "Why didn't I know you had a brother?"

"Long story," I say.

"Don't you think that's something your therapist should know about?"

"You haven't been here all week," I say.

"I had math practice after school every day," he says.

"Math practice? How does one practice math?"

Josh pipes in. "Wait. Theo is your *therapist*?"

Theo answers him with, "Yeah, but he doesn't pay me. Hey, did you get Trent for math?"

"No, I got Sully," Josh says.

"Bummer." Theo looks over at me, and then back at Josh. Then back at me. "How have you never mentioned you have a brother?" Theo can't seem to get past that fact, but I don't have time to explain it to him right now. The kitchen is running behind.

"Josh can tell you. I have a kitchen to run." I leave them in the office and head back to help out with all the chits we're behind on.

I like that they know each other, but I like it even more that Theo seemed comfortable around him. I know Theo much better than I know my little brother, and I feel like Theo would have had some sort of reaction if he was displeased to see Josh.

. . .

About an hour later, the kitchen is fully staffed, and I have a few minutes to break free. When I walk into the office, Josh and Theo are having what looks like an intense discussion about a manga Theo is holding. "Sorry to interrupt." I motion for Josh to follow me. "You finish your homework?"

"Sure," he says.

"'Sure'?" I don't know him well enough to know what kind of answer *sure* is. "Is that a yes? A no? A mostly?"

"Yes." He sighs, following me out of the kitchen. "Mostly. I'll finish it tonight; my brain hurts."

I introduce him to a few people in the kitchen, finishing with Brad. "Josh, this is Brad. He's Theo's father." I gesture toward Josh. "This is Josh, my little brother." Brad wrinkles his forehead in confusion but says nothing. "Josh has a debt to pay off. You have any work for him?"

"I have debt?" Josh asks, befuddled.

"Crouton debt."

"Oh. That."

Brad immediately puts two and two together. He nods slowly, and then says to Josh, "You ever washed dishes?"

Josh rolls his eyes and follows Brad to the sink.

I feel bad making him work, but I'd feel even worse if there weren't any consequences to the thousands of dollars he cost me. I'll let him do dishes for an hour and then we'll call it even.

I mostly just wanted him out of my office so I could talk to Theo about him. I haven't had a chance to talk to him without Josh in the room.

Theo is at my desk, stuffing papers into his backpack. I sit on the couch, prepared to ask him about Josh, but Theo speaks first. "You kiss Lily yet?"

Always about me, never about him.

"Not yet."

"What the heck, Atlas? I swear, you are so lame sometimes."

"How well do you know Josh?" I ask, changing the subject.

"He's only been in school for two days, so not super well. We have a couple of classes together."

"How's he doing in that school?"

"No clue. I'm not his teacher."

"I don't mean his grades. I mean his interactions. Is he making friends? Is he nice?"

Theo tilts his head. "You're asking *me* if your brother is nice? Shouldn't you know?"

"I just met him."

"Yeah, me too," Theo says. "And you're asking me a loaded question. Kids are mean sometimes. You know that."

"Are you saying Josh is mean?"

"There are different kinds of mean. Josh is the better kind of mean."

I'm not following at all. Theo can see that, so he expands. "He's like a bully to the bullies, if that makes sense."

This conversation is making me uncomfortable. "So Josh is . . . *king* of the bullies? That sounds bad."

Theo rolls his eyes. "It's hard to explain. But I'm sure it's not surprising that I'm not the most popular kid in that school. I'm on the math team, and I'm . . ." He shrugs off the last word. "But I don't have to worry about kids like Josh. When you ask me if he's nice, I don't know how to answer that, because he isn't nice. But he isn't mean, either. Or at least he isn't mean to the nice people."

I don't speak up immediately because I'm trying to absorb all this information. I might be more confused than I was before this conversation. But it does make me feel good to know that Theo isn't scared of Josh.

"Anyway," Theo says, zipping his backpack. "You and Lily. Did it fizzle out already?"

"No, we're just busy. I'm going to a wedding with her tomorrow, though."

"You finally gonna kiss her?"

"If she wants me to."

Theo nods. "She probably will as long as you refrain from saying anything cheesy, like, *Look at the ships, let's lock lips!*"

I grab one of the couch pillows and throw it at him. "I'm getting a new therapist who doesn't bully me."

Chapter Twenty
Lily

It's challenging being the florist for a wedding *and* a guest.
I've been running all day to make sure the flowers at the
venue were set up the way Lucy wanted them. And on top of
that, we're closing early for the wedding, so Serena needed
help getting all the deliveries completed and onto the truck.

By the time Atlas makes it to my apartment to pick me
up, I'm not even close to being ready. I just received a text
from him asking if he should come up. I'm sure he's cautious
because everything is so new with us, and he doesn't know
who might be here if he were to knock on the door, and if I'd
want them to know Atlas is my date to the wedding.

I was hesitant to invite him to the wedding for that very
reason, but I'm confident no one at Lucy's wedding would
even know Ryle. We run in different circles. And on the off
chance they do know Ryle, and it might get back to him that I
was with someone, the risk is worth the reward. I've been looking forward to this night since Atlas agreed to come with me.

Come up, I'm still getting ready.

Atlas knocks at my door moments later. When I open
the door to let him in, my eyes feel like they might double
in size like they do in the cartoons. "Wow." I'm staring at
him all dressed up in his black designer suit. He stands in

the hallway for longer than I'd normally make someone wait before inviting them in because I forget basic things like hospitality when I'm in his presence.

He's holding a bouquet, but it isn't flowers. It's *cookies.*

He hands them to me. "Figured you get enough flowers," he says. He leans in and kisses my cheek, and I want to tilt my face just enough so that his lips land on mine, but hopefully I won't have to be patient for much longer.

"These are perfect," I say, motioning for him to enter. "Come in. I need, like, fifteen minutes to get dressed."

I've been so busy today, I haven't even had a chance to eat. I open one of the cookies and bite into it. Then, with a mouthful, I say, "I'm sorry if this is tacky. I'm starving." I point toward my bedroom. "You can wait in my room with me while I get ready; it won't take me long."

Atlas is looking around, taking everything in as he follows me to my bedroom.

My dress is laid out on the bed, so I pick it up and walk to my bathroom. I leave the door cracked a bit so that I can talk to him while I change. "Where's Josh?"

"You remember Brad from that poker night?"

"I do, actually."

"His son, Theo, is at my house with Josh. They go to school together."

"How's he liking school?"

I can't see Atlas, but he's closer to the bathroom when he says, "Fine, I guess." It sounds like he's right next to the door. I slip the dress over my head and open the door farther. I chose a merlot-colored fitted dress with spaghetti straps. It has a matching shawl, but it's still hanging in the closet.

Atlas looks me over when I appear in the doorway. His eyes journey up the length of me, but I don't give him time to compliment me.

"Can you zip me up?" I give him my back and lift my hair, but I can feel him hesitate. Or maybe he's soaking in the moment.

A couple of seconds later, I feel his fingers press against my back as he raises the zipper. It sends chills rolling over my skin. When he's finished, I drop my hair and turn and face him. "I need to put on makeup." I start to back into the bathroom, but Atlas grips my waist.

"Come here," he says, pulling me until I smush against him. He admires my face for a couple of seconds, smiling appreciatively. Seductively. Like he's about to kiss me. "Thank you for inviting me."

I return the smile. "Thank you for coming. I know you've had a busy week."

Atlas's eyes look tired. The usual glimmer has dulled a little, like he's been stressed and could use a night of relaxation. I can't help but touch his cheek when I say, "We can Uber there if you want. You seem like you could use a drink."

Atlas touches my hand that's cupping his cheek. He tilts his face so that he can kiss the inside of my palm. Then he pulls my hand away and threads his fingers through it. He opens his mouth to say something else, but I see it the second his eyes get a glimpse of my tattoo.

Atlas has never seen the heart tattoo on my shoulder— the one I got because he always used to kiss me there. He touches it softly with his fingers, tracing the shape of it. His eyes flicker up to mine. "When did you get this?"

My voice catches, and I'm forced to clear my throat. "In college." I've thought about this moment a lot—what he would say if he ever saw it, how it would make him feel.

He quietly regards me and then looks at the tattoo again. He's so close, I can feel his breath trickling across my collarbone. "Why'd you get it?"

I got it for so many reasons, but I choose to say the most obvious one. "Because. I missed you."

I wait for him to lower his head and press a kiss there like he's done so many times before. I wait for him to kiss *me*. To press his mouth to mine in a silent thank-you.

Atlas doesn't do any of those things. He continues staring at the tattoo for a beat, but then he releases his hold on me and turns away. His voice is detached when he says, "You should probably finish getting ready or we'll be late." He takes a couple of steps toward my bedroom door, and then, without looking back, he says, "I'll wait in the living room."

I feel like I just got the breath knocked out of me.

His entire demeanor changed. It wasn't at all what I expected from him. I stand frozen in place for a few depressing seconds, but then I force myself to finish getting ready. Maybe I'm misreading his reaction and it wasn't a negative one. Maybe he liked it so much, he needed alone time to process.

Whatever the reason is for his unexpected reaction, I fight back the sting of tears the entire time I'm trying to do my makeup. I can't help it. I think my feelings might be hurt, and that's not something I expected to happen tonight at all.

I go to my closet and find my shoes and grab my shawl, and I half expect Atlas to be gone when I walk out of my bedroom, but he's still here. He's standing by the wall in the hallway looking at pictures of Emmy. When he hears me exit the bedroom, he looks in my direction, and then full-on turns to face me.

"Wow." He looks genuinely pleased when I'm back in his presence, so the whiplash is a little confusing. "You're beautiful, Lily."

I appreciate his compliment, but I can't move past what just happened. And if there's one thing I've learned from the relationship I was in before and the relationship I witnessed between my parents, it's that I refuse to be someone who brushes everything under a rug. I don't even want there to be a rug.

"Why did my tattoo upset you?"

My question catches him off guard. He fidgets with his tie, and seems to be looking for an excuse, but nothing comes to him, and the hallway remains silent, other than a ragged, slow breath he pulls in. "It wasn't the tattoo."

"What is it? Why are you mad at me?"

"I'm not mad at you, Lily." He says that convincingly, but he's not the same after seeing the tattoo, and I don't want us to start out with lies. Apparently, he doesn't, either, because I can see him working through what to say to me next. He looks uncomfortable, like he doesn't want to have this conversation, or at least he doesn't want to have it right now.

He shoves his hands in the pockets of his pants and sighs. "That night I took you to the emergency room . . . they bandaged up your shoulder while we were there." His voice sounds pained, but when he makes eye contact with me, that pained sound is nothing compared to the turmoil in his expression. "I heard you tell the nurse he bit you, but I wasn't close enough to see that . . ." Atlas pauses midsentence and swallows hard. "I wasn't close enough to see that you had the tattoo, and that he bit . . ." Atlas stops speaking again. He's so upset, he can't even finish his sentence. He just moves on to another one. "Is that why he did it? Because he read your journals and knew you got the tattoo for me?"

My knees feel shaky.

I can see why Atlas didn't want to have this conversation. It's too much for a casual chat while we're on our way out the door. I press a hand flat against my nervous stomach, prepared to answer him, but it's hard to talk about. Especially knowing how upset it's making Atlas on my behalf.

I don't want to hurt him, but I also don't want to lie to him, or protect Ryle in any way. Because Atlas is right. That's exactly why Ryle did what he did, and I hate that Atlas will now forever pair my tattoo with that awful memory.

My lack of response is enough confirmation for him. He winces and turns away from me. I can see the deep breath he forces himself to take in order to remain calm. He looks like he wants to explode, but Ryle isn't here for him to explode on.

Atlas is so angry, but this is an anger I'm not afraid of.

I realize the significance of this moment. I'm alone with an angry man in my apartment, but I'm not in fear for my life, because he isn't angry at me. He's angry at the person who *hurt* me. It's a protective anger, and there's a world of difference between my reactions to Ryle's anger versus my reaction to Atlas's anger.

When Atlas turns to me again, I can see the hard set of

his jaw and the veins in his neck when he says, "How am I supposed to be civil around him, Lily?" There's guilt in his voice when he whispers, "I should have been there for you. I should have done more."

I can understand the anger, but Atlas has absolutely nothing to feel guilty for. I wasn't at a point in my life where Atlas could have said or done anything to change my views of Ryle. I had to get to that point on my own.

I walk closer to Atlas and press my back into the wall across from him. He does the same on the opposite wall until we're facing each other. He's working through a lot of emotions right now, and I want to give him the space to do that. But I also have a lot to say about the guilt Atlas is holding on to.

"The first time Ryle hit me, it was because I laughed at him. I was tipsy, and I thought something was funny that wasn't funny, and he backhanded me."

Atlas has to break eye contact after hearing me say that. I don't know if he wants these details, but I've been wanting to say all this to him for a long time. He remains still against the wall, but it looks like it's taking everything in him not to run straight to wherever Ryle is right now. His eyes are sharp when he looks back at me, waiting for me to finish.

"The second time, he pushed me down the stairs. That argument started because he found your number hidden in my phone case. And when he bit me on my shoulder . . . You're right. It was because he read the journals and found out my tattoo was because of you, and that the magnet I kept on my refrigerator was from you." I look down briefly because it's hard seeing how much this is affecting him. "I used to think the things I did somehow warranted his reactions. Like maybe if I wouldn't have laughed, he wouldn't have hit me. Maybe if I didn't have your number in my phone, he wouldn't have gotten angry enough to push me down a flight of stairs."

Atlas isn't even looking at me anymore. His head is leaned back against the wall, and he's staring at the ceiling, taking everything in, frozen in his anger.

"Every time I would start to take on the guilt and justify Ryle's actions, I would think about you. I would ask myself what your reaction would have been compared to Ryle's. Because I know it would have been different. If I would have laughed at you under the same circumstances that I laughed at Ryle, you would have laughed *with* me. You never would have backhanded me. And if any man on this planet gave me their phone number as a way to protect me from someone they feared was dangerous, you would *appreciate* them for that. You wouldn't have pushed me down a flight of stairs. And if the journals I let you read were about another boy in high school besides you, you would have teased me. You probably would have highlighted lines you thought were cheesy and laughed about them with me."

I stop speaking until Atlas brings his focus back to mine, and then I finish. "Every time I would doubt myself and think that what Ryle did to me was in any way deserved, all I had to do was think about you, Atlas. I think about how differently each scenario would have been if it were you, and that helped me remember that none of it was my fault. You're a big part of the reason I got through it, even though you weren't there."

Atlas silently soaks up everything I've said for maybe five seconds, but then he closes the distance between us and kisses me. Finally. *Finally.*

His right hand curls around my waist as he tugs me against him, his tongue sliding gently and warmly against my lips, coaxing his way past them. His left hand snakes its way through my hair until he's molding his palm to the back of my head. A spool of yearning begins to unravel inside me.

He doesn't kiss me with any trepidation. His mouth meets mine with confidence, and mine responds to his with relief. I pull at him, wanting his warmth to sink into me. His mouth and his touch are familiar since we've done this dance before, but completely new at the same time because this kiss is made up of a whole new set of ingredients. Our first kiss was made of fear and youthful inexperience.

This kiss is hope. It's comfort and safety and stability. It's everything I've been missing in my adult life, and I am so happy Atlas and I have each other again, I could cry.

Chapter Twenty-One
Atlas

There have been a lot of things in my life that have made me angry, but nothing filled me with rage like seeing Lily's tattoo and the faded scars that circled it in the shape of a bite mark.

How any man can do that to a woman, I'll never understand. How any *human* can do that to a human they're supposed to love and want to protect, I will never understand.

But what I do understand is that Lily deserves better. And I get to be the one to *give* her better. Starting with this kiss that we can't seem to stop. Every time we pause to look at each other, we go right back to kissing like we have to make up for all the lost time in this one kiss.

I trail kisses down her jaw until I meet her collarbone. I've always loved kissing her there, but until I read her journal, I didn't know she was aware of how much I loved kissing her there. I press my lips to her tattoo, determined to make sure she remembers the good parts of us in all the future kisses I'm going to give her in this spot. If it takes a million kisses for her not to think about the scars that surround her heart tattoo, then I'll kiss her there a million and *one* times.

I press kisses up her neck, then her jaw. When I'm looking at her again, I slide the shoulder strap of her dress back in place because as much as I could stay right here for hours,

I'm supposed to be taking her to a wedding. "We should go," I whisper.

She nods, but I kiss her again. I can't help it. I've been waiting for this moment since I was a teenager.

• • •

I can't really say how the wedding went because I was more focused on Lily than anything else. I didn't know anyone there, and after finally kissing Lily tonight, it was hard to focus on anything other than wanting it to happen again. I could tell Lily craved to be alone with me as much as I wanted to be alone with her. Being forced to patiently sit next to her after what happened between us in her hallway was torture.

As soon as we got to the reception and Lily saw how crowded it was, she was relieved. She said Lucy would never know if we left early, and I don't even know Lucy, so I wasn't about to argue with her when, after less than an hour of mingling, she grabbed my hand and we slipped out.

We've just pulled back up to Lily's apartment complex, and while I'm almost positive she wants me to go upstairs with her, I'm not going to assume. I open her door and wait for her to put her shoes back on. She took them off in the car because they were hurting her feet, but they look difficult to fasten. There are strings, and Lily is struggling with them in the passenger seat. I doubt she wants to walk barefoot on the parking garage floor, though.

"I can carry you on my back."

She glances up at me and laughs like I'm joking. "You want to give me a piggyback ride?"

"Yeah, grab your shoes."

She stares at me for a moment, but then she grins like she's excited. I turn around and she's still laughing when she wraps her arms around my neck. I help her hoist herself onto my back and then I kick the car door shut.

When we make it to her apartment, I lean forward so she can use her key to unlock her door. Once we're inside, she's laughing when I lower her to her feet. I turn around just as she drops her shoes and starts to kiss me again.

Picking up right where we left off, I guess.

"What time do you need to be home?" she asks.

"I told Josh ten or eleven." I look at the clock and it's just after ten. "Should I call him and tell him I might be late?"

Lily nods. "You're definitely gonna be late. Call him and I'll make us drinks." She walks to the kitchen, so I take out my phone and call Josh. I video-chat him so I can make sure he's not throwing a party at my house. I doubt Theo would let him, but I'm not taking any chances with either of those two.

When Josh answers the video call, the phone is lying on the floor. I can see his chin and the light from the TV. He's holding a controller. "We're in the middle of a tournament," he says.

"Just checking in. Everything okay?"

"It's fine!" I hear Theo yell.

Josh starts shaking his remote, hitting buttons, but then he yells, "Shit!" He tosses the controller aside and picks up the phone, bringing it closer to his face. "We lost."

Theo appears behind him. "That doesn't look like a wedding. Where are you?"

I don't answer him. "I might be a little late tonight."

"Oh, are you at Lily's?" Theo says, moving closer to the phone screen. He's grinning. "Did you finally kiss her? Can she hear me? What line did you use to get her to invite you in? *Lily! We watched people wed, let's hop into—*"

I immediately end the call before he finishes that rhyme, but Lily heard that whole conversation. She's standing a few feet away from me, holding two glasses of wine. Her head is tilted in confusion. "Who was that?"

"Theo."

"How old is he?"

"Twelve."

"You talk to a twelve-year-old about us?"

She seems amused by this. I take a glass of wine from her, and right before I sip it, I say, "He's my therapist. We meet every Thursday at four."

She laughs. "Your therapist is in junior high?"

"Yeah, but he's about to get fired." I wrap my hand around Lily's waist and pull her to me. When I kiss her, she tastes like the red wine she poured. I kiss her deeper to get more of that taste. More of her.

When she pulls back, she says, "This is weird."

I don't know what she's referring to as weird. I hope she's not referring to us, because *weird* is the last word I'd use to describe this. "What's weird?"

"Having you here. Not having a kid here. I'm not used to free time, or . . . guy time." She takes another sip of her wine and then separates from me. She sets her wineglass on the counter and walks toward her bedroom. "Come on, let's take advantage of it."

I follow her lead entirely too quickly.

Chapter Twenty-Two
Lily

I'm trying to act confident about this, but as soon as I walk into my bedroom, I lose every bit of the confidence that got me in here.

It's just that it's been so long since I've been with anyone. Probably since right after getting pregnant with Emmy. I haven't had sex postbaby, and I haven't had sex with Atlas since I was sixteen, and both of these thoughts start swirling together to create this monstrous invasive-thought tornado in my mind.

I'm standing in the middle of my bedroom when Atlas appears in the doorway a few seconds later. I put my hands on my hips and just . . . stand here. He's staring at me. I feel like I'm supposed to make the next move since I'm the one who just invited him into my bedroom.

"I don't know what to do next," I admit. "It's been a while."

Atlas laughs. Then he saunters toward the bed because of course he can't just walk in an unattractive way. Every move he makes is sexy. Him removing his suit jacket right now is sexy. He tosses it onto my dresser and then kicks off his shoes. *God, even that was sexy.* Then he sits down on my bed.

"Let's talk." He leans against my headboard and then crosses his ankles. He looks very relaxed. *And sexy.*

I can't imagine lying down on that bed in this dress. It would be uncomfortable, and probably not very much fun to try to remove if we get to that point. "Let me change clothes first." I walk into my closet and close the door.

I turn on the light, but nothing happens. The bulb is out. *Shit.* I can't get dressed in the dark. I don't have my phone on me, so I can't use the flashlight app to help.

I do my best, but it takes a minute to get the zipper down. When I finally do, instead of stepping out of the dress, for some reason I pull the dress over my head, and of course it snags in my hair. I try to set my hair free, but the dress is heavy, and it's taking forever in the dark, and I can't walk out to find a mirror because Atlas is out there. I keep trying to untangle it. After a few defeating minutes, Atlas finally taps on the door.

"You okay in there?"

"No. I'm stuck."

"Can I open the door?"

I'm standing in my bra and panties with a dress halfway over my head, but this is what I deserve. This is closet karma. "Okay, but I'm not really dressed."

I hear Atlas laugh, but when he opens the door and sees my situation, he immediately springs into action by flicking the light switch. It does nothing, of course.

"The bulb is out."

He moves toward me to inspect my situation. "What happened?"

"My hair is stuck."

Atlas pulls out his phone and uses the light to help him see what I'm tangled on. He tugs my hair and my dress in opposite directions, and then, magically, my dress is on the floor.

I smooth out my hair. "Thank you." I fold my arms over myself. "This is embarrassing."

The light from Atlas's phone is still on, so he can see that I'm standing in my bra and panties. He turns off his phone light, but the closet door is open, and there's a lamp on in the bedroom, so I'm still very visible to him.

There's a moment of hesitation on both our parts. He can't tell if he should walk away and let me finish getting dressed, and I can't tell if I want him to.

And then suddenly we're kissing.

It just happened, as if we moved toward each other at the same time. One of his hands slips around to the back of my head, and the other goes directly to my lower back, so low that his fingers are skimming over my panties.

I wrap both my arms around his neck and pull him to me so hard, we stumble into a line of clothes. Atlas rights us again, but I can feel his smile in his kiss. He pulls far enough away from my mouth so that he can speak. "What is it with you and closets?" Then he kisses me again.

We make out in the closet for a few minutes, and it's everything I remember about all the times we used to sneak make-out sessions when we were younger. The desire, the thrill, the newness of doing things you've never done, or in this case, haven't done in a long time.

It reminds me of how much I loved being in a bed with him. Whether we were kissing or talking or doing other things, the memories I made with him in my bedroom are some of my absolute favorite memories. He's kissing my neck when I whisper, "Take me to my bed."

He doesn't hesitate. He slides his hands down my ass and grips my thighs, hoisting me up. He carries me out of the closet, across the bedroom, and then plants me onto my mattress where he proceeds to climb on top of me.

The feel of him against me only makes me more desperate for him, but he treats this like he used to treat our make-out sessions. With patience and appreciation—like making out is enough, and that it's a privilege just to be kissing me.

I don't know where he finds that patience, because I kind of want him to take off his clothes and treat me like this is his only chance to have me.

Maybe he would if he thought that—but we both know this is just the beginning. He's taking it slow because I asked him to. I'm sure if I asked him to go faster, he would do that, too.

Considerate Atlas.

We eventually come to a point where we have to make a decision. I have a condom in my drawer, and he probably has a little time before he needs to leave, but when we stop kissing long enough to look at each other, he shakes his head. We're both breathing heavily, and a little worn out from being so worked up for so long, so he rolls off me and falls onto his back.

He's still dressed. I'm still in my bra and underwear. We never got further than that.

"As much as I want to," he breathes, "I don't want to have to leave right after." He rolls onto his side and places a hand on my stomach. He's looking down at me with eyes that are unsatisfied, like he wants to say, *Never mind*, and ravish me.

I sigh and close my eyes. "Sometimes I hate responsibility."

Atlas laughs, and then I feel him move closer. He kisses the corner of my mouth and says, "I don't have to leave *yet*." When he says that, his index finger slips beneath the hem of my panties, right below my belly button. He drags it back and forth, waiting for a reaction.

I lift my hips, hoping that's enough of a conversation.

Every part of my body feels like it's on fire when he slips two more fingers into my underwear. Then, when his entire hand makes the move, I'm a goner. I release a trembling breath and grip the sheet at my sides, arching my back and my hips up and against his hand.

He brings his mouth to mine, but he doesn't kiss me. He remains close to my lips, using the movement of my hips and the sounds of my moans to guide him toward the finish.

He's extremely intuitive. It doesn't take me long at all before I'm tensing around his hand, pulling his neck down so that I can kiss him through the end of it.

When it's over, he slides his hand out of my panties but then cups me there, leaving his hand over me while I recover. My chest is heaving as I try to catch my breath.

Atlas is breathing heavily, too, but I need a minute to recover before I can do anything about it.

"Lily." Atlas kisses me gently on the cheek. "I think you . . ." He pauses, so I open my eyes and look at him. He shifts his eyes to my breasts, and then back at my face.

Then he pulls at his white shirt and looks down at it and I see there's some kind of stain on it.

Oh, shit.

I look down at my bra and it's soaking wet. *Oh my God.* Breast milk. Everywhere. I am such an idiot.

Atlas doesn't seem at all fazed by it. He rolls off the bed and says, "I'll give you some privacy."

I'm a little mortified that my bra is covered in breast milk, so I grab the sheet and cover my chest with it before meeting Atlas at the foot of my bed. It kind of killed the mood. "Are you leaving?"

"Of course not." He kisses me and then leaves the room as if it's completely normal for a man to make out with a woman who is breastfeeding a baby that isn't even his. It has to be at least a little awkward for him, but he covers it well.

I spend the next several minutes in the bathroom pumping, and then I take a quick ten-second shower. I throw on an oversized T-shirt and some pajama shorts before heading back into my living room.

Atlas is sitting on my couch, waiting patiently with his phone in his hand. When he hears me enter the living room, he glances up at me and looks me up and down. I'm still a little embarrassed, so when I sit next to him, I don't sit *right* next to him. I sit, like, two feet from him, and then I mutter, "Sorry about that."

"Lily." He can sense my embarrassment, so he reaches for me. "Come here." He settles against the couch and pulls my leg over his so that I'm straddling him. He slides his hands up my thighs, to my waist, and lets his head fall lazily against the couch. "Everything about tonight was perfect. Don't you dare apologize."

I roll my eyes. "You're being nice. I got breast milk on you."

Atlas slides a hand around the back of my neck and pulls me to him. "Yeah, while we were making out. Trust me, I don't mind one bit." He kisses me after that, which might be a mistake because *here we go again.*

It's going to be impossible for him to leave at this rate. I probably should have put on another bra, but I honestly thought I was going to the living room to tell him goodbye. I didn't know we were going to pick up where we left off on the couch, but I don't mind it at all.

We're situated so perfectly, we don't even have to adjust to get the most out of this position. He groans during our kiss, and that just urges me on even more.

One of Atlas's hands slides up the back of my shirt, and I can feel him hesitate when his hand never meets a bra. He pauses our kiss and looks me in the eye. I'm still moving against him, and the way he's looking at me is piercing my core. He starts to move his hand from my back around to my breast. When he cups it in his hand, that seems to flip a switch in him. In both of us.

Our kiss turns feverish as I start to unbutton his shirt. Nothing else is said. We just frantically remove every piece of clothing left between us, and we don't even bother moving to the bedroom. We barely pause the kissing when he reaches for his wallet and pulls out a condom and puts it on.

And then, as if it's the most natural thing in the world, Atlas kisses me while he pushes into me, and I feel every bit as loved as I did the first time this happened between us. There are so many feelings that come out in this moment, I'm not sure I've ever experienced anything so chaotically beautiful when we're finally connected.

He sighs against my neck, like the same feelings are running through him. He starts to move in and out, slowly, kissing me gently the whole time. But several minutes later, the kisses are frantic and we're both sweaty, and I am so completely and wholly in the moment, nothing else matters to me other than the fact that we're together again, and it's right. Everything about this is so right.

I'm exactly where I belong, being loved by Atlas Corrigan.

Chapter Twenty-Three
Atlas

I should definitely go home, but it is so hard to crawl out of this bed after the last couple of hours with her. Once the couch happened, then the shower happened. Now we're both too tired to do anything other than talk.

She's lying on her back, her arms folded beneath her head. She's staring at me, listening intently as I tell her about my meeting with a lawyer yesterday. "He says I did the right thing by taking him to the hospital. They were legally obligated to notify Child Protective Services. I'm not sure how I feel about that, though. It puts the power in the hands of the state, and what if they don't think I'm the best place for him?"

"Why wouldn't they?"

"I work a lot. I'm not married, so Josh will be alone some of the time. And I have no experience raising kids. They might think Tim is a better fit since he's the biological father. They could even give him back to my mother; I'm not even sure what she did is enough to have him removed from her custody."

Lily leans toward me and presses a kiss against my forearm. "I'm going to tell you what you told me the first time you FaceTimed me. You said, 'You're stressing over things that haven't even happened yet.'"

I fold my lips together momentarily. "I did say that."

"You did," she says. She tucks herself against me, wrapping a leg over my thigh. "It'll work out, Atlas. You're the best thing for him, and anyone who has vested interest will see that. I promise."

I fold myself around her, fitting her head under my chin. It's incredible how much we've both changed physically since we were teens, but we somehow still fit together just as perfectly as we did back then.

"I've been wanting to ask you something," she says, pulling back far enough to look at me. "Remember our first time? What happened after that night? After my father hurt you."

I'm not surprised she's thinking about that, because I've thought about it as well tonight. This is the first time we've been intimate since that night that ended so terribly, so it's hard not to compare them.

That was what her very last journal entry was about. It was painful to read, seeing how much she was hurting. I wish more than anything it could have ended better than it did.

"I don't remember a lot from that night," I admit. "I woke up in the hospital the next day, confused. I knew your father was the one who had hurt me, I remembered that much, but I had no idea if he did to you what he had done to me. I hit the call button several times, and when no one came to my room, I somehow hobbled into the hallway with a broken ankle. I was frantic, asking if you were okay, but the poor nurse had no idea what I was talking about."

Lily tightens her grip around me as I talk.

"She finally calmed me down enough to get your information from me, and then she came back to let me know that I was the only one brought in with injuries. She asked me if your father was Andrew Bloom. I told her yes, and I told her I wanted to press charges. When I asked her if she could have an officer come to the room, she looked at me sympathetically. I remember her exact words. She said, 'The law is on his side, honey. No one turns him in. Not even his wife.'"

Lily exhales against my chest, so I pause and press a kiss against the top of her head. "Then what?" she whispers.

"I did it anyway," I say. "I knew if I didn't report him, your mother would never get out of that situation. I made the nurse contact an officer, and when one finally arrived that afternoon, he wasn't there to listen to my statement. He was there to make it clear that if anyone was going to be arrested, it wouldn't be your father. He said your father could have me arrested for breaking into houses and forcing myself on his daughter. Those were the officer's exact words, like the relationship you and I had was something criminal. I felt guilty about that for years."

Lily looks up at me and places a hand on my cheek. "What? Atlas, we're only two and a half years apart. You did absolutely nothing wrong."

I appreciate that she says that, but it doesn't change the fact that I felt guilty for bringing stress into her life. But I also felt guilty for leaving her once I did bring stress into her life. "I don't know that any choice I made back then would have felt right. I didn't want to stay and put you in more danger by showing up at your house again. And I didn't want to be arrested because then I wouldn't have been able to go to the military. I thought the best thing would be to put space between us, and then someday I would contact you down the line and see if you ever still thought of me like I thought of you."

"Every day," she whispers. "I thought of you every single day."

I run my hand over her back for a while, and then I stroke my fingers through her hair, wondering how in the world she can make me feel so whole when I had no idea I was only half of myself without her.

Of course I've missed her all these years, and if I could have snapped my fingers and brought her back into my life, I would have in a heartbeat. But we had built lives without each other, her with Ryle and me with my career, and I assumed that was our fate. I had grown used to not living life with her. But now that she's back, I don't know that I could ever feel whole again without her. Especially after tonight.

"Lily," I whisper.

She doesn't respond. I pull back a little and can see that her eyes are closed, and her arm has gone limp around me. I'm scared if I move, I'll wake her up. But I told Josh I'd only be a couple of hours later than the time I initially gave him, and I'm at three hours now. I'm not even sure I'm allowed to leave twelve-year-olds by themselves.

Brad was okay with it when I asked if they were fine by themselves, and if he doesn't even allow Theo to have a phone, I doubt he'd let me leave them alone while I went on a date unless Brad has left Theo alone before.

Maybe I should google what the age limit is in Boston for a kid to stay by themselves.

I'm overthinking this. Of course, they're fine. Neither of

them has called or texted with any kind of emergency, and twelve-year-olds even babysit other kids sometimes.

I think I'm fine, but I still need to get home. I don't know Josh well enough yet to be convinced he isn't throwing a rager in my house right now. I slowly remove my arm from beneath Lily's head and ease out of her bed. I dress as quietly as I can, and then I go in search of a pen and paper. I don't want to wake her up, but I don't want to leave without saying anything. Especially after the night we had.

I find a notebook and a pen in her kitchen drawer, so I sit at the table to write her a letter. When I finish, I take it back to her bedroom and I set the note on the pillow next to her. Then I kiss her goodnight.

Chapter Twenty-Four
Lily

There's a pounding in my head.

And *outside* my head.

I lift my face off my pillow and feel drool on my chin. I wipe it away with the corner of my pillowcase. I sit up and see that Atlas left a note beside me. I grab for it, but then hear the knock again, so I tuck the note under my pillow for later and force myself to clear space in my foggy brain to make room for what's happening in this moment.

Emmy is at my mother's.

I just had the best night of sleep I've had in two years.

Someone is at my door.

I reach for my phone on my nightstand and try to focus on the screen. I have several missed calls from Ryle, which makes me concerned something is wrong. But the only thing I have from my mother is a picture of Emmy eating breakfast from half an hour ago.

Phew. Emmy is okay. I immediately relax, but knowing Ryle is probably the one knocking on my door doesn't allow for much relaxation.

"Hold on!" I yell.

I throw on something quick—a T-shirt and jeans—and then I open the door to let him in. He moves past me, into the apartment, without being invited in. "Is everything okay?" He looks panicked, but also relieved to see that I'm alive.

"I was asleep. Everything is fine." He can tell I'm annoyed. He glances around the room for Emmy. "She spent the night at my mother's."

"Oh." He's disappointed. "I tried calling because I wanted to pick her up for a few hours. You weren't answering your phone, and you're always awake by now . . ." Ryle's voice trails off when he sees the couch. I don't have to look at the couch to know what he's staring at. My T-shirt and panties are still tossed haphazardly over the back of it, I'm sure.

"Let me call my mother and let her know you're coming." I go get my phone from my room, hoping Ryle isn't about to question me. He's ruining the good mood Atlas left me in last night.

When I walk back into the living room, I pause while searching for my mother's contact on my phone. Ryle is holding a wineglass in his hand, inspecting it. It's the one Atlas drank from. Mine is on the counter next to it—a clear indication that someone was here *with* me drinking wine last night.

Before my underwear got removed and left on the couch.

I can see Ryle's jealousy bubbling over when he sets down the wineglass and looks straight at me. "Did someone stay the night?"

I don't bother denying it. I'm an adult. A single adult. *Well, possibly not single anymore, but that's another matter.* "We're divorced, Ryle. You can't ask me questions like that."

Maybe that was the wrong thing to say, because Ryle immediately responds by taking two quick steps toward me.

"I can't ask you if someone spent the night in the home my daughter *lives* in?"

I take a step back. "That's not what I meant. And I wouldn't bring anyone around her without your approval; that's why she's at my mother's."

Ryle's eyes are narrowed, accusing. He looks disgusted by me. "You won't leave her with me overnight, but you'll drop her off somewhere else when you want to get fucked?" He laughs. "Great parenting, Lily."

Now I'm getting angry. "This is only the second time I've ever left her overnight since she was born almost a year ago. Don't shame me for taking a night for myself. And when I do take a night for myself, what I do during that time is not your business."

Ryle has that look in his eye—the distant void that always took over right before he'd go too far.

My anger instantly turns to fear, and when Ryle can see that I'm backing away from him, he releases this sound of rage. A guttural, angry noise of frustration that reverberates in the room.

He leaves my apartment, slamming the front door shut behind him. I hear him yell the word *fuck* in the hallway.

I'm not sure which angle his rage is coming at me from. Is he mad I'm moving on? Is he mad my mother has Emmy? Or is it that I allow my mother overnights with her but I'm still not comfortable with Ryle having over-nights? Maybe he's angry about all three things presenting at once.

I blow out a calming breath, relieved he's gone, but before I can think about what to do next, Ryle is opening my door again. He's looking at me from the hallway with a very flat affect when he says, "Is it him?"

I can feel my heart catch in my throat when he asks that. He doesn't say Atlas's name, but who else could he be referring to? I don't immediately deny it, which is enough of a confirmation for him.

Ryle looks up at the ceiling briefly, and then shakes his head. "So I had a right to be concerned about him the whole time?"

The entire past few minutes have been a roller coaster of emotions, but nothing has been as tumultuous as the question that just left his mouth. I take a few steps until I'm standing in my doorway, prepared to close the door on him as soon as I say my piece.

"If you truly believe that I would have been unfaithful to you, then go ahead and believe that. I don't have the energy to keep convincing you otherwise. I've explained this to you before, so I'm not saying it again. I never would have left you for Atlas. I didn't *leave* you for Atlas. I left you because I deserve to be treated better than the way I was treated by you."

I go to close the door, but before I can take a step back, Ryle moves forward and pushes me until my back is flat against the open living room door. His eyes are filled with fury when he slides his left hand to the base of my throat, applying pressure as if he wants to hold me in place. He slaps his right palm flat against the door by my head, and it scares me so much, I immediately squeeze my eyes shut, not wanting to see what's about to come next.

A huge wave of anxiety and fear rolls over me so intensely, I'm scared I might pass out. I can feel Ryle's breath crashing against my cheek as it moves through his clenched teeth because his face is so close to mine. My heart is pounding so hard, there's no way he can't feel that fear beating against his palm with the way his hand is pressed against me. I want to scream, but I'm terrified if I make a noise, it'll make him even angrier.

Several seconds pass between the moment Ryle pins me against the door and the moment he starts to realize what he's done. What more he was likely *about* to do.

My eyes are still shut, but I can feel the remorse in the way he leans forward and presses his forehead against the door, right next to my head. He still has me caged in, but he's released the pressure in the hand that was gripping my neck, and there's a struggling sound coming from him, as if he's trying not to cry.

It takes me back to the last night he hurt me. The apologies he was whispering as I drifted in and out of consciousness. *I'm sorry, I'm sorry, I'm sorry.*

My heart is shattered, because Ryle hasn't changed at all. As much as I hoped he had, and as much as I know he wanted to, he's still the same man he's always been. I somehow held on to a sliver of hope that he had become stronger for Emmy, but this is absolute confirmation that I'm making the right choices for her.

Ryle is clinging to me like I can make this better, and at one point in time I thought I could. He's a broken man, but he isn't broken because of me. He was broken before he met me. Sometimes people think if they love a broken person enough, they can be what finally repairs them, but the problem with that is the other person just ends up broken, too.

I can't afford to allow anyone to break me anymore. I have a daughter I need to be whole for.

I gently press my hands against his chest and urge him back into the hallway. When I'm finally in a position where there's enough space between us to shut the door, I close it and lock it, and then I immediately call my mother and tell her to put Emmy in the car and meet me at the park. I don't want them to be at her house if Ryle still plans on showing up there.

After I end the call, I move with purpose through my apartment. If I stop and allow myself to get lost in what just happened, I might cry. I don't have time to cry right now. I get dressed to go to the park because I need to be present for my daughter in every way that I can be.

Before I walk out the door, I grab the note Atlas wrote me and tuck it into my purse. I have a feeling his words are going to be the only bright spot to this day.

• • •

My premonition is coming true. I hear a loud clap of thunder as soon as I pull into the parking lot of the park. There's a storm brewing to the east, and it's heading this direction. *Fitting.*

It's not raining yet, though, so I scan the playground until I spot my mother. She's holding Emmy, and they're going down the slide together. She hasn't spotted me yet, so I take a moment to pull Atlas's letter out of my purse. I'm still reeling from my interaction with Ryle. I'd like to read something that can hopefully put me in a better mood before I greet my daughter.

Dear Lily,

I'm sorry I had to leave without saying goodbye, but you fall asleep so easily. I don't mind it—I like watching you sleep. Even when it's in a car in the middle of a date.

I used to watch you sleep sometimes when we were younger. I liked how peaceful you looked, because when you were awake, there was always a quiet fear in you. But when you slept, the fear was gone, and it always put me at ease.

I can't begin to tell you what tonight meant to me. I don't think I have to put it into words because you were here. You felt it, too.

I know I mentioned earlier that I carried a lot of guilt about what happened between us, but I don't want you to think I carry regret for loving you back then. If there's anything at all I regret, it's that I didn't fight harder for you. I think that's where the majority of my guilt stems from— knowing if I didn't leave you, you never would have met a man who would end up hurting you the way your father hurt your mother.

But no matter how we got here, we're here. I had to get to a point where I realized I was always worthy of being loved by you. I hate that we didn't get here sooner, because there are so many things in your life I wish you didn't have to go through, or that I could have prevented. But any other path wouldn't have given you Emerson, so I'm grateful this is where we ended up.

I love watching you talk about her. I can't wait to get to know her. But that'll come in time, along with all the other things I'm looking forward to. We'll continue to take this at whatever pace you're comfortable with. Whether I get to talk to you every day or see you once a month, anything is better than the years I had to go not knowing anything about you.

I'm so happy you're happy. That's all I've ever wanted for you.

But I will say, nothing beats knowing I'm the one you get to be happy with now.

Love,
Atlas

I flinch so hard, I almost rip the letter in two when someone bangs on my window. I gasp and glance up to see my mother standing next to my car. Emmy lights up when she sees me through the window, and that smile is all it takes to make me smile in return.

Well, her smile and the letter in my hand.

I fold it up and tuck it back into my purse. My mother opens my door. "Is everything okay?"

"Yeah, it's fine." I take Emmy from her, but my mother's eyes are squinting with suspicion.

"You sounded scared when you asked me to meet you at the park."

"It's fine," I say, wanting to brush it off. "I just didn't want Ryle to pick her up today. He's not in a very good mood, and he knew she was with you, so . . ."

I blow out a breath and walk over to the empty swing set. I take a seat in one of the swings and place Emmy on my lap, facing out. I kick the ground and give the swing a little push, watching as my mother takes a seat in the swing next to us.

"Lily." My mother is looking at me with concern. "Just tell me what happened."

I know Emerson is only one and can't understand me yet, but it still makes me uncomfortable to talk about her father in her presence. I'm convinced babies and toddlers can sense moods, even if they can't understand what you're saying.

I attempt to explain my situation without mentioning names. "I'm sort of seeing someone?" That confession comes out like a question because we haven't made it official, but I don't think Atlas and I have to put a label on it to know where this is headed.

"Really? Who?"

I shake my head. I'm not about to tell her it's Atlas, even though she probably wouldn't know who I was talking about. She saw him twice when I was younger, and we never once spoke about him. And if she does remember him, I'm sure she doesn't want to, considering her husband put him in the hospital.

There may come a day when I officially introduce Atlas to my mother, and I don't want her to know him from my past or she might feel mortified.

"Just someone I met. It's early. But . . ." I sigh and kick the ground again to give us another small push. "Ryle found out, and he isn't happy."

My mother winces, like she knows all too well what *he isn't happy* implies.

"He came by this morning, and his reaction was scary. I

panicked, thinking he was going to show up at your place to get her, so I didn't want you to be home."

"What did he do?"

I shake my head. "I'm not hurt. It's just been a while since I've seen that side of him, so I'm a little shaken, but I'm okay." I kiss Emmy on top of her head. I'm surprised to feel a tear skating down my cheek, so I quickly wipe it away. "I just don't know what to do about his visits now. I almost wish something *would* have happened so I could have reported him this time. But then I feel like an awful mother for thinking that way about her father."

My mother reaches over and squeezes my hand. It makes my swing come to a still, so I twist until we're facing her. "No matter what you decide to do, you are *not* an awful mother. Precisely the opposite." She releases my hand and grips the chains, staring at Emmy. "I admire the choices you've made for her. Sometimes I get sad that I couldn't be that strong for you."

I immediately shake my head. "You can't compare our situations, Mom. I had a lot of support that enabled me to make the choice I made. You had no one."

She gives me a sad, appreciative smile. Then she leans back and kicks at the ground to give herself a little shove. "Whoever he is, he's a lucky guy." She glances over at me. "Who is he?"

I laugh. "No, you don't. I'm not talking about him to you until he's a for-sure thing."

"He already is a for-sure thing," she says. "I can see it in your smile."

We both look up at the same time when it starts sprinkling. I tuck Emmy under my chin and we begin to head back toward the parking lot. My mother kisses Emmy before I put her in the car seat. "I love you. Gamma loves you, Emmy."

"Gamma?" I ask. "Last week it was Nannie."

"I still haven't settled on one yet." My mother kisses me on the cheek and then rushes to her car.

I climb into my car right when the bottom falls out of the sky. Huge drops of rain assault the windshield, the pavement, the hood of my car. They're so fat, they sound like acorns hitting my car.

I sit for a moment, waiting to figure out where I'm going before I start the car. I don't want to go home yet because Ryle might show back up. I definitely don't want to go to Allysa's because I'll absolutely run into him in the apartment building where he lives.

I feel very protective of Emmy right now because Ryle has every right on paper to show up and take her from me for the day, but I'm not allowing my daughter around him on a day I know his fuse is nonexistent.

I look in my rearview mirror, and Emmy is just sitting peacefully, looking out the window at the rain. She has no idea the kind of chaos that surrounds her existence, because to her, *I'm* her entire existence. Every ounce of her trust is in me. She depends on me for everything, and she's just sitting there happy and comfortable, as if I have it all under control.

I don't feel like I have it under control, but the fact that she assumes I do is good enough for me. "Where do we go today, Emmy?"

Chapter Twenty-Five
Atlas

"What time did you get home last night?" Josh asks. He's shuffling into the kitchen wearing two different socks: one of them a new one I bought him and one of them mine. Theo and Josh were asleep when I got home, but I still woke up three hours before they did. Brad just left with Theo about twenty minutes ago.

"That's none of your business." I point at the table, where Josh's homework sits unfinished. He promised he would do it yesterday if I let Theo spend the night, but I have a feeling the video games and manga and anime got in the way. "You didn't do your homework?"

Josh looks at the pile of papers and then back at me. "No."

"Get to it." I say that with confidence, but I have no idea how to do this. I've never had to tell a kid to do homework before. I don't even know how to ground him if he *doesn't* do his homework. I feel like I'm acting. I am. I'm an imposter.

"I'm not avoiding it," Josh says. "I just can't do it."

"Is it too hard? What is it, math?"

"No, I did the math. Math is easy. It's this stupid shit I have to do for computer class."

"Stupid *crap*," I say, correcting him. *I think.* Maybe "stupid crap" is just as bad. I sit down next to Josh to see what it is he's having trouble with. He slides the assignment in front of me, and I look over it.

It's a research assignment about ancestry. There are five things required for the term, and one of them is a family tree that was due on Friday. The other is a generational assignment using an ancestry website that's due next Friday.

"We're supposed to find our relatives using some website. I don't know any of their names or even where to start," he says. "Do you?"

I shake my head. "Not really. I met Sutton's father once, but he died when I was a kid. I don't even remember his name."

"What about my dad's parents?" Josh asks.

"I don't know anything about his family, either."

Josh takes the papers from me. "They really should stop having kids do these things; no one has normal families anymore."

"You're right, actually." I hear a text ping on my phone in the kitchen, so I stand up to go check it.

"Did you ever try to find my dad for me?" Josh asks.

I did try, but Tim never responded to the voice mail I left him. I just don't want to tell Josh that because I know it'll be disappointing. I pick up my phone but walk back to Josh before looking at my texts. "I haven't had a chance to really look into it yet. You sure you want me to?"

Josh nods. "He might want to hear from me. I'm sure Sutton has done everything she can to keep us apart."

I feel a stab of concern in the center of my chest. I was hoping Josh would be comfortable enough here to not want to find his dad, but that was a ridiculous hope. He's a twelve-year-old boy. Of course he wants to find his father.

"I'll help you try to find him." I point to the papers. "But do what you can with that for now. As long as you try, they can't give you a bad grade for not knowing your grandparents."

Josh leans over his work, and I finally look down at the text. It's from Lily.

Can I call you?

She should know she can call me any second of the day, and I would answer. I take my phone to my room and call her without texting her back. She picks up in the middle of the first ring.

"Hey," she says.

"Hi."

"What are you doing?"

"Helping Josh with his homework. Trying to pretend I'm not thinking about you." She's quiet after I say that, and I immediately sense something is off. "Are you okay?"

"Yeah, I just. I don't want to go home. I was wondering if I could come to your place?"

"Sure. Is Emmy still with your mom?"

She sighs. "That's the thing. I have her with me. I know that's weird, but I'll explain when I get there."

If she's bringing Emerson to my house, something is definitely off. She's been adamant she didn't want to bring her around me before Ryle knew about us. "I'll text you my address."

"Thank you. I'll be there in a little while." She ends the call, and I fall back onto my mattress wondering what in the hell happened in the time between slipping out of her bed last night and this phone call.

Did she get my letter? Did I say something wrong?

Is she about to break things off with me?

All those concerns swirl in my gut as I wait for her, but my biggest concern is one I don't even want to allow my mind to entertain. *Did Ryle hurt her?*

.   .   .

I'm watching for them when she pulls into my driveway, so I meet her outside. I can immediately tell something is wrong when she gets out of the car. But I don't think it's related to me because she seems relieved to see me. I pull her in for a hug because she looks like she needs one. "What happened?"

She places her hands on my chest and pulls back to look up at me. She seems hesitant to say anything. She glances into the back window to check on her daughter, who is asleep in the car seat.

Then Lily just starts to cry. She drops her face against my chest and sobs into my shirt, and it's the most heartbreaking thing. I press my lips into her hair and give her a moment.

She doesn't need long. She composes herself fairly quickly and then wipes at her eyes. "I'm sorry," she says. "I've been holding that in all morning since Ryle left."

The mention of his name makes my spine stiffen. I knew this had to do with him.

"He knows about us," she says.

"What happened?" It's taking everything in me to stand where I am and not run to find him. My bones feel as if they're crackling with anger. "Are you hurt?"

"No. But he's really upset, and I don't want to be home alone right now. I know I shouldn't be bringing Emmy around you yet, but I feel safer with her here than if Ryle tried to show up and take her today. I'm sorry, I just don't want to be anywhere he might find me."

I tilt her chin up until she's looking at me. "I'm happy you're here. *Both* of you. Stay the whole day if you want."

She exhales and presses her lips against mine. "Thank you." She moves to the back door to grab her daughter out of her car seat. Emerson doesn't even wake up. She's limp in Lily's arms, passed out. "She's been at the park for an hour; she's exhausted."

I stare at Emerson in wonder, still amazed by how much she looks like Lily. She's the spitting image of her mother, and I'm not at all upset that she looks nothing like her father. "Do you need me to grab anything?"

"Her diaper bag is in the passenger seat."

I grab it, and we make our way into the house. Josh looks over his shoulder when he hears me walk inside. Lily waves at him, and he nods his head, but then when he notices Emerson, he turns completely around in his chair.

"That's a baby," he says.

"It is," Lily replies. "Her name is Emerson."

Josh looks at me. "Is it yours?" He uses the Sharpie in his hand to point at Emerson. "Is that my niece?"

Lily laughs uncomfortably.

I probably should have warned Josh before they showed up. "No, I am not a dad, and you are not an uncle."

Josh stares at us for a minute, then shrugs and says, "Okay." He turns around and gives his attention back to his homework.

"Sorry about that," I say quietly. I set Emerson's diaper bag near the couch. "Want me to get a blanket for her?"

Lily nods, so I grab a thick quilt from the hallway closet and lay it on the floor next to the couch. I double it over to give it more cushion, and she places Emerson on it. Emerson sleeps through the entire transfer.

"Don't let her fool you—she's a very light sleeper." Lily kicks off her shoes and sits on the couch, pulling her feet beneath her. I sit down next to her, hoping she feels like talking about what happened, because I need to know why she's scared.

Josh can't see us from the dining room, so I give Lily a quick kiss. I doubt he can hear us from where he is, but I whisper anyway. "What happened?"

She sighs with her entire body and leans against the couch, facing me. "He showed up to get Emmy, and I wasn't expecting him. He saw our wineglasses. My clothes. He put two and two together, and he had the exact reaction I was afraid he would have."

"What reaction was that?"

"He got angry. But he left before it got too bad."

Too bad*? What does that even mean?* "Does he know it was me who was there?"

Lily nods. "That's practically the first thing he asked. He got angry, and I asked him to leave. And he did . . . but . . ."

She stops talking, and for the first time, I notice her hand is trembling. God, I hate him so much. I pull her to me so that her cheek is pressed against my chest and I hold her. "What did he do that scared you, Lily?"

Her palm is pressed right over my heart. She whispers, "He pushed me against the door, and he got close to my face, and I thought he was going to hit me or . . . I don't know. He didn't, though." She must feel my heart hammering twice as fast against my chest now, because she lifts her head and looks at me. "I'm fine, Atlas. I promise. Nothing happened after that; it's just been a long time since I've seen him that angry."

"He pushed you against the door. That's not nothing."

Her eyes flick away, and she lays her head back on my chest. "I know. I *know*. I just don't know what to do about it. I don't know what to do about Emmy. I was actually getting close to letting him have an overnight with her, and now I don't even want him to have unsupervised visits."

"He doesn't deserve unsupervised visits. You need to take him back to court."

Lily sighs, and I can tell this is probably the part of her life that causes her the most stress. I can't imagine what it must be like for her to watch him drive off with her little girl in his car, knowing what he's capable of. I'm glad she came here today. I know it's important to her that she waited to bring Emmy around me, but she made the right decision. Ryle might show back up to apologize and get Emmy, and he'll find her at all her usual places.

He won't find her here. Besides, Lily and I know this thing that's been brewing between us is absolutely a long-term situation. She doesn't have to worry about me forming an attachment to Emmy and then disappearing. As long as Lily wants me around, I'm not going anywhere.

She lifts her face to look at me again, and there's a smudge of mascara near her temple. I wipe it away. "This conflict with him," she says. "This is what I tried to warn you about. It could be a constant thing, especially now that he knows you're back in my life."

She's saying this like she's giving me the opportunity to bow out of this thing with her. I can't believe she assumes that's even crossing my mind. "You could have fifty ex-husbands who try to make our lives hell, but as long as I have you, I will be absolutely unaffected by anyone else's negativity. That's a promise."

That makes her smile for the first time since she showed up here. I don't want to do or say anything that could steal that smile, so I change the subject away from her weak-ass ex-husband.

"Are you thirsty?"

She pushes off my chest and grins even bigger. "Yes. I'm thirsty *and* I'm hungry. Why else would I show up at a chef's house?"

. . .

Lily and Emerson have been here for about four hours now. Once Josh did as much of his homework as he could, he started playing with Emerson. Lily said she's been taking steps for a few weeks now, and Josh finds it hilarious that she follows him everywhere. He moved around for an hour while she stumbled after him, but now she's asleep again. She fell asleep on the floor next to me with her head on my leg. Lily offered to move her, but I wouldn't let her.

I would be lying if I said this wasn't a little surreal. Deep down, I know that Lily and I are going to work out. She's my person, and I am hers, and that's something I've known since the first week we met. But looking at Emerson, knowing this child is likely going to end up becoming a huge part of my life—that's a lot to take in. I could be her stepfather someday. I'll likely be more of an influence in her life than her biological father, because Lily and I will eventually move in together. We'll likely marry someday.

I'd never admit any of this out loud because people like Theo would say I'm getting ahead of myself, but the truth is, I'm years behind where I want to be with Lily. Where I could have been with her.

This is a hugely significant day, even if I don't see Emerson again for months. This could be the first day I'm spending with someone who might one day end up becoming my daughter.

I brush thin strands of strawberry hair behind Emerson's ear and try to understand where some of Ryle's anger is coming from. He can't be clueless to what Lily moving on would mean for his relationship with Emerson. Lily has Emerson the majority of the time, so whoever Lily chooses to bring into her life will also be around Emerson that same amount of time.

I'm not excusing Ryle's behavior by any means. If I had my way, he'd get a job offer in Sudan, and we'd only have to deal with him once a year.

But that's not the reality here. Ryle lives in the same city as his daughter, and his ex-wife is moving on with someone else. That can't be easy on anyone. While I can understand how difficult it probably is for him, I'll never understand his failure to recognize that it's no one's fault but his own. If he would have been a more mature, more rational man, Lily never would have left him. He'd have his wife and his daughter, and me and Lily wouldn't even be in contact.

I'm worried for Lily. I'm worried Ryle is a little bit like

my mother, and that he's going to retaliate by fighting for the sake of fighting, and for no other reason.

"Have you ever made a report against Ryle?" I ask, looking at Lily. She's sitting on the floor next to me, watching Emerson sleep on my leg.

"No." There's a drop of shame in Lily's response.

"Do the two of you have a custody agreement?"

She nods. "I have full custody, but it comes with stipulations. Because of his schedule, I'm required to be flexible, but technically he gets her two days a week."

"He pays child support?"

She nods. "He does. He's never been late."

I'm relieved he at least provides her that, but knowing the answers to these questions is making Lily's situation seem even more precarious.

"Why?" she asks.

I shake my head. "It's not my business." *Is it?* I don't even know. I'm trying to take things slow and give Lily space, but that part of me is warring with the part of me that wants to protect her.

Lily lifts a hand and pulls my focus to hers. "It is your business, Atlas. We're together now."

Her response makes my heart stutter. Did she just make us official? "Are we? Together?" I smile and urge her closer to me, my pulse thrumming. "Are me and you a thing, Lily Bloom?"

Her lips grin against mine. She's nodding when she kisses me.

I think we both knew it was official long before last night, but if her daughter weren't asleep on my leg right now, I'd probably pick Lily up and spin her around. I am that happy.

And that much more invested.

My quick burst of adrenaline begins to slow again, bringing me back to my thoughts from before Lily declared us official.

Ryle. Custody. Immaturity.

Lily's head is on my shoulder and her hand is on my chest, so she feels it when I exhale all the air from my lungs. She lifts her head and looks at me anxiously. "Just say it."

"Say what?" I ask her.

"Your thoughts about my situation. Your eyebrows are all scrunched together like you're worrying about something." She lifts her hand and uses her thumb to smooth out my serious expression.

"Is it too late to tell the court he was a danger to you in the past? Maybe that would help prevent him from getting overnights with her."

"Once two people agree on a custody arrangement, you can't use past evidence to modify an arrangement. Unfortunately, I never reported him, so I can't use the abuse as a defense at this point."

That is unfortunate. But I can understand her attempting to keep things civil with him at the time. I'm just worried it might come back on her in a negative way.

"He's too busy to have her half the time, or even overnights, really. I doubt he would ever try to get joint custody of her."

I press my lips together and nod, hoping she's right. I don't know him like she does, but from what I do know of him, he seems to hold grudges. And people who hold grudges tend to need retaliation. Parents do this all the time.

They don't like what another parent is doing, or who they're seeing, so they use their child as a weapon. And that worries me. I could absolutely see Ryle making the decision to take her to court, simply to get back at her for being with me. And he would likely get what he wants. He's never hurt Emerson, he's never been reported for hurting Lily, he's never been late on child support. And he has a successful career. All these things are in his favor.

When I glance at Lily, it looks like she's about to sink into the floor. I didn't mean to upset her even more by talking about this.

"I'm sorry. I'm not trying to be a pessimist. We can change the subject."

"You aren't a pessimist, Atlas. You're a realist, and I need that from you." She lifts her head off my shoulder and peeks over at Emmy, who is still asleep on my leg. Then Lily settles against me again, releasing a quiet sigh. "You know, even if I had reported Ryle and fought for sole custody, my chances were slim. He has no criminal history, and he has money for the best lawyers. Almost every lawyer I spoke to encouraged me to work it out civilly with him because they've seen cases like ours, and the arrangement Ryle was agreeing to at the time was my best option."

I grab her hand and lace my fingers through hers. She wipes away a tear that skates down her cheek. I hate that I even brought it up, but these fears are already in her. I'm just glad to know she's thinking about it because she needs to stay a step ahead of Ryle. "Whatever happens, you aren't alone in this anymore."

Lily smiles appreciatively.

Emerson begins to stir awake on my leg. She opens her eyes and looks at me, and then immediately searches for Lily. She makes a beeline for her, right across my lap. When she's in Lily's arms, I lift my leg and stretch it. I haven't been able to move it for over half an hour and it's asleep.

"We should go," she says. "I feel guilty for even being here with her. I'd be livid if Ryle took her around a girlfriend without me knowing."

"I think your situations are a little different. Ryle isn't having to find a safe place to hide your daughter for the day because he's scared of your temper. Don't be so hard on yourself."

Lily shoots me a grateful look.

I help her gather their things and I walk her to the car. Once Emerson is in her car seat, Lily moves close to say goodbye. I burrow my fingers in her hips and tug her closer. I dip my head, grazing her nose, and then I catch her lips with mine. I kiss her deeply, wanting her to still feel it on her drive home.

I slide my hands into the back pockets of her jeans and squeeze her ass. It makes her laugh. Then she sighs wistfully. "I already miss you."

I nod in agreement. "There's been a lot of that on my end," I admit. "I'm kind of obsessed with you, Lily Bloom." I kiss her cheek and then force myself to release her.

This is the only negative aspect to finally being with the person you're meant to be with. You go years aching to be with them, and when they finally become a significant part of your life, it somehow hurts even *more*.

Chapter Twenty-Six
Lily

You disappoint me Lily.

I'm staring at my phone in shock.

Is this a joke?

You treat me like a monster im her goddamn father

It's five in the morning. I woke up to use the bathroom, and naturally, I glanced at my phone before attempting to get the last hour of sleep before my alarm goes off.

All the texts are from Ryle. I haven't heard from him since he showed up at my house on Sunday. It's been four days, and he never even bothered to reach out and apologize for losing his temper on me. He was silent for four days and then *this?*

I was happier before I met you.

I read through the barrage of text messages, knowing full well he was drunk when he sent them last night. The first one was sent at midnight, and the last one, from two in the morning, reads, **have fun fucking the homeless guy.**

I drop my phone onto my bed, my hands trembling. I can't believe he sent these. I was hoping the four days of silence was a stretch of remorse on his part, but it's obvious he's been stewing in his anger.

This is so much worse than I thought.

I try to go back to sleep, but I can't. I get up and make myself a cup of coffee, but my stomach is too upset to drink it. I spend the next half hour standing in my kitchen, staring at nothing, replaying those texts over and over in my mind.

When Emerson finally wakes up, I'm relieved. I am more than welcoming to the distraction of our chaotic morning routine.

• • •

By the time I drop her off with my mother and make it to work, it's eight o'clock sharp. I'm the first one at the flower shop, so I distract myself with as much as I can until Serena and Lucy show up. Lucy can tell something is wrong with me, she even asks me if I'm okay at one point, but I reassure her that I'm fine.

I pretend I *am* fine, but I'm watching the front door every chance I get, expecting Ryle to angrily burst through it. I wait for another mean text from him. I wait for the phone to ring.

Hours go by and there's nothing. Not even an apology.

I don't tell Atlas, I don't tell Allysa, I don't say anything to anyone throughout the day about what he's done. It's embarrassing. It's insulting to Atlas; it's insulting to me. I have no idea what to do about it, but I know that this isn't something I'm willing to tolerate. I refuse to go the next seventeen years of my daughter's life being abused in any way, even through text messages.

Serena has gone for the day, and it's just Lucy and me when the inevitable finally happens. It's after five, and we're just getting ready to close up shop so I can pick up

Emerson from my mother's when Ryle walks through the front door.

My anxiety shoots through me like an explosion of lava.

Lucy has never been Ryle's biggest fan, so she groans under her breath when she sees him and says, "I'll be in the back if you need me."

"Lucy, wait," I whisper. I look down at my phone like I'm busy with something so Ryle can't see my lips moving. "Stay." I glance at her so she can see the concern in my eyes. She just nods and finds something to make herself look busy.

My heart is hammering against my chest when Ryle approaches. I don't even try to hide behind a fake expression when I look him in the eye.

He holds my stare for a few seconds and then side-eyes Lucy. He nudges his head toward my office. "Can we talk?"

"I was just leaving." My words come out quick and firm. "I have to pick up our daughter."

I can see Ryle's left hand grip the edge of the counter. He squeezes it, and the muscles in his arm flex. "Please. It won't take long."

I look at Lucy. "Wait for me to lock up?" She gives me a reassuring nod, so I turn on my heels and walk to my office. I can hear him right behind me. I fold my arms over my chest and suck in a breath before I can face him.

I'm so sick of his remorse. I want to wipe that stupid frown off his face, I'm so angry.

"I'm sorry." He runs a hand through his hair and winces, coming closer. "I had too much to drink at an event last night and . . ."

I say nothing.

"I don't even remember sending those texts, Lily."

I still say nothing. He begins to fidget, growing uncomfortable in my silent anger. He slides his hands into his pockets and stares at his feet. "Did you tell Allysa?"

I don't answer that question. If anything, it infuriates me even more. He's worried what his sister will think of him more than what kind of damage he's doing to me? "No, but I told a lawyer." I'm lying, but it'll be the truth as soon as he leaves this building. From this point forward, I'm documenting everything he does to me. Atlas is right. Ryle looks perfect on paper, and if he's going to continue with abusive tactics, I need to protect myself and Emerson.

Ryle's eyes slowly journey to mine. "You *what*?"

"I sent them to my lawyer."

"Why would you do that?"

"Seriously? You pinned me against a door on Sunday, and then you sent me threatening texts in the middle of the night. I have done nothing to deserve this, Ryle!"

He pulls his hands from his pockets and squeezes the back of his neck as he spins to face the other direction. He stretches his back while he sucks in a breath. He seems to be holding that breath in while he silently counts in an attempt to subdue the anger building in him.

We both know how those techniques have worked in the past.

When he turns around, the remorse is gone. "You don't see the pattern, here? Are you really that blind?"

Oh, I definitely see a pattern, but I think we're looking at different ones.

"We've been fine for a *year*, Lily. We didn't have a single issue until he showed back up. Now we're fighting all the time, and you're getting lawyers involved?" He looks like he wants to punch the air.

"Stop blaming your behavior on other people, Ryle!"

"Stop ignoring the common fucking denominator for all of our problems, *Lily*!"

Lucy appears in the doorway of my office. She looks from me to Ryle, and then back to me. "Are you okay?"

Ryle lets out an exasperated laugh. "She's fine," he says, irritated. Ryle walks toward the door, and Lucy has to press herself against the doorframe to avoid being bumped into. "A fucking *lawyer*," I hear him mutter. "Let me take one guess as to whose idea that was." Ryle is walking toward the door like he's on a mission. Lucy and I both exit my office, most likely for the same reason. To lock him out once he exits the shop.

When Ryle reaches the front door of the building, he spins around and stabs me with a sharp glare. "I am a neurosurgeon. You work with *flowers*, Lily. Remember that before your lawyer does anything stupid to threaten my career. I pay for that fucking apartment you live in." His threat is punctuated by his hands slamming open the door.

Lucy is the one to lock it after he finally leaves because I'm frozen from the impact of that last insult. She walks back to me and pulls me in for a sympathetic hug.

I realize in this moment that the hardest part about ending an abusive relationship is that you aren't necessarily putting an end to the bad moments. The bad moments still rear their ugly heads every now and then. When you end an abusive relationship, it's the good moments you put an end to.

In our marriage, the few terrifying incidents were blanketed by so many good ones, but now that our marriage is over, the blanket has lifted and all I'm left with are the worst pieces of him. Where our marriage was once full of heart and flesh that cushioned the skeleton, all that's left is the skeleton now. Sharp, bony edges that slice right through me.

"You okay?" Lucy asks, smoothing her hands down my hair.

I nod. "Yeah, but . . . did it seem like he left here with a purpose? Like he was going somewhere else?"

Lucy's eyes scan the door again. "Yeah, he peeled out of the parking lot pretty fast. Maybe you should warn Atlas."

I immediately grab for my phone and call him.

Chapter Twenty-Seven
Atlas

It's only been half an hour since I checked my phone, so I'm alarmed when I see several missed calls and three texts from Lily.

Please call me.

I'm okay but Ryle is angry.

Did he show up there? Atlas, please call me.

Shit.

"Darin, can you take over?"

Darin moves to finish plating for me, and I immediately walk to my office and call her. Her phone goes straight to voice mail. I try her again. Nothing.

I'm preparing to head out back to my car when my phone finally rings. I answer immediately with, "Are you okay?"

"I'm fine," she says.

I stop rushing toward the door and lean my shoulder into a wall. I release a breath, my heart rate plummeting back to normal.

It sounds like she's driving. "I'm going to pick up Emmy. I just wanted to warn you that he's angry. I was worried he might show up there."

"Thanks for the warning. You sure you're okay?"

"Yes. Call me when you get home. I don't care how late it is."

Ryle bursts through the kitchen doors in the middle of her sentence. He makes enough of a ruckus that everyone notices and pauses what they're doing. Derek, my head waiter, is right behind Ryle.

"I said I would *get* him," Derek is saying to Ryle. Derek looks at me and throws up his hands to let me know he tried to prevent the intrusion.

"I'll call you on my way home," I say. I fail to mention Ryle just showed up. I don't want her to be concerned. I end the call right as Ryle's eyes land on me.

I don't think he's here to congratulate me.

"Who is that?" Darin asks.

"My biggest fan." I nudge my head toward the back door, so Ryle starts walking in that direction.

The kitchen begins to buzz again, everyone ignoring Ryle's intrusion. Everyone but Darin. "You need me to do something?"

I shake my head. "I'll be fine."

Ryle pushes open the back door so hard, it slams against the outside wall.

What a piece of work. I head in that direction, but as soon as I open the back door and walk onto the back steps, Ryle comes at me from the left. He knocks me off the steps, and then, when I try to stand up, he punches me.

It's a good punch, too. I'll give him that.

Fuck.

I wipe my mouth and stand up, thankful he's at least giving me room to do that. It's not really a fair advantage when one person is on the ground when the punching begins. But Ryle doesn't seem like the type to play fair.

He's about to hit me again, but I back up and he ends up tripping. He pushes off the ground, and when he's back on his feet, he stares at me, fuming. He doesn't seem to be in attack mode in the moment.

"You done?" I ask him.

He doesn't respond, but I don't think he'll lunge for me again. Ryle straightens his shirt and smirks. "I liked it better when you fought back last time."

I struggle not to roll my eyes. "I have no desire to fight you."

He pops his neck and starts to pace. He has so much anger in him, I can't imagine what this must be like for Lily when she has to witness it. He's breathing heavily, his hands on his hips, his eyes piercing me like knives. I don't just see anger in his expression. I see a hell of a lot of pain.

I sometimes try to put myself in Ryle's shoes, but as much as I struggle to stand in them, they don't fit. They never will, because there isn't a single human in history with a past misfortunate enough to excuse beating the person you're supposed to protect.

"Just say whatever it is you came here to say."

Ryle wipes blood away from his knuckles with his shirt, and I notice his hand is swollen. It looks like he was punching things before he showed up and hit me. I'm glad I know Lily is okay, or he wouldn't be walking away in the same condition he showed up in.

"You think I don't know the lawyer was your idea?" he says.

I try to hide my surprise, but I have no idea what he's talking about. *Did she speak to a lawyer about her situation?* It makes me want to smile, but I'm sure a smile would antagonize Ryle, and I do enough of that simply by existing.

My lack of response is getting under his skin. Ryle's face twists in anger. "You might have her fooled right now, but you'll have your first fight with her. And your second. She'll see that marriage isn't fucking rainbows all the goddamn time."

"I could have a million arguments with her, but I can promise you they'll never end with her in the hospital."

Ryle laughs. He's trying to spin this to look like I'm the ridiculous one. I'm not the one who barged into his place of work because I couldn't control my emotions.

"You have no idea what Lily and I have been through," he says. "You have no idea what *I've* been through."

It's like he showed up wanting a fight, but I'm not giving him that, so he's using it as a venting session. Maybe I should give him Theo's number. I'm seriously at a loss here.

I don't want to come back to this moment tomorrow and see it as a lost opportunity. My only goal is to make Lily's life with this man more peaceful. The last thing I want to do is make things more difficult between us all, but until he gets it through his head that he's the only one in control of his reactions, I'm just as confused as Lily as to how to deal with him.

"You're right, Ryle." I nod slowly. "You're right. I have no idea what you've been through." I take a seat on the stairs to let him know he has no reason to feel threatened by me. And if he tries to attack me again while I'm sitting, I'm not going to respond to him with as much composure this time. I clasp my hands together and do my very best to speak in a way that might get through to him.

"Whatever happened in your past helped make you a great neurosurgeon, and the world needs that side of you. But your past also—for whatever reason—made you a shitty husband. The world doesn't need that side of you. Just because we get the opportunity to be something, that isn't a guarantee that we'll be good at it."

Ryle rolls his eyes. "That's dramatic."

"I watched them stitch her up, Ryle. Wake the fuck up, man. You were a horrible husband."

He stares at me for a beat, then says, "What has you convinced you'll be any better?"

"Treating Lily the way she deserves to be treated is the easiest part of my life. I think you should be relieved she's with someone like me."

He laughs. "Relieved? I should be *relieved*?" He takes several steps toward me, his anger ascending again. "*You're* the reason we aren't together!"

It takes everything in me to remain on these steps, and every ounce of patience I have not to return his shouts with my own. "*You're* the reason you aren't together. It was *your* anger and *your* fists that got you here. I was barely an acquaintance in Lily's life when she was with you, so do the mature thing and stop blaming me, and Lily, and everyone else for your actions." I stand up, but not to hit him. I just need to make room in my chest to exhale because if I don't, I'm not sure how much longer I can do this without raising my voice to his level. It's hard looking at him and remaining composed, knowing what he's done to Lily. "*Dammit*," I mutter. "This is ridiculous."

Ryle and I are both quiet for a moment. Maybe he can

tell I'm at my limit because I'm not keeping my frustration as under control anymore. I spin and face him, looking at him pleadingly. "This is our life now. Yours, mine, Lily's, *your daughter's.* We have to deal with this. Forever. Holidays, birthdays, graduations, Emerson's wedding. All these things are going to be difficult for you, but you're the only one who can make sure they aren't difficult for the rest of us, too. Because none of us owes you our happiness. *Especially* Lily."

Ryle shakes his head. He paces like he's trying to erase the asphalt and uncover earth. "You expect me to what—to cheer you two on? To wish you well? To encourage you to be a good father to *my* fucking daughter?" He laughs at the absurdity he finds in the idea of that, but I keep a very straight face.

"Yes. *Exactly* that."

I think my response throws him off. He pauses and threads his hands at the nape of his neck.

I take a step closer to him, but not in a threatening way. I don't want to yell. I want Ryle to hear the absolute sincerity in my voice. "As happy as I know I can make Lily, she'll never be fully happy until she has your acceptance and coopera-tion. And you're making it difficult, even though you know she deserves a good life. They both do. If you want your daughter to grow up with the best version of Lily, then please work with her. This is possible for all of us."

Ryle rolls his neck. "What are we, some kind of *team* now?"

I hate that he's trying to make any of this sound beyond the realm of possibility. "A team is the *only* thing people should be when kids are involved."

That hits him. I can see it in the way he flinches, and then subtly swallows. He turns around and faces away from me, taking a few steps while he contemplates everything I've said. When he turns back around and looks at me, there's a little less vitriol there.

"When things don't work out between the two of you and Lily needs somewhere to run, I'm not picking up the pieces this time." With that, Ryle walks away. He doesn't go through the restaurant this time. He heads down the alley, toward the street.

I can do nothing but stare at him with pity as he walks away. He truly doesn't know Lily at all.

At all.

Lily doesn't *run* to people. She didn't run after me when I left Maine. She didn't run *to* me when she left Ryle. She focused on being a mother. Yet that's what he expects her to do if things don't work out between us? *Run* to him like he's her home base?

Lily's home base is Emerson, and if he still can't see that, he's clueless.

If Lily had stayed with him, he would have spent the rest of their lives inventing issues in order to justify his excessive anger. Because I was never an issue in their marriage, and I never would have been.

I thought I pitied him before, but he's fighting for a woman he barely even knows, which means he's just fighting for the sake of fighting. He's got a very similar personality to my mother, and sometimes there's no fixing that. You just have to learn to live your life around it.

Maybe that's what Lily and I are going to have to do. Learn to live our lives the best we can while occasionally having to deal with the ridiculous wrath of Ryle.

That's fine. I'd go through this shit every day if it means I'm the one who gets to fall asleep next to her every night.

I walk up the steps and return to the hustle of the kitchen, and I get right back to work like he was never even here. I don't know if my response tonight made this situation better, but I definitely don't think I made it worse.

Darin hands me a wet rag. "You're bleeding." He points to the left side of my mouth, so I hold the rag there. "Was that her ex?"

"Yeah."

"Everything okay now?"

I shrug. "I don't know. He might get mad and come back. Hell, this could go on for years." I look at Darin and smile. "But she's worth it."

•   •   •

Three hours later, I'm knocking softly on Lily's apartment door. I texted her to let her know I was coming. I thought she might need another drive-by hug.

When she opens her door, it's clear that's exactly what she needs. And what *I* need. As soon as we're inside her living room, she slips her arms around my waist and I fold myself around her. We remain embraced for a couple of minutes.

When she lifts her face, her eyebrows draw apart when she sees the small cut on my lip. "He's such an immature asshole. Did you put ice on it?"

"I'll be fine. It didn't even swell."

Lily lifts up onto her toes and kisses my cut. "Tell me what happened."

We sit on the couch and I try to recall everything that

was said, but I'm sure I leave a few things out. When I'm finished speaking, she's leaning against the back of the couch with a leg draped over mine, concentrating. She's threading her fingers in and out of my hair.

She's quiet for a long time. Then she just looks at me with a sweetness that melts over me. "I'm convinced you're the only man on the planet who could get punched and then offer the aggressor *advice*." Before I can respond, she's sliding onto my lap, bringing her face close to mine. "Don't worry, I find it so much more appealing than if you would have fought him back."

I slide my hands up her back, surprised she's in such a good mood. I don't know why I thought this conversation would be a weight on her. But I guess this is the best possible outcome. Ryle knows we're a thing, I had a chance to say my piece, and we all came out of it relatively unharmed.

"I can't stay long, but I can probably stretch this hug out for another fifteen minutes before Josh notices I'm late."

She raises an eyebrow. "When you say 'hug,' do you mean . . ."

"I mean get naked—we're down to fourteen minutes." I push her onto her back and kiss her, and we don't stop for fourteen minutes. Then seventeen. Then twenty.

It's thirty minutes later before I finally walk out of her apartment.

Chapter Twenty-Eight
Lily

Allysa has the bright idea of just setting them on the floor on a layer of trash bags, so it'll be an easy cleanup. Emmy and her cousin, Rylee, are both covered in cake now.

Emmy has no idea what's going on, but she's enjoying herself. We ended up having a small party for her here at Allysa's. My mother is here, Ryle's parents, Marshall, and Allysa.

Ryle is also here, but he's about to leave. He snaps a couple of photos on his phone before giving both the girls a quick kiss goodbye.

I heard him telling Marshall it's been a busy day with work, but he made the party. I was happy he made it in time for presents, and he stayed until the cake was mostly demolished. I know it'll mean something to Emmy someday when she sees the pictures.

We haven't spoken the entire time he's been here. We've circled around each other, pretending everything is fine in front of everyone, but Ryle is anything but fine. I can feel the tension radiating from him while standing across the room. Being ignored by him is better than being blamed by him, though. I'd take the silent treatment over the alternative any day.

Unfortunately, I don't get the silent treatment for long.

Ryle is making eye contact with me for the first time today. I made the mistake of standing alone, so he takes this as an opportunity to walk over and stand beside me. I stiffen, not wanting to do this right now. We haven't spoken since he insulted me while walking out of my flower shop last week. I know we need to have a conversation, but our daughter's birthday party is not the time or place.

Ryle slips his hands into his pockets. He tucks his chin against his chest and stares at the floor. "What did your lawyer say?"

Anger climbs up my chest. I side-eye him and give my head a shake. "We aren't having this conversation right now."

"Then when?"

It's not really a matter of when, but *who with*? Because I'm not going to discuss anything while we're alone ever again. He's proven to me that I'm not safe when I'm alone with him, so that privilege is over.

"I'll text you," I say, and then I walk away, leaving Ryle standing alone. My mother is holding Emmy, wiping cake off her face and hands, so I head in their direction, but Allysa pulls me aside before I reach them.

"Let's chat," she says. I follow her to her bedroom, where she sits on her bed.

She only brings me to her bedroom when she wants to confront me about something, and her timing is always impeccably intuitive. I roll my eyes as soon as I walk into her room, and then I sit down on her bed. "What do you want to know?" It's been a couple of weeks since we've caught up alone. There's a lot she could be wondering about my life. It's been pretty eventful here lately.

Allysa falls back onto the bed. "Things between you and Ryle feel kind of off today."

"It's noticeable?"

"I notice everything. Are you okay?"

I think long and hard about that question. *Are you okay?* I used to hide from that question because I wasn't okay. Even months after Emerson's birth, when someone would ask me that, I would put on a smile while I shriveled up inside.

This is the first time I'm not lying when I say, "Yes. I'm okay."

Allysa regards me silently. There's a reassurance in her expression, like she might even believe me this time. She grabs my hand and pulls me until I'm lying on the bed next to her. She locks our arms at the elbows, and we just stare up at the ceiling, enjoying a moment of silence in a house full of people.

I'm glad I still have Allysa. That would have been the most heartbreaking thing of all to have to lose in my divorce. I'm grateful she's so full of forgiveness and positivity.

I wish I could say the same for her brother. Sometimes I feel like Ryle has a monster inside him that is on a constant search to be offended. His dark side feeds off drama, and if no one gives him any, he makes it up. But I can't be a player in his game anymore. I know my intentions were pure when I was married to Ryle, no matter how much Ryle wanted his delusions to be true so they could excuse his behavior.

"How are things with Adonis?"

I laugh. "You mean Atlas?"

"I said what I said. Adonis, the beautiful Greek god you're in love with."

I laugh again. "Wasn't Adonis a product of incest?"

Allysa shoves me. "Stop deflecting. How are things going?"

I roll onto my stomach and lift up on my elbow. "Good, if we'd ever get to spend time together. His restaurant doesn't open until my flower shop closes. We haven't even spent an entire night with each other yet."

"What's Atlas doing right now? Working?"

I nod.

"You should see if he can take off early and I'll keep Emerson tonight. We don't have plans tomorrow; you could come get her whenever."

My eyes widen at her offer. "For real?"

Allysa climbs off the bed. "Rylee loves it when she's here. Go spend the night with your Adonis."

.　　.　　.

I didn't text Atlas to let him know I was on my way to Corrigan's. He told me he'd be working there tonight, and I thought it might be fun to surprise him, but when I walk through the doors that lead to the kitchen, I'm amazed at how busy it is. No one even hears me enter, so I look around until I spot him.

Atlas is inspecting each plate as they're given to him to place on trays, then the waitstaff quickly disappear with the food through the double doors. This place is more upscale than Bib's, and I thought Bib's was upscale. All the waiters are dressed in formal attire. Atlas is in a white chef's coat that matches a couple of the others in the kitchen.

They've got such a groove going, I question whether I

should have shown up. I feel like I'll be in the way if I walk over to him, but I suddenly feel very awkward that I just showed up without letting him know.

I recognize Darin as soon as he spots me. He smiles and nods his head, then gets Atlas's attention. He motions toward me, and when Atlas turns around and sees me in his kitchen, his eyes light up. But only momentarily. The fact that I'm here instantly changes his excitement to concern. He makes a beeline for me, sidestepping around a waiter who is walking back into the kitchen with an empty tray.

"Hey. Everything okay?"

"It's fine. Allysa decided to keep Emmy for the night, so I thought I'd stop by."

Atlas smiles hopefully. "Is she keeping her for the whole night?" There's a flicker of flirtation in his eyes.

I nod.

"Hot behind!" someone yells from behind me. *Hot behind?* My eyes widen just as Atlas pulls us out of the way of a waiter carrying a tray of food.

"Kitchen slang," he says. "Means you're in the way of hot food."

"Oh."

Atlas laughs, and then looks over his shoulder at all the plates he's falling behind on. "Give me about twenty minutes to get us caught up?"

"Of course. I didn't come here to ask you to leave early. I thought I could watch you work for a while; it's kind of fun."

Atlas points to a metal counter. "Sit there. It's the best view, and you won't get knocked over. Gets pretty busy back here. Be done soon." He lifts my chin and bends to kiss me, then he backs away and returns to what he was doing before I walked in.

I take a seat on the counter and pull up my legs, crossing them so that I'm completely out of the way. I notice a few of the employees stealing glances at me, which makes me somewhat uncomfortable. Out of all the people back here right now, I've only met Darin, so I have no idea who any of them are. I do wonder what they're thinking of the random girl Atlas just kissed who is now watching them work.

I don't know if Atlas normally brings women around, but I get the feeling he doesn't. Everyone is looking at me like this is an anomaly.

Darin comes over to greet me as soon as he gets a chance. He gives me a quick hug and says, "Good to see you again, Lily. You still hustling unassuming poker players?"

I laugh. "Not for a while now. Do you guys still have your poker nights?"

He shakes his head. "Nah, we're too busy now that Atlas has both restaurants. It was difficult finding a night we could all meet up."

"That's a shame. Are you working here now?"

"Not officially. Atlas wanted to see how I work with the menu here; he's thinking of promoting me to head chef." He leans in and smiles. "He said he wants more time off. I guess now I know why." Darin tosses a rag over his shoulder. "It was good seeing you. Sounds like you'll be around more often." He winks before walking away.

Knowing Atlas is making an effort to spend less time at work makes my stomach swirl with happiness.

I spend the next fifteen minutes silently watching Atlas

work. Every now and then he'll glance at me and give me a warm smile, but the rest of the time, he's focused on his job. His intensity and confidence are mesmerizing.

No one seems intimidated by him, but everyone appears to want his opinion. He's constantly being asked questions, and he responds to each one of them with patience. In between those moments of teaching, there's a lot of yelling. Not the kind of yelling I'd expect to find in a kitchen, but people calling out food orders and cooks yelling their acknowledgments. It's loud and busy, but the vibe is a rush.

It's honestly not at all what I expected to find. I thought I'd see a whole new side to Atlas—one where he barked orders with anger and behaved like all the chefs I've seen on television. But, thankfully, that's not at all what is happening in this kitchen.

After a thrilling half an hour goes by, Atlas finally steps away from his station. He washes his hands before walking over to me. I get this knot of excitement in my stomach when he leans forward and presses his mouth to mine, like he doesn't care that all his staff can see us.

"Sorry that took so long," he says.

"I enjoyed it. It was different than I expected."

"How so?"

"I thought all chefs were assholes and screamed at their staff."

He laughs. "No assholes in this kitchen. Sorry to disappoint." He uncrosses my legs so he can stand between them. "Guess what?"

"What?"

"Josh is staying over at Theo's tonight."

I can't hold back my grin. "What a wonderful coincidence."

Atlas's eyes sweep over me, and then he leans his head against mine, pressing his lips lightly against my ear. "Your place or mine?"

"Yours. I want to be in a bed that smells like you."

He nips at my ear, sending chills down my neck. Then he takes my hands and helps me down from the counter. He gives his attention to someone passing by. "Hey, can you take over the pass?"

The guy says, "You bet."

Atlas looks back at me and says, "Meet you at my house."

. . .

I stopped by my apartment before going to his restaurant to pack a bag just in case this was a possibility, so I get to his place before he does. While I wait for Atlas, I use the time in my car to check in with Allysa.

Did she fall asleep okay?

Just fine. How's your night going?

Just fine. ;)

Have fun. I expect a full report.

Atlas's headlights shine through my car as he pulls into his driveway. I'm still gathering my things when he opens my car door. As soon as I climb out of the car, Atlas dips an impatient hand into my hair and kisses me. It's the kind of kiss that screams *I've missed kissing you.*

When he pulls back, he studies my face with a gentle smile. "I liked you watching me in the kitchen tonight."

A shiver passes over me. "I like watching you." I can't say

it without grinning. I grab my bag from the passenger seat, and Atlas takes it from me and hoists it over his shoulder. I follow him through the garage. He still has moving boxes piled up along one wall. There's a weight bench in pieces on the floor next to the unpacked boxes. There are two full baskets of laundry sitting in front of a washer and dryer.

Seeing a little bit of disarray in his garage is comforting. I was beginning to think he was too good to be true, but Atlas Corrigan is behind on life and behind on laundry like the rest of us.

He unlocks his house and holds the door open for me. It's smaller than his last one, but it's more him. And it's not a cut-and-paste brick building in a subdivision of similar-looking homes. The houses in this neighborhood have character. Each one is vastly different, from the pink two-story house on the corner to the modern boxy glass one at the other end of the street.

Atlas's house is a bungalow-style home nestled in between two larger homes. When I was here last time, I noted that he somehow got the biggest backyard of the three. *Plenty of room for a garden someday . . .*

Atlas enters his security code into his keypad. "It's nine five nine five," he says. "If you ever need in."

"Nine five nine five," I repeat, noting it's the same number combination as his phone. He's a man of commitment. I like it.

His security code isn't a key to his house, but it feels almost as significant. He places my bag on his couch and then flips on the living room light. My back is to the wall, and I'm standing out of the way, watching him. It's a good thing he informed me that he liked it when I was watching him at work, because watching Atlas is my favorite pastime. I could live my life as a fly on his wall and be content. "What's your routine when you get home at night?"

Atlas tilts his head. "What do you mean?"

I gesture at the room. "What do you do when you get home at night? Pretend I'm not here."

He regards me silently. Then he walks toward me, pausing right in front of me. He presses a hand onto the wall beside my head and leans in. "Well," he whispers. "First, I take off my shoes."

I hear one of his shoes being kicked off, then the other. He's suddenly an inch lower and even closer to my mouth. He feathers his lips lightly across mine, sending fireworks popping beneath my skin. "Then . . ." He kisses the corner of my mouth. "I take a shower." He pushes off the wall and backs away, his eyes locked on mine in a dare.

He disappears into his bedroom.

I'm inhaling a steadying breath when I hear his shower start running. I slip off my shoes and leave them next to his, then I follow the path he took down the hallway. I gently push open the half-closed door and take in his bedroom in person for the first time. I've seen it in our video chats, but I didn't come in here when I came to his house the first time. I recognize his black headboard and the denim-blue accent wall behind it, but the rest of his bedroom is new to me. I pass over everything in search of the bathroom door.

He left it open. His shirt is on the floor by the doorway.

I don't know why my heart is pounding like it'll be my first time seeing Atlas without clothes. It's not like I'm brand-new to this, or him, or even to showering with him. But every time I'm with him, it's like my heart gets amnesia.

I make it to the doorway of his bathroom, disappointed to see that his shower is hidden behind half of a stone wall. I can hear the breaks and splashes in the shower stream, and I feel a tightening in every curve of my body.

I don't leave my clothes with his. I stay dressed and slowly make my way over to the shower. I press my back flush against the long wall of his bathroom, and I inch closer to the shower opening, leaning my head in just enough to get a peek at him.

Atlas is standing under the stream of water, his eyes closed, the water coming down directly on his face as he runs his fingers through his hair. I stay quiet and still and continue leaning against the wall while I watch him.

He knows I'm here, but he ignores my presence and allows me to soak up the sight of him. I want to run my hands over the rise and fall of muscles across his shoulders, and I want to kiss the dimples in his lower back. He is absolutely beautiful.

Once he rinses all the soap out of his hair and off his face, he looks toward me. His eyes catch mine, and they narrow. Darken. Then he faces me, my gaze falling, falling . . .

"Lily."

My eyes move back up to his, and he's smirking. Then, so quickly, he strides across the wet tile and yanks me away from the wall until I'm wrapped in his arms. He pulls me into the shower with him, and I gasp from the rush of it all.

He catches my gasp in his mouth as he grips my thighs, pulling my wet-blue-jean-covered legs around him. My back meets the shower wall, taking some of my weight off Atlas so that he can free up a hand.

He uses that free hand to unbutton my shirt.

I use both of mine to help him. We stop kissing long enough for him to lower me to my feet so that he can slip the shirt down my arms. The shirt plops against the shower floor with a small splash just as Atlas's fingers meet the button on my jeans.

His mouth is hungry and back on mine as he slides his hands between my hips and my panties, tugging my clothes down one difficult inch at a time.

He grips the waistband on the sides of my jeans and lowers himself down my body as he works to slide them off me. Once they're around my ankles, I help him by kicking them off, then he places his hands on the backs of my calves and slowly works his way back up me.

When he's fully standing again, his fingers gather behind my back at the clasp of my bra. My stomach clenches as he begins to unfasten it. His mouth finds mine again, but this kiss is gentle and slow, like the removal of this last piece of clothing deserves to be savored.

I feel his hands slide to my shoulders, and then he tucks his fingers beneath the straps and slips them down my arms. My bra begins to fall away from me, and Atlas pulls away from my mouth long enough to admire me. His hand curves over my hip, and then slides over my ass, squeezing me.

I wrap my arms around his neck and slide my lips across his jaw, settling my mouth over his ear. "Then what?"

I watch as chills break out over his arms. He groans, and then lifts me higher up the wall until we're aligned at the waist. I roll my hips into him, wanting to feel him hard against me, and he meets my movement with a quick thrust, forcing me to gasp. It's obvious we both want this, but he still looks at me for permission before he takes me right here in the shower. We've had the proper conversations about my being on birth control, and both of us having been tested, so I just nod and whisper a desperate "Yes."

I grip his shoulders tighter in an attempt to take more weight off his arms so that he can position himself to push into me. He uses his left arm to hold me up and his right hand to grip himself, and then he rolls his hips forward and up until I feel the pressure of him inside of me.

He sighs into my neck at the same time I release all the breath in my chest. It comes out like a moan, and that sound encourages Atlas to get that noise out of me again.

My legs are tight around his waist, but he thrusts against me hard enough for them to unlock at the ankles. I start to slip down him, but he hoists me back up and repositions himself until I'm filled with him all over again.

I release another moan, and he rolls into me a second time, and a third time, and it may not be as graceful against a water-soaked shower wall as it is in a bed, but I can't get enough of the unruly side of him.

He gives me that unruly side of him for several minutes before we're both too weak and breathless to continue this without the support of a bed. He doesn't say anything after he pulls out of me and lowers me to my feet. He just turns off the water and then grabs a towel. He starts at my hair, squeezing water out of it with both his hands, and then he slowly works his way down my body with the towel until I'm dry enough.

He does a quick swipe of himself with the towel before grabbing my hand and walking me out of the bathroom.

I don't know how something as simple as him holding my hand on our way to the bedroom can make my heart expand.

Atlas lifts the blanket and motions for me to climb into his bed. It's so comfortable, it feels like I'm nestling into a cloud. He scoots in next to me, stopping only when he can't come even a centimeter closer to me. He's on his side, but he rolls me so that I'm flat on my back, tucked against him.

I like this position. I like the way he's holding himself up on his elbow, hovering over me. I like the slight grin in his eyes, as if I'm a reward he's earned.

Atlas lowers himself and we're no longer easing into these kisses. It's an immediate deep and hungry kiss that starts with the dive of his tongue and ends with him impressively reaching for a condom and putting it on without interrupting the strength of his kiss. Atlas grips the inside of my thigh and pushes my leg aside to make room for himself.

Then he's above me, pushing into me, and he moves against me until I find myself in the middle of a beautiful falling apart.

• • •

Atlas is on his back on the bed, and I'm curled into him, my leg draped over his thigh. These are the moments I look forward to sharing with him the most. The quiet minutes we get to steal from the chaos of our lives, where it's just the two of us, satiated, content. My head is resting on his chest, his fingers are trailing back and forth over my arm.

He kisses the top of my head and says, "How long has it been since we ran into each other on the street?"

"Forty days," I say. *I've been counting.*

He makes a *huh* sound, like that surprises him.

"Why? Does it feel longer?"

"No, I just wanted to know if you've been counting like I have."

I laugh and press my lips against his skin, right over his heart.

"How were things at the party today?" he asks me. I know what he's asking without him having to say it. He wants to know how Ryle treated me.

"The party was good. I spoke to Ryle for maybe five seconds."

"Was he unkind?"

"No. We just stayed out of each other's way, mostly."

Atlas runs his fingers through my hair, pulling them through the strands and letting them fall over my back. He takes another handful and repeats the movement. "That's progress. Hopefully it'll just get easier from here."

"Hopefully." I do hope things between Ryle and I continue to get easier, but I'm no longer letting his reactions control my happiness. I'm all-in with Atlas, and I want to be present in that part of my life. If that makes Ryle upset or uncomfortable, Ryle is going to have to bear the burden of those feelings. "I might ask Allysa to have a sit-down with me and Ryle this week. I want to discuss what happened, and what to do going forward, but I don't want to discuss it with him alone."

"That's smart."

Ryle and I may never get to a point where we can be more than merely civil. But I'd be okay with civil. What I'm not okay with are the insults, the threatening texts, the outbursts. He's got a lot of work to do, and I'm finally willing to hold him to task.

I probably should have been firmer earlier on, but I've been trying to make it work in the least dramatic way possible. But I'm done bending my own life for Ryle's sake.

My loyalty is to the people who bring positivity into my life. My loyalty is to the people who want to build me up and see me happy. Those are the people I'm going to make decisions about my life for.

I'm going to continue doing the best I can, and that's all I can do. I may not have made all the right decisions in the right time frames, but the fact that I found the courage to make those decisions at all is what I'm going to keep focusing on.

Atlas slips a finger beneath my chin, tilting my head back so that I'm looking at him. He's got this look on his face like he's right where he wants to be. "I can't tell you how much I've enjoyed this," he says. He pulls me closer, sliding me up his chest so that I'm eye to eye with him. He caresses the side of my head. "I wish I could have you in my bed like this every night. I want to shower with you and cook with you and watch TV with you and go grocery shopping with you. I want *everything* with you. I hate that we have to pretend like we don't already know we're spending the rest of our lives together."

It's incredible how fast a heart rate can double. I slide my fingers over his lips. "We aren't pretending. We *are* going to spend the rest of our lives together."

"How long do we have to wait until we start?"

"From the looks of it, we've already started," I say.

"How long do I have to wait before I ask you to move in with me?"

Heat swirls in my stomach. "Six months, at least."

He nods as if he's taking mental notes. "And how long before I'm allowed to propose?"

A thickness forms in my throat, making it hard to swallow. "A year. Year and a half."

"A year from when we move *in* together or a year from *now*?"

"From now."

He grins, pulling me flat against him. "Good to know."

I can't help but laugh into his neck. "That was a surprising conversation."

"Yeah, my therapist is going to kill me when I tell him about it."

I'm smiling as I roll off him and lay on my side. I snuggle into the crook of his arm and run my fingers over Atlas's chest, and then trail them over the ridges of his stomach. His muscles clench and twitch beneath my fingernails. "Do you work out?"

"When I can."

"It shows."

Atlas laughs lightheartedly. "Are you trying to flirt with me, Lily?"

"Yes."

"I don't need compliments. You're naked and in my bed. Not much else you need to do; you won me over years ago."

I lift my head and smirk, like that's a challenge. "You don't think so?"

He shakes his head, smiling lazily. He runs his thumb over my bottom lip. "Pretty sure I am filled to capacity. I think I may have even reached enlightenment tonight."

I keep my eyes locked with his, but I readjust myself, and then I slowly start to slide down his body. "I think I can still impress you," I whisper. He releases a deep exhale when I press a kiss to his stomach. My gaze is still on his face, and I love that his expression begins to tighten while he watches me.

He swallows when I start to move the sheet aside, until he's no longer covered below the waist. His eyes darken. "*Fuck*, Lily."

He allows his head to fall back against his pillow as soon as my tongue slides up the length of him.

He groans when I take him in my mouth, and then I prove him *very* wrong.

Chapter Twenty-Nine
Atlas

I can't get enough of her, but I think it's okay because she can't seem to get enough of me. She woke me up this morning by sliding on top of me and kissing my neck.

She ended up on her back seconds later with my mouth between her thighs.

Maybe we're so hungry for each other because we know it's rare that we'll get days like this. Or maybe it's because we've missed each other for so many years.

Or maybe this is just what things are like when you're in love. I've been with women aside from Lily, but I'm convinced she's the only one I've ever truly loved.

My feelings for Lily are amplified unlike anything I've ever experienced. They're even more amplified than the feelings I had for her when we were younger. It's different now—stronger, deeper, more exciting. There's no way in hell I'd walk away from her now like I did back then.

I know I was in a different headspace entirely at the age of eighteen, and that had a lot to do with why I didn't feel like I should stick around for her. But I'm all-in now. I absolutely hate the idea of taking it slow. I get why we need to, but I don't have to like it. I want her near me every day, because I feel absolutely unfulfilled on the days I can't see her.

Now that we've stayed the night together, I have a feeling the ache is going to get worse. I'm going to grow irritable when I have to go too long without seeing her. She's standing right next to me while we brush our teeth, but I'm already dreading that she's about to leave.

Maybe if I offer to cook her breakfast, I'll get her for at least another hour.

"Why do you have a spare toothbrush?" Lily asks me. She spits her toothpaste into my sink and winks at me. "You have overnight guests a lot?"

I smile at her and rinse my mouth, but I don't answer that question. I have that toothbrush for her, but I don't want to admit it. I've made a lot of small moves over the years that were all excused with *just in case Lily* . . .

After she left my place a couple of years ago while she was hiding from Ryle, I went out and bought a lot of things just in case she needed to come back. An extra toothbrush, more comfortable pillows for my guest room, a change of clothes in case she showed up in an emergency.

I had a Lily emergency kit, if you will. I guess now it's more of a Lily *sleepover* kit. And yes, I brought it all to the new house with me when I moved. I've always had a little bit of hope that we'd end up together someday.

Hell, if I'm being honest with myself, I've had a great deal of hope. I've based a lot of my decisions on the possibility that Lily might come back into my life. I even chose this house over another one I was considering, simply because of the backyard. It looked like a backyard Lily would fall in love with.

I wipe my mouth on a hand towel and then hand it to her to use. "Can I make you breakfast before you go?"

"Yeah, but kiss me first. I taste better than I did this morning." She stands on her tiptoes and I wrap my arms around her and lift her the rest of the way to my mouth. I kiss her while I walk her out of the bathroom and then drop her onto my mattress. I hover over her.

"You want pancakes? Crepes? An omelet? Biscuits and gravy?" Before she can answer me, my doorbell rings. "Josh is home." I give her a quick peck. "He likes pancakes. Will that work?"

"I love pancakes."

"Pancakes it is." I walk to the living room and unlock the door for Josh. I open it, and then I immediately freeze at the sight of my mother.

I sigh, frustrated I didn't use the peephole.

She looks at me flatly, her arms folded across her chest. "I got a visit from a caseworker yesterday." Her eyes are accusing, but at least she isn't yelling.

I am not about to do this with Lily here. I step outside and try to close the door, but my mother slaps it open. "Josh, get out here!" she yells into the house.

"He isn't here." I keep my voice low.

"Where is he?"

"At a friend's house." I pull my phone out of my pocket and check the time. Brad said he'd have Josh here by ten, and it's ten fifteen. *Please don't let him show up while Sutton is here.*

"Call him," she demands.

The door is wide open from when Sutton pushed it, so I can see out of the corner of my eye when Lily emerges from the hallway.

This is not how I wanted my morning with Lily to end. I can feel the regret slide all the way through me. I shoot her an apologetic look, and then give my attention back to Sutton.

"What did the caseworker say?" I ask her.

Her mouth screws into a tight twist, and then she looks to her left. "They're not even opening an investigation. If you don't return him to me today, I'll file charges."

I know the steps Child Protective Services has to take during an investigation, and they haven't even contacted Josh for an interview yet. "You're lying. I'd like you to leave."

"I'll leave when I have my son."

I exhale. "He doesn't want to live with you right now." *Or ever*, but I save that sting.

"He doesn't want to *live* with me," she repeats with a laugh. "What kid that age *wants* to live with their parents? And how many parents *haven't* slapped a kid that age? They don't end custody over that. *Jesus* Christ." She folds her arms over her chest again. "The only reason you're doing this is to get back at me."

If she knew me, she would know I'm not vengeful like she is. But of course, the conclusion she comes up with is something that only fits her own personality. "Do you miss him?" I ask her, my voice calm. "Honestly. Do you miss him? Because if you're doing this to prove something to someone, just let it go. *Please*."

Brad's car turns onto the street, and I wish there were a way I could ask him to keep driving. But he's pulling up to the curb before I can even reach my phone. Sutton follows my line of sight and sees Josh opening the back door of Brad's car.

She immediately walks toward the car, but Josh pauses when he sees her. More like *freezes*. He doesn't know what to do.

Sutton snaps her fingers and points at her car. "Let's go. We're leaving."

Josh immediately looks at me. I shake my head and motion for him to come inside. Brad can sense something is off, so he puts the car in park and opens his door.

Josh ducks his head and walks directly across the yard, past Sutton, and rushes toward me. Sutton is hot on his trail, so I try to get Josh inside quick enough to close the door on her, but she's too fast. I'm not about to injure her with the door, so I just let her inside.

I guess we're doing this now.

I wave to Brad to let him know he can go, and then I look at Lily, who is standing against a wall, watching everything unfold with a surprised look on her face.

I mouth, *I'm sorry.*

Josh tosses his backpack on the floor and sits down on the couch, firmly folding his arms. "I'm not going with you," he says to Sutton.

"This isn't up to you."

Josh looks directly at me, pleading. "You said I could stay here."

"You can."

Sutton shoots daggers at me like I'm out of line. Maybe I am. Maybe it's not my business to be getting in the way of a mother and her child, but she should have thought twice about that before she made me that child's brother. I can't turn the other way and just hope he makes it out okay.

"If you don't come with me, I'll have your brother arrested."

Josh slaps his hands on the couch and pushes himself up. "Why can't it be *my* choice?" he yells. "Why do I have to live with either one of you? I've told you both I want to live with my dad, but no one will help me *find* him!" Josh's voice cracks, and then he's marching down the hallway. The slam of his door makes me flinch . . . or maybe it was what he said before running to his room.

Either way, I feel punctured.

Sutton can see the sting because she's staring at me, assessing my reaction to that.

Then she starts to laugh. "Oh, *Atlas*. You thought you were doing something here? Forming a *bond* with him?" She shakes her head and throws up her hand in defeat. "Take him to his daddy. You'll be running back to me next week, just like you did the last time you needed my help."

She walks to the door and leaves, and I'm too dazed by everything that just happened to walk over and lock it.

Lily does it for me.

She starts to walk toward me with a face full of sympathy, but as soon as she pulls me in for a hug, I shake my head and separate myself from her. "I need a minute."

Chapter Thirty
Lily

Atlas closes his bedroom door behind him, and I find myself alone in his living room.

I feel awful for both of them. I can't believe that was his mother. *Or maybe I can.* After hearing stories of her, I imagined her to be that unhinged, but I guess I expected her to look different. Both Atlas and his brother look so much like her that it makes it difficult to see that kind of behavior come from someone Atlas is related to. They are polar opposites.

I take a seat on the edge of the couch, shocked that I just witnessed all of that. I've never seen Atlas that affected. I want to go hug him, but I can absolutely understand that he needs a moment alone.

Josh, too. The poor kid.

I don't want to leave before saying goodbye to Atlas, but I also don't want to disturb him until he's had a moment to recover. I walk to the kitchen and open the refrigerator. I look for the ingredients to make breakfast for them.

• • •

I kept it simple because that's all I really know how to do. I made scrambled eggs and bacon and put a pan of biscuits in the oven. When the biscuits are almost ready, I go tap on

Josh's bedroom door. I can at least offer him something to eat while I wait for Atlas to come out of his room.

Josh opens the door about two inches and looks at me.

"You want some breakfast?" I ask him.

"Is Sutton gone?"

I nod, so he opens the door and follows me down the hall. Josh gets himself something to drink while I pull the biscuits out and make us both a plate of breakfast. I sit across from him at the table, and he eyes me while he eats. I feel like I'm being sized up.

"Where's Emerson?" he asks.

"She's with her aunt."

Josh nods and takes a bite of his food. Then: "How long have you and my brother been together?"

I shrug. "That depends. I've known him since I was fifteen, but we started dating about a month and a half ago."

There's a flash of surprise on Josh's face. "Really? Were you, like, friends back then or something?"

"Or something." I take a sip of my coffee, and then set it down carefully. "Your brother didn't have anywhere to live when I met him, so I helped him for a while."

Josh leans back in his chair. "Really? I thought he lived with our mom."

"When she and your dad would allow it," I say. "But he spent a lot of time trying to survive without their help." I hope I'm not saying too much, but I feel like Josh needs a better understanding of Atlas. "Go easy on your brother, okay? He cares a lot about you."

Josh stares at me for a beat, then nods. He leans over his plate again, taking a bite of bacon. He drops the bacon back onto the plate and wipes his mouth with a napkin. "His cooking is normally better than this."

I laugh. "That's because I made it."

"Oh, shit," Josh says. "Sorry."

I don't take offense at all because I'm sure he's getting used to Atlas's cooking. "Do you think you want to be a chef like him? He told me you like helping out at the restaurants."

Josh shrugs. "I don't know. It's fun. Maybe. But I feel like I'll get tired of it. He works a lot of nights. I feel like I'll get tired of *any* career after a few years, though, so I don't know what I'll do."

"Sometimes I feel like I still don't know what I want to be when I grow up."

"I thought you owned a flower shop or something. That's what Atlas told me."

"I do. Before that, I used to work at a marketing firm." I push my plate aside and fold my arms on the table. "I still feel like you do, though. Worried about boredom. Why are we expected to pick one thing to try and be successful at? What if I want to do something completely different every five years?"

Josh nods like he's in complete agreement. "The teachers at school talk like we have to decide on one thing we love and stick with it, but I want to do a hundred things."

I love how animated he is right now. He reminds me so much of a younger Atlas. "Like what?"

"I want to be a professional fisherman. I don't know how to fish, but it sounds fun. And I want to be a chef. And sometimes I think it would be fun to make a movie."

"Sometimes I dream of selling my flower shop and opening a clothing boutique."

"I want to make pottery and sell it at fairs."

"I'd like to write a book someday."

"I want to be the captain of a ship," he says.

"I think it would be fun to be an art teacher."

"I think it would be fun to be a bouncer at a strip club."

I sputter laughter at that, but I'm not the only one laughing. Josh and I glance up at Atlas, who is leaning in the doorway, laughing at our conversation.

I'm relieved to see him in a better mood than the one his mother left him in. Atlas smiles at me warmly.

"Lily made us breakfast," Josh says to him.

"I see that." Atlas walks over and kisses me on the cheek, then picks up a piece of bacon and takes a bite.

"Kind of sucks," Josh mutters in warning.

"Don't insult my girlfriend or I'll stop cooking for you." Atlas steals the last slice of bacon off Josh's plate.

"These eggs are great, Lily," Josh says with fake enthusiasm.

I laugh while Atlas takes a seat next to me. As much as I want to spend the entire day here with him, I've already stayed longer than I intended.

It also feels like he and Josh have a lot to work out today.

"I have to go," I say regretfully. Atlas nods, and I scoot back from the table. "I'm gonna go grab my stuff." I walk to the bedroom, but I don't close Atlas's door, so I hear their conversation as I'm packing my bag.

Atlas says, "You feel like taking a road trip today?"

"Where to?" Josh asks.

"I found your dad's address."

I pause gathering my things and walk closer to the door so I can hear Josh's response.

"You did?" There's a new excitement in Josh's voice. "Does he know we're coming?"

"No, I only got his address. I don't know how to get in touch with him. But you were right: He's in Vermont." I can hear the dread Atlas is attempting to cover up in his voice all the way from his bedroom. *God, I hate this for him.*

I hear Josh running toward his room. "He is going to be so shocked!"

I finish packing with a heavier heart. When I walk back into the kitchen, Atlas is standing in front of the sink, staring out the window into his backyard. He doesn't hear me, so I put my hand on his shoulder.

He immediately pulls me in and kisses me on the side of my head. "I'll walk you to your car."

He carries my bag to the car and places it in the backseat. I open my door, but we hug again before I climb inside.

This is the kind of hug Atlas gave me when he showed up at my apartment needing a hug that night. It's long and sad, and I don't want to let go of him. "What do you think is going to happen when you get there?" I ask.

Atlas finally releases me, but keeps his hand on my hip while he leans against my car. He sighs, threading his finger through a belt loop on my jeans. "I don't know. Why do I feel so worried for him?"

"Because you love him."

Atlas's eyes scroll over my face. "Is that why I always feel worried for you? Because I love you?"

My breath hitches at his question. "I don't know. Do you?"

Atlas digs his fingers into my waist, and he pulls me to him. He lifts his hand and traces a finger down my neck, until it meets my tattoo. "I've loved you for years and years and years, Lily. You know that." He moves his finger and then kisses me there, and that move coupled with his words takes everything in me to keep my composure.

"I've loved you for just as long."

Atlas nods. "I know you have. No one on this earth loves me like you do." He cradles my head in both of his hands, and he tilts my face up to his and he kisses me. When he pulls back, he looks at me longingly, like I've already left and he's already sad about it. Or maybe that's just what I'm imagining he feels, since that's what *I* feel.

"I'll call you tonight. I love you."

"I love you, too. Good luck today."

I drive home with such conflicted feelings. Every moment with him over this last day was more than I could have hoped for, but knowing what he's about to face makes my heart feel like a piece of it broke off and stayed with him.

I'm going to be thinking about him all day. I'm hoping they don't find Tim, but if they do, I hope Josh makes the right decision.

Chapter Thirty-One
Atlas

It's a three-hour drive there. Josh hasn't said much. He's been reading, although if he's as nervous as I am about this, I'm not sure he's actually absorbing anything he's reading. He's been on the same page for five minutes. It's a drawing of what looks like a battle scene, but mostly all I see is cleavage.

"Is that manga appropriate for a twelve-year-old?" I ask him.

He shifts ever so slightly so that the cover of the book is all I can see. "Yes."

His voice dropped an entire octave on that lie. At least he's a horrible liar. If he ends up staying with me, detecting when he is or isn't telling me the truth should be easy.

If he ends up staying with me, maybe I should buy him a few self-help books for balance. I'll stock his bookshelves with whatever graphic novels he wants, and then secretly slip in a few of my own to supplement my lack of skills as a guardian. *Untamed, Man Enough, The Subtle Art of Not Giving a F*ck.* Heck, maybe even some sacred text from every major world religion. I'll take whatever help I can get.

Especially after today. As much as Josh may think this is a one-way trip, I know in my heart he's coming right back to Boston with me. I just hope he doesn't come back kicking and screaming.

When the GPS says we're turning onto the street, Josh's hand tightens around his manga. He doesn't look up from it, though, even though he still hasn't turned the page. When I spot Tim's address on the curb in front of a run-down frame house, I pull the car over. The house is across the street on the driver's side, but Josh pretends to be sunk into his story.

"We're here."

Josh drops his book and finally looks up. I point to the house, and Josh stares at it for a good ten seconds. Then he puts the book in his backpack.

He brought most of his things with him. The clothes I bought him, some of the books. They're all stuffed so tight in a backpack that barely zips, and he holds it in his lap with the hope that he has at least one parent that will take him.

"Can we wait a little bit?" he asks.

"Sure."

While he waits, he fidgets with everything. The air vents, his seat belt, the music on his Bluetooth. Ten minutes pass while I patiently give him the time to work up whatever courage he's in need of that will help him open the door.

I look at the house, taking my attention off Josh for a while. There's an old white Ford in the driveway, which is probably why Josh hasn't worked up the courage to walk across the street and knock on his door yet. It's an indicator that someone is probably home.

I haven't tried to talk him out of this because I know what it's like to want to know your father. He's going to live in this fantasy until he's able to confront his reality. As a kid, I had the highest hopes for family, too, but after years of being disappointed, I realized that just because you're born into a group of people, that doesn't make them your family.

"Should I just go knock?" Josh finally asks. He's scared, and to be honest, I'm not feeling the bravest right now, either. I went through a lot with Tim. I'm not looking forward to seeing him again, and I am absolutely dreading the potential outcome of this meeting.

I don't think this is the best place for Josh, and I'm in no position to tell him he can't reconnect with his father. But my biggest fear is that he's going to choose to stay here. That Tim is going to be like my mother and welcome Josh with open arms, simply because he knows it's the one thing I don't want to happen.

"I can go with you if you want," I say, even though it's the last thing I want to do. I'll have to stand in front of that man and pretend I don't want to punch him for the sake of my little brother.

Josh doesn't move for a while. I'm staring at my phone, attempting to appear patient as he works up courage, but I want to throw the car in drive and get him out of here.

I eventually feel Josh's finger briefly graze an old scar on my arm, so I look over at him. He's staring at my arm, taking in the faded scars that remain from the shit I endured living with Sutton and Tim. Josh has never asked me about the scars, though.

"Did Tim do that to you?"

I clench my arm and nod. "Yeah, but it was a long time ago. How he treats a son might be completely different from how he treated a stepson."

"That shouldn't matter, right? If he treated you like that, why should he get another chance with me?"

It's the first time Josh has come close to admitting his father isn't a hero.

I don't want to be the person he blames in the future for not having a relationship with his dad, but I want to tell him he's right. His father *shouldn't* get another chance. He left and never looked back. There's no excuse good enough to walk away from your son.

There's this toxic belief that family should stick together simply because they're family. But the best thing I ever did for myself was walk away from them. It scares me to think of where I might be had I not done that. It scares me to think of where Josh might end up if he *doesn't* do that.

Josh looks past me, toward the house. His eyes grow a little wider, prompting me to turn and look.

Tim is outside, making his way from the front door to his truck. Josh and I watch in mutually stunned silence.

He looks fragile—older and smaller. Or maybe that's because I'm no longer a kid.

He's swigging from the last of a beer can when he opens the front door to his truck. He tosses the empty can into the bed and then leans inside his cab in search of something.

"I don't know what to do," Josh whispers. He seems all of the twelve years old that he is right now. It kind of breaks my heart to see him so nervous. Josh's eyes are pleading for truth when he looks back at me, like he needs me to guide him in this moment.

I've never said a bad word about Tim to Josh, but knowing I'm not being completely honest with him about my feelings feels like I'm doing a disservice to him as a brother. Maybe my silence on the matter is more damaging than my truth would be.

I sigh and set my phone down, giving this moment my full attention. Not that it didn't have my full attention before, but I was trying to give Josh space. It doesn't seem like he wants it, though. He wants brutal honesty, and what else is an older brother good for if not for that?

"I don't know my dad," I admit. "I know his name, but that's about it. Sutton said he left when I was young, probably about the same age you were when Tim left. It used to bother me, not knowing my father. I used to worry about him. I imagined there was something awful that was keeping him away, like he was locked up in a prison somewhere on a wrongful conviction. I used to come up with these wild scenarios that would excuse how he could know I existed but not be in my life. Because what kind of man could have a son and *not* want to know him?"

Josh is still staring across the yard at Tim, but I can see that he's soaking up every word I'm saying.

"My father never sent a penny of child support. He never made an effort at all. My father never bothered to do a Google search, because if he had, he would have easily found me. Hell, *you* did that at the age of *twelve*. You found me, and you're a kid. He's a grown-ass adult."

I move so that I have Josh's full attention. "So is Tim. He is a capable, grown man, and if he cared about anything more than himself, he would have made an effort. He knows your name, he knows what city you live in, he knows how old you are."

Josh's eyes are starting to tear up.

"It blows my mind that this man has you for a son, and you *want* to be in his life, yet he still hasn't made an effort. You're a privilege, Josh. Believe me, if I'd known you existed, I would have knocked over buildings to find you."

As soon as I say that, a tear trickles out of his eye, so Josh quickly looks out his passenger window, away from Tim's house, away from me. I see him wipe at his eyes, and it breaks my heart.

It also makes me angry as hell that they kept him from me knowingly. My mother knew I would have been a good brother to him, which is why she chose not to let us be a part of each other's lives. She knew my love for him would outweigh the love she was capable of, so she selfishly kept us apart.

But I don't want my anger for my mother or Tim or even my father to bleed into Josh's decision. He's old enough to make up his own mind, so he can take my honesty and his hope, and I'll support him in whatever he decides to do with those things.

When Josh finally looks back at me, his eyes are still filled with tears and questions and indecision. He's looking at me like I need to be the one to make this decision for him.

I just shake my head. "They took twelve years from us, Josh. I don't think I can forgive them for that, but I won't be upset if you do want to forgive them. I only ever want to be honest with you, but you are your own person, and if you want to give your father a chance to get to know you, I'll put a smile on my face and walk you straight to his front door. You just let me know how to be here for you and I'll be here."

Josh nods and uses his shirt to wipe away another tear. He inhales, and on his exhale, he says, "He has a truck."

I don't know what he means by that, but I follow his line of sight back to Tim's truck.

"All this time I imagined him to be really poor, without a way back to Boston," he says. "I even thought maybe he never came because he wasn't physically able to drive, like maybe his vision was too bad or something. I don't know. But he has a truck and he never even tried."

I don't interfere with his thought process. I just want to be here for him when he finalizes it.

"He doesn't deserve me, does he." He says it like a statement rather than a question.

"Neither of them deserves you."

He doesn't move for an entire minute as he stares past me out the window. But then he looks at me firmly, sitting a little taller. "You know that homework I'm behind on? The family tree?" Josh pulls at his seat belt and begins to fasten it. "They never said how big the tree needed to be. I'll just draw a baby seedling. They don't have branches." He pats the dash. "Let's go."

I laugh hard at that. I wasn't expecting it. The way this kid weaves humor into the most depressing moments gives me hope for him. I think he's gonna be okay.

"A seedling, huh?" I start the car and pull on my own seat belt. "That might work."

"I can draw a seedling with two tiny branches. Yours and mine. We'll be on our own brand-new, tiny family tree—one that starts with us."

I feel heat behind my eyes, so I grab my sunglasses off

the dash and put them on. "A whole new family tree that starts with us. I like it."

He nods. "And we'll do a much better job of keeping it alive than our shitty parents did."

"That shouldn't be too hard." I am absolutely relieved by this decision. Josh may change his mind in the future, but I have a strong suspicion that even if he contacts his father going forward, he's never going to choose him over me. Josh reminds me a lot of myself, and devotion is a trait we have in spades.

"Atlas?" Josh says my name right as I put the car in drive.

"Yeah?"

"Can I flip him off?"

I stare back at Tim and his truck and his house. It's an immature request, but one I happily respond to with, "Please do."

Josh leans as far toward my window as his seat belt will allow. I roll down the window and honk the horn. Tim looks over at us right as I start to drive away.

Josh flips him off and yells, "Ass hole," out my window. Once we're out of Tim's eyesight, Josh falls back against his seat, laughing.

"It's *asshole*, Josh. *One* word."

"Asshole," he says, pronouncing it the correct way.

"Thank you. Now stop saying it. You're twelve."

Chapter Thirty-Two
Lily

Are you at home?

The text is from Atlas, so I respond to it with, **For a minute. Why?**

I pack baby food into Emmy's diaper bag and then rush around the room, grabbing her a change of clothes. I throw a can of formula in as well, since I'm no longer breastfeeding, and then I scoop her up. "You ready to go see Rylee?"

Emmy smiles when I say Rylee's name.

When I picked her up this morning from Allysa's, I had a talk with both her and Marshall about everything that's happened with Ryle. Allysa agreed that it was smart to show my lawyer the texts he sent me. She also agreed that it's time we have a serious sit-down with Ryle. I'm nervous, but knowing she and Marshall have my back is extremely reassuring.

As soon as we make it to my front door, there's a knock. I glance through the peephole, relieved to see Atlas standing there. But Josh isn't with him, so my heart immediately sinks. *Did he actually choose to stay with his father over Atlas?* I swing open the door.

"What happened? Where's Josh?"

Atlas smiles, and the assurance in his smile fills me with instant relief. "It's fine. He's at my house."

I blow out a breath. "Oh. Why are you here, then?"

"I'm on my way to my restaurant. I was driving by and thought I'd run up and steal a hug."

I smile, and he holds the door open for me. He can't give me a full-on hug since I have Emerson perched on my hip, so he gives me a quick kiss on the side of my head. "Liar. My apartment isn't on your way. And it's Sunday—your restaurant is closed."

"Details," he says, waving off my point. "Where are you headed?"

"Allysa's. We're having dinner with them tonight." I hoist the diaper bag onto my shoulder, but he takes it from me.

"I'll walk you out." He slings the diaper bag over his shoulder. Emmy reaches for him, and I think we're both a little surprised when she willingly transfers from my arms to his. She tucks her head against his chest, and the sight of it makes me pause for a second. It makes Atlas take a pause, too. But then he smiles at me and begins walking down to my car. He holds my hand the whole way.

I take Emmy from him and buckle her into her car seat. We're finally in a position where Atlas can give me an actual hug, so he pulls me to him. His hug feels like an entire conversation. He's holding me in a way that makes it feel like he's needing strength—like he wants to take a piece of me with him. "Where are you going again?" I ask him, pulling back.

"I really am going to my restaurant," he says. "I asked Sutton to meet me there. We need to have a serious discussion about Josh, and I'd like to do it when it's just me and her. She feeds off an audience, so I refuse to give her one."

"Wow. I'm actually on my way to Allysa's to have that

sit-down with Ryle I told you I wanted. What is this, problem-solving Sunday?"

Atlas laughs softly. "Hopefully."

I kiss him. "Good luck."

He smiles gently. "You too. Be safe, and call me as soon as you can." He presses his mouth to mine one last time, and then when he pulls away, he says, "Love you, babe."

He walks to his car, and I don't know why his words leave me so flustered, but I'm smiling as I get into my car. *Love you, babe.* I'm still smiling as I drive away. My good mood surprises me, considering what I'm on my way to do, and how it's more of a spontaneous intervention than a planned sit-down. I *am* going to Allysa and Marshall's for dinner, but Ryle has no idea I'm heading over there with a purpose.

· · ·

"Lasagna?" I ask Marshall when he opens the front door. I could smell the garlic and tomatoes from the hallway.

"Allysa's favorite," he says, closing the door behind me. He reaches for Emmy. "Come to Uncle Marshall," he says, pulling her to him.

She's giggling as soon as he makes a face at her. Marshall is one of Emmy's favorite people, but I think we'd be hard-pressed to find a kid who doesn't love Marshall. "Is Allysa in the kitchen?"

Marshall nods. "Yeah. He's in there, too," he says, whispering. "We didn't mention you were coming."

"Okay." I set Emmy's diaper bag down and head for the kitchen. I see Ryle and Allysa's mother sitting with Rylee in the living room when I pass by. I wave at her, and she smiles, but I don't stop to chat. I go in search of Allysa.

When I walk through the kitchen door, I find Ryle leaning over the bar, chatting casually with Allysa, but as soon as he makes eye contact with me, his spine stiffens and he stands up straight.

I don't react at all. I don't want Ryle to think he holds any sort of control over me anymore.

Allysa has been expecting me. She acknowledges me with a nod and then she closes the lasagna in the oven. "Perfect timing." She drops the pot holders on the counter and points at the table. "We have forty-five minutes until it's ready," she says, guiding both Ryle and me toward the table.

"What is this?" Ryle asks, looking back and forth between the two of us.

"Just a conversation," Allysa says, urging him to take a seat. Ryle rolls his eyes but reluctantly takes a seat across from both Allysa and me. He leans back in his chair, folding his arms over his chest. Allysa looks over at me, giving me the floor.

I'm not sure why I'm not scared right now. Maybe Atlas already having had a conversation with Ryle has put most of my concerns to rest. Having Allysa and Marshall in the apartment with us also feels like a layer of protection. And Ryle's mother, even though she has no clue what's about to transpire. Ryle keeps his behavior in check when his mother is around, so I'm grateful for her presence.

Whatever is giving me strength right now, I don't sit and question it. I take advantage of it. "You asked yesterday if I spoke to my lawyer," I say to Ryle. "I did. She had some suggestions."

Ryle chews on his bottom lip for a few seconds. Then he lifts a brow, indicating he's listening.

"I want you to undergo anger management."

As soon as the words come out of my mouth, Ryle laughs. He stands up, prepared to push in his chair and end this conversation, but as soon as he does, Allysa says, "Sit down, please."

Ryle looks at her, and then me, and then back at her. Several seconds pass as he takes in what's happening. It's apparent he feels deceived right now, but I'm not here to give him empathy, and neither is his sister.

Ryle loves and respects Allysa, so he eventually returns to his seat, despite his current anger.

"While you're undergoing anger management, I would prefer for your visits with Emerson to take place here, or somewhere Marshall or Allysa are present."

Ryle swings his eyes to Allysa, and the look of betrayal he shoots her would have given me chills at one point in our past, but right now that look does nothing to me.

I continue. "Depending on your interactions with me going forward, we'll decide as a family when we feel comfortable with you having unsupervised visits with the girls."

"The *girls*?" Ryle repeats incredulously, looking at Allysa. "Did she convince you I'm not safe around my own niece?" His voice is louder now.

The kitchen door swings open, and Marshall walks in. He takes a seat at the head of the table and looks from Ryle to Allysa. "Your mom has the girls in the living room," he says to Allysa. "What'd I miss?"

"Are you aware of this?" Ryle asks Marshall.

Marshall stares at him for a beat, and then leans forward. "Am I aware you lost your temper with Lily last week and pinned her against a door? Or am I aware of the texts you sent her? Or the threats you made when she said she was talking to her lawyer?"

Ryle stares blankly at Marshall. His face reddens, but he doesn't immediately react. He's trapped in a corner, and he knows it. "A goddamn intervention," Ryle mutters, shaking his head. He's annoyed, irritated, a little bit betrayed. Understandable. But he can either agree to cooperate, or he can fracture the few remaining relationships left in his life.

Ryle pegs me with a jaded stare. "What else?" he asks, somewhat smugly.

"I've given you more than enough grace, Ryle. You know I have. But from this point forward, please know that Emerson is what matters to me. If you do anything threatening or harmful to me or our daughter, I will sell everything I own to fight you in court."

"And I'll help her," Allysa says. "I love you, but I'll help her."

Ryle's jaw is twitching. His expression is blank otherwise. He looks at Allysa and then at Marshall. The tension in the room is palpable, but so is the support. I could cry, I'm so grateful for them.

I could cry for all the victims who don't *have* people like them.

Ryle stews over everything for a long beat. It's so quiet, but I've made the point I wanted to make, and I've made it obvious that there's no room for negotiation.

He eventually scoots back from the table and stands. He

brings his hands to his hips and stares down at the floor. Then he drags in a long inhale before he heads for the kitchen door. Before he leaves, he looks back toward us, but makes eye contact with none of us. "I'm off this Thursday. I'll be here around ten if you want to make sure Emerson is here."

He leaves, and as soon as he does, my shield of armor collapses, and I shatter. Allysa puts her arms around me, but I'm not crying because I'm upset. I'm crying because I am so, so relieved. It actually feels like we accomplished something significant. "I don't know what I'd do without you two," I say through my tears, hugging Allysa.

She runs her hand over my hair and says, "You'd be so miserable, Lily."

We both start to laugh. Somehow.

Chapter Thirty-Three
Atlas

I called Sutton after I dropped Josh off at my house and asked her to meet me at Bib's. I got here an hour before we agreed to meet. I've never cooked for her, so I'm hoping my making her a meal does something to her. Pleases her, puts her in a decent mood. Anything to make her less combative.

My phone pings, so I step away from the stove and look at the screen. I told her to text me when she arrived so I could let her in. She's five minutes early.

I walk through the dark restaurant and flip on some lights on my way through. She's standing near the front, smoking a cigarette. When she sees the door open, she flicks the cigarette into the street and then follows me inside.

"Is Josh here?" she asks.

"No. It's just me and you." I gesture toward a table. "Have a seat. What do you want to drink?"

She regards me silently for a moment, then says, "Red wine. Whatever you have open." She takes a seat in a booth, and I head back to plate our food. I made coconut shrimp because I know it's her favorite. I saw her fall in love with it when I was nine years old.

It was on the one and only road trip she took me on. We went to Cape Cod, which isn't all that far from Boston, but it's the only time I remember my mother ever doing something with me on a day off. She usually slept or drank her way through her days off, so the day trip to Cape Cod where we tried coconut shrimp for the first time is not something that went unappreciated by me.

I place our plates and drinks on a tray and walk it out to the table she's seated at. I set the food and wine in front of her, then take a seat across from her. I slide silverware to her side of the table.

She stares at her plate for a beat. "You cooked this?"

"I did. It's coconut shrimp."

"What's the occasion?" she asks, opening her napkin. "Is this an apology for assuming you could actually parent a kid like him?" She laughs like she told a joke, but the lack of noise in the restaurant makes her laugh fall flat. She shakes her head and picks up her glass of wine, sipping from it.

I know she has twelve years on me with Josh, but I'm willing to bet I already know him better than she does. Josh probably knows *me* better than she knows me, and I lived with her for seventeen years. "What was my favorite food growing up?" I ask her.

She stares back at me blankly.

Maybe that was a tough one. "Okay. What about my favorite movie?" Nothing. "Color? Music?" I give her a few more, hoping she can answer at least one of them.

She can't. She shrugs, setting down her wineglass.

"What kind of books does Josh like to read?"

"Is that a trick question?" she asks.

I settle back against the booth, attempting to hide my agitation, but it's living and breathing in every part of me.

"You don't know anything about the people you brought into this world."

"I was a single mother to both of you, Atlas. I didn't have time to worry about what you liked to read when I was busy trying to survive." She drops the fork she was about to use. "Jesus Christ."

"I didn't ask you to come here so I could make you feel bad," I say. I take a sip of my water, and then run my finger around the rim of my glass. "I don't even need an apology. Neither does he." I look at her pointedly, shocked that I'm about to say what I'm about to say. It's not what I came here to say to her at all, but the things I selfishly came here for aren't what's nagging at me. "I want to give you an opportunity to be a better mother to him."

"Maybe the issue is that he should be a better son."

"He's twelve. He's as good as he needs to be. Besides, the relationship you have with him isn't his responsibility."

She scratches her cheek and then flicks a hand in the air. "What is this? Why am I here? Do you want me to take him back because he's too much for you to handle?"

"Not even close," I say. "I want you to sign your rights over to me. If you don't, I'll take you to court, and it'll cost us both a ridiculous amount of money that neither of us wants to pay. But I'll pay it. If that's what it takes, I will drag this in front of a judge, who will take one look at your history and force you to undergo a year of parenting classes that we both know you have no interesting in completing." I lean forward, folding my arms together. "I want legal custody of him, but I'm not asking you to disappear. I don't want you to. The last thing I want is for that boy to grow up feeling as unloved by you as I felt."

She sits frozen in my words, so I pick up my fork and take a casual bite of my dinner.

She stares at me while I chew, and she's still staring at me as I wash down the food with a sip of water. I'm sure her brain is running a mile a minute, searching for an insult or a threat of her own, but she's got nothing.

"Every Tuesday night we're going to have dinner here, as a family. You are more than welcome to come. I'm sure he would enjoy that. I'll never ask you for a penny. All I ask is that you show up one night a week and be interested in who he is, even if you have to fake it."

I notice Sutton's fingers are shaking as she reaches for her wineglass. She must notice, too, because she makes a fist before grabbing it and pulls her hand back to her lap. "You must not remember Cape Cod if you think I was such a horrible mother to you."

"I remember Cape Cod," I say. "It's the one memory I try to hold on to so that I don't completely resent you. But while you feel like you did this wonderful thing by giving me that one memory of us that one time, I'm offering to give that to Josh every day of his life."

Sutton looks down at her lap when I say that. For the first time, she looks like she might be experiencing an emotion other than anger or irritation.

Maybe I am, too. When I decided to have this conversation with her on the drive home from Tim's house today, I fully planned on cutting her out of our lives forever. But even monsters can't survive without a heart beating inside their chest.

There's a heart in there somewhere. Maybe no one in

her life has ever let her know they're appreciative that it still beats.

"Thank you," I say.

Her eyes flicker up to mine. She thinks I'm testing her with that comment.

I shake my head, conflicted by what I'm about to say. "You were a single mother, and I know neither of our fathers helped you in any way. That must have been really difficult for you. Maybe you're lonely. Maybe you're depressed. I don't know why you can't look at motherhood like the gift that it is, but you're here. You showed up tonight, and that effort is worth a thank-you."

She looks down at the table, and it's a completely unexpected reaction when her shoulders begin to shake, but she fights back the tears with all that she is. She brings her hands up to the table and fidgets with her napkin, but never has to use it because she doesn't allow a single tear to fall.

I don't know what she went through that made her so hard. So unwilling to be vulnerable. Maybe one of these days she'll share that with me, but she has a lot to prove as a mother to Josh before she and I will ever get to that point.

She pulls her shoulders back, sitting up straighter. "What time will the dinner be on Tuesdays?"

"Seven."

She nods and looks like she's about to scoot out of the booth.

"I can get you a to-go box if you want to take it with you."

She nods quickly. "I'd like that. It's always been my favorite dish."

"I know. I remember Cape Cod." I take her plate to the kitchen and prepare it to go.

. . .

Josh is asleep on the couch when I finally make it back home. Anime is playing on the television, so I hit pause and set the remote on the coffee table.

I watch him sleep for a little while, overcome with relief after the day I've had. Things could have gone a lot differently. I press my lips together, choking back the emotional exhaustion as I watch him sleep in peace. I realize as I'm staring at him that I'm looking at him the same way Lily looks at Emerson, like she's so full of pride.

I pull the blanket off the back of the couch and drape it over him, then I walk to the table where Josh's homework is laid out. Everything is completed, even the family tree assignment.

He drew a tiny seedling sprouting from the ground with two small branches. One says *Josh* and one says *Atlas*.

Chapter Thirty-Four
Lily

I almost missed the note, I was in such a rush this morning. It was shoved under my front door and was caught on the entry rug.

I had Emmy on my hip, a purse and a diaper bag on my shoulder, and coffee in my free hand. I managed to bend and pick up the note without spilling any of it. *Supermom.*

I had to wait until I got a quiet moment at work to open it. When I unfold the note and see Atlas's handwriting, I feel a shiver of relief run through me. Not because I thought the note would be from anyone other than Atlas. We've been together several months now, and he leaves me notes all the time. But this is one of the first notes he's left that a small part of me hasn't dreaded opening, in the off chance the note *was* from Ryle.

I make a mental note of the significance of this moment.

I do that a lot. Mentally note significant things that are clues my life is finally getting back to normal. I don't do it as often as I used to, but that's a good thing. Ryle is such a small part of my life now, I sometimes forget how eternally complicated I used to believe it would be.

He's still a part of Emmy's life, but I've been demanding more structure from him. He sometimes tries to push back on how strict I am with her visits, but I'm never going to be comfortable until she can tell me in her own words what her visits with Ryle are like. I'm hoping anger management is helping, but only time will tell.

The contact Ryle and I do have is still sometimes terse, but all I've ever wanted out of our divorce was my freedom from fear, and I truly feel like I have that.

I'm hiding in my office storage closet, sitting cross-legged on the floor because I wanted to read this letter uninterrupted. It's been months since I forced Atlas to hide out in here, but it still smells like him.

I unfold the note and trace the little open heart he drew at the top left-hand corner of the first page. I'm already smiling as I begin to read.

Dear Lily,

I don't know if you're aware of the date, but we have officially been dating for half of an entire year. Do people celebrate half-year anniversaries? I would have gotten you flowers, but I don't like to make the florist work too hard.

I decided to give you this note, instead.

They say there are two sides to every story, and I've read a couple of stories of yours that, even though they happened the way you said they did, I had an entirely different experience.

You kind of brushed over this moment in your journals, even though I know it meant enough for you to get a tattoo. But I'm not sure you're aware of how much that moment meant to me.

You say our first kiss happened on your bed, but that's not the one I count as our first kiss. Our first kiss happened on a Monday in the middle of the day.

It was that time I got sick and you took care of me. You noticed I was ill as soon as I crawled through your window. I remember you taking immediate action. You gave me medicine, water, and blankets, and forced me to sleep on your bed.

I don't remember ever being sicker than that in my entire life. I do believe you witnessed the most awful day I've ever lived through. And I've lived through some awful days. But when you're in it, there seems to be nothing worse in the moment than a horrible stomach bug.

I don't remember a lot of that night. I remember your hands, though. Your hands were always near me, either checking my temperature or wiping my face with a rag or holding my shoulders steady while I repeatedly had to fold over the side of your bed throughout the night.

That's what I remember: your hands. You had a light pink polish on, I even remember the name of the color because I had been with you when you painted your nails. It was called Surprise Lily and you told me you picked it because of the name.

I could barely open my eyes, but every time I did, there they were, your slender helping hands with your Surprise Lily fingernails, holding up my water bottle, feeding me medicine, tracing my jaw.

Yes, Lily. I remember that moment, even though you didn't write about it.

After hours of being ill, I remember waking up, or at

least becoming more aware of my surroundings. My head was pounding and my mouth was parched and my eyelids were too heavy to open, but I felt you.

I felt your breath on my cheek. Your fingertips were on my jaw and you traced them all the way down to my chin.

You thought I was asleep—that I couldn't feel you touching me, watching me, but I had never felt more than I did in that moment.

It was the exact moment I realized that I loved you. I kind of hated realizing something that monumental in the middle of such a shitty day, but it hit me so hard I thought I was going to cry for the first time in years and I didn't know what to do with that feeling.

But, man, Lily, I had gone my whole life not knowing what love felt like. I didn't have the love a mother and son should have, or a father and son, or a sibling. And until you, I had never spent that kind of time with anyone unrelated to me, especially a girl. Not long enough to truly get to know a girl, or for them to get to know me, or for us to connect and deepen that connection, and then for that girl to prove to be caring and helpful and kind and worried and everything that you were to me.

I'm not even saying it was the moment I realized I was IN love with you. It was just the first moment I realized I loved something, anything, anyone, ever. It was the first time my heart had ever reacted. At least in a positive way. People had done things to me in the past that made my heart shrink, but never expand like that. When your fingers were trickling over my chin like soft drops of rain, I thought my heart was going to swell so big it might pop.

I pretended to slowly wake up in that moment. I put my arm over my eyes, and you quickly pulled your hand back. I remember craning my neck and looking at your window to see if it was light outside. It almost was, so I started to pull myself out of your bed, pretending not to know you were awake. You sat up and asked me if I was leaving, and I had to swallow before I could get my voice to work. It barely did. I said something like, "Your parents will be up soon."

You told me you were going to skip school and come back for me in a couple of hours. I nodded without speaking, because I was still sick, but I had to get out of your bedroom before I said something or did something to embarrass myself. I didn't trust the feeling that was buzzing beneath my skin. It was creating this burning need to look at you and say, I love you, Lily! *It's funny how, as soon as you feel love for the first time, you suddenly have this huge desire to profess it. The words felt like they were forming right in the center of my chest, and even though I was weaker than I'd probably ever been, I had never lifted your window and crawled out of it that fast before.*

I shut it and flattened my back against the cold wall of your house, and I exhaled. My breath turned to fog, and I closed my eyes, and after the absolute worst eight hours of my life, I somehow cracked a smile.

I thought about love the rest of the morning. Even after you'd come back to get me once your parents were gone and I spent several more hours being sick at your house, I was thinking about love. When your Surprise Lily fingernails would flash across my line of sight every time you checked my temperature, I'd think about love. Every time you'd walk into your room and adjust the covers, tucking them under my chin, I'd think about love.

And then when I finally started to feel a little better around lunchtime, I stood in the shower, weak and dehydrated from being sick, yet I somehow felt like I was standing taller than I ever had before.

That whole morning and into the rest of the day, I knew something significant had happened. For the first time, I had felt a flicker of what I knew life could be. Before that moment, I never gave much thought to falling in love, or having a family someday, or even the idea of cultivating a successful career. Life to me had always felt like a burden I had to bear. Something heavy and murky that made waking up difficult and falling asleep a little bit scary. But that's because I had gone eighteen years not knowing what it felt like to care about someone so much, you want them to be the first thing you see when you open your eyes. I even felt a desire to make something of myself because you were the first person I ever wanted to become something better for.

That was the day we laid on your couch together and you told me you wanted me to watch your favorite cartoon with you. It was the first time you had ever snuggled up to me, your back to my chest as we lay under the blanket with my arm wrapped over you. It was hard to focus on the television because the words I love you were still tickling their way up my throat, and I didn't want to say it, couldn't say it, because I didn't want you to think it was too fast, or that those words held no weight for me. They were the heaviest damn thing I'd ever carried.

But I think about that day so much, Lily, and I have no idea if that's what love feels like for everyone, like it's an airplane that just fell from the sky and crashed right through you. Because most people, they have love seeping in and out their whole lives. They're born being wrapped in it and they go their whole childhood being protected by it, and they have people in their lives that welcome their love in return, so I'm not sure it hits people like it hit me—in one small moment, in such a colossal way.

You were wearing this shirt I loved. It was too big for you, and the sleeve was always falling off your shoulder. I should have been watching the cartoon, but I couldn't stop staring at that stretch of exposed skin between your neck and your shoulder. As I was looking at it, I once again felt that incredible pull to say I love you, *and the words were there, right on the tip of my tongue, so I leaned forward and pressed them against your skin.*

And that's where they stayed, hidden and quiet, until I worked up the courage to speak them out loud to you six months later.

I had no idea you remembered that kiss, or all the times I kissed you in that spot after that day. Even when I read it in your journal, you rushed past it in a hurry to get to what you considered our actual first kiss, so I had no idea that it even meant anything to you until the moment I saw your tattoo. I can't tell you what that means to me, knowing that you have our heart placed in the very spot where I once secretly buried the words I love you.

I want you to promise me something, Lily. When you look at that tattoo, I don't want you to think about anything other than the words I've written in this letter. And every time I kiss you there, I want you to remember why I kissed you there the first time. Love. *Discovering it, giving it, receiving it, falling in it, living in it,* leaving *for it.*

I'm writing this letter while sitting on the floor of Josh's bedroom. My experience with Josh tonight is kind of what sparked my memory. He's sick with a stomach bug. Maybe not as sick as I was the day I first realized I loved you, but very, very sick nonetheless. He caught it from Theo, who had it a few days ago.

I've never taken care of a sick person before, so I have no medicine at all. I think I'm about to make a pharmacy run. I might slip this letter under your apartment door on my way there.

It isn't fun taking care of a sick person. The sounds, the smell, the lack of sleep—it's actually almost as bad for the person doing the caring. Every time I check his temperature or force him to drink water, I think about you and how you cared for me with such a gentle parental instinct. I'm trying to replicate that in my care for Josh, but I don't think I'm as good at this as you were.

You were so young, just a few years older than Josh is now. But I'm sure you felt much older than you were. I know I did. We had been through things no kid should have to experience. It makes me wonder if Josh feels his age, or if he feels older than he should because of all he's been through.

I want him to feel young for as long as he can. I want him to enjoy his time with me. I want him to know what love is long before I did. And I hope that love has been seeping slowly into him so that it doesn't hit him all at once like it did me. I want him to grow up with it, wrapped in it, surrounded by it. I want him to witness *it.*

I want to be an example for him. I want us *to be an example for him, and for Emerson. Me and you, Lily.*

It's been six months.

Move in with me.

Love,
Atlas

As soon as I finish reading the letter, I set it down and wipe my eyes. If this is how much I cry when he asks me to move in with him, I have no idea how I'll survive a proposal.

Or wedding vows, for that matter.

I pick up my phone and call Atlas over video chat. It rings for ten long seconds, and when Atlas finally answers it, he's lying on his living room couch. He's smiling through his obvious exhaustion from being up all night with Josh.

"Hey, beautiful." His voice is barely awake.

"Hi." My hand is curled into a fist, and I'm resting my cheek on it, pushing down my huge smile. "How's Josh feeling?"

"He's okay," Atlas says. "He's sleeping, but I think I stayed up so long, my brain is too overwhelmed to shut off now." He puts a fist to his mouth and stifles a yawn.

"Atlas." I say his name sympathetically because he does look absolutely drained. "Do you need me to come over and give you a hug?"

"You mean do I need you to come *home* and give me a hug?"

I smile when he says that. "Yes. That's exactly what I meant. Do you need me to come *home* and give you a hug?"

He nods. "I do, Lily. Come home."

Chapter Thirty-Five
Atlas

"Aren't you rich?" Brad asks. "Couldn't you hire people to do this for you?"

"I own two restaurants. I'm not even close to rich. And why would I hire someone when I have you guys?"

"At least we're going *down*stairs," Theo says.

"Take notes from your son, Brad. Silver lining."

We don't have much left to move. Lily didn't need a lot of her stuff since my house is already furnished, so she donated most of it to a local domestic violence shelter. We should have her apartment completely cleared out by this afternoon.

Brad is the only person I know with a truck, so he and Theo have been helping us load the things we can't fit into our cars. Emerson's crib, Lily's living room television, some of the artwork hanging on her walls.

Josh lucked out. He's at baseball practice, so he didn't have to help with the move.

I was surprised when he came home a few months ago and told me he had signed up for tryouts. He made the team and has been giving it everything he has. Between Lily and I, we haven't missed a single game.

I texted our mother his schedule, but so far she hasn't shown up to a game. She's only shown up once to the dinners we started having every Tuesday night. I was hoping she would want to be more involved, but I'm not surprised she isn't. I doubt Josh is surprised, either. We don't focus too much on what isn't working out in our lives. We focus on what *is*, and there's a lot to be grateful for. The two main things being that I was able to get custody of Josh, and Lily and Emerson are moving in with us. Funny how drastically life can change on a dime.

The Atlas of last year wouldn't know what to think of the Atlas of this year.

Lily is heading up the stairs right as I reach the bottom of them. She grins and gives me a kiss in passing, then runs up the rest of the steps.

Theo shakes his head. "Still can't believe you made it this far with her." He hoists his box up with his knee and then presses his back against the exit door to push it open. He holds it open for me and Brad, but I pause once we're in the parking garage.

There's a car that resembles Ryle's pulling into a parking spot a few spaces away from Brad's truck.

A sense of dread washes over me. I haven't had a single interaction with him since that day he attempted to fight me at my restaurant, but that was months ago. I have no idea how much he's warmed up to the idea of me and Lily, but from the look he's shooting in my direction, it doesn't seem like he's warmed up much.

Someone else is with him. A man gets out of the passenger seat, and from what Lily has told me, it looks like he could be Ryle's brother-in-law. I've met Lily's mother, and I've met Allysa and Rylee, but I've never met Marshall.

I walk over to Brad's truck and load up the box I'm carrying, but I'm watching Ryle's car the whole time. Theo and Brad head back inside, unaware of Ryle's presence. Marshall lifts Emerson out of the backseat and closes the door. Ryle remains in the car as Marshall walks Emerson in my direction.

He holds out a hand. "Hey. Atlas, right? I'm Marshall."

I return his handshake. "Yeah, good to meet you."

He nods, but when Emerson sees me, Marshall has to clasp a tighter hand around her because she lunges for me. I step forward and take her from him.

"Hey, Emmy. Did you have fun today?"

Marshall watches me with her for a moment, then says, "Be careful. She puked on Ryle twice today."

"Is she not feeling well?"

"She's fine, but she's been with the two of us all day. Both the girls had sugar for breakfast. And snack. *And* lunch *and* second snack and . . ." He waves a dismissive hand. "Lily and Issa are used to it."

Emerson reaches up and pulls the sunglasses off my head. She tries to put them on her own face, but they're crooked, so I help her adjust them until she's wearing them right. She grins at me, and I smile back at her.

Marshall glances over at the car that Ryle's sitting in, and then back to me. "Sorry he's not getting out. This is all still a little weird for him. Her moving in with you."

When Marshall says "her," he doesn't mean Lily. He's looking at Emerson. I nod in understanding, because I do understand. "It's fine. I can't imagine this is easy for him."

Marshall ruffles Emmy's hair and then says, "I'll get out

of here so you guys can finish up. It was good finally meeting you."

"You too," I say. And I mean that. Marshall seems like someone I could be friends with if the circumstances were different.

He turns to head back to Ryle's car, but he pauses and faces me again before he gets very far. "Thank you," he says. "Lily means a lot to my wife, so . . . yeah. Thanks for making Lily happy. She deserves it." As soon as Marshall says that, he shakes his head and holds up his hands, taking a step back. "I'll go now before it gets too awkward." He makes a beeline for Ryle's car, but I kind of wish he wouldn't have run off so fast. I would have thanked him, too. I know his support has meant a lot to Lily.

Marshall shuts the passenger door, and Ryle puts his car in drive and heads out.

I glance at Emmy, who is now chewing on my sunglasses. "You want to go say hi to Mommy?" I start to walk in the direction of the building, but I pause when I see Lily standing in the doorway to the stairwell.

As soon as she sees me, she spins around and wipes quickly at her eyes. I'm not sure why she's crying, but I walk a little bit slower so she can erase the tears before she greets her daughter. Sure enough, several seconds later, she spins around with a big grin and takes Emmy from me.

"Did you have fun with your daddy today?" she asks, right before she smothers Emmy with several kisses.

When she looks at me, I shoot her a curious look, wondering why she was crying. She gestures to the parking lot, where Ryle's car was moments before.

"That was a big thing," she says. "I mean, I know Marshall was with him, but the fact that he felt okay enough to leave her with you . . ." She's starting to tear up again, which makes her sigh and roll her eyes at her own reaction. "It feels good knowing the men in her life can at least *pretend* to get along for her sake."

It honestly makes me feel good, too. I'm glad she was upstairs when they showed up. I know Ryle sat in the car while Marshall handed her over, but it was a step in the right direction. Maybe Ryle and I needed an exchange like that just as much as Lily did.

We just proved cooperation is possible, even if it stings.

I wipe at Lily's wet cheek, and then I give her a quick kiss. "I love you." I put my hand on Lily's lower back and guide her toward the stairs. "One more trip before you're stuck with me forever."

Lily laughs. "I can't wait to be stuck with you forever."

Chapter Thirty-Six
Lily

I'm curled up on Atlas's couch, exhausted from moving.

Our couch.

This is going to take some getting used to.

I had Theo and Josh help me unpack the rest of Emerson's and my things because Atlas has a late night at work. I wake up early, he gets home late, but it's exciting that we'll now get more pieces of each other, even when it's in passing. And we have Sundays together.

But tonight is a Friday, and tomorrow is a Saturday, Atlas's busiest days, so I'm entertaining Josh and Theo until my mother returns with Emerson. The three of us have been watching *Finding Nemo*, but it's almost over.

I honestly didn't think they would sit through it because they're at the age when preteens tend to want to separate themselves from Disney cartoons. But I'm learning that Gen Z is a different breed. The more time I spend with these two, the more I think they're unlike any generation that came before them. They're less prone to peer pressure and more supportive of individuality. I'm a little bit jealous of them.

Josh stands when the credits begin to roll.

"Did you like it?"

He shrugs. "It was pretty funny, considering it started

with the brutal slaughter of all that caviar." He takes his empty bag of popcorn toward the kitchen, but Theo is still staring at the television. He's shaking his head slowly.

I'm still stuck on Josh's description of the beginning of the movie . . .

"I don't get it," Theo says.

"The caviar comment?"

Theo looks between me and the television. "No. I don't get why Atlas said that to you about finally reaching the shore. It wasn't even a quote in the movie. He told me he said it because of *Finding Nemo*. I waited for someone to say it through the entire movie."

I'm sure I'll have to get used to a lot of things now that I live with Atlas, but knowing he talks to this kid about our relationship is probably not one of the things I'll ever get used to.

The confusion in Theo's eyes flips like a light switch. "Oh. *Oh*. Because when life gets them down, they keep swimming, so Atlas was saying life will no longer . . . *okay*." His mind is still going a mile a minute behind those eyes. He starts to shake his head as he pushes himself off the floor. "I still think it's cheesy," he mutters. Theo's phone buzzes right as he stands. "I gotta go—my dad's here."

Josh is back in the living room. "You aren't staying over?"

"I can't tonight; my parents are taking me to a thing in the morning."

"I want to go to a thing," Josh says.

Theo is pulling on his shoes when he hesitates. "Yeah, I don't know."

"Where are you going?"

Theo's eyes flash briefly to mine, and then back to Josh. "It's a parade." He says it quietly, but also like it's a warning.

"A parade?" Josh tilts his head. "Why are you being weird? What kind of parade is it? A pride parade?"

Theo swallows like maybe him and Josh haven't had this conversation, so I'm nervous on Theo's behalf. But I've been around Josh enough over the last several months to know that he values his friendship with Theo.

Josh grabs his shoes and sits next to me on the couch and starts putting them on. "What are you saying? I'm not allowed to go to a pride thing because I like girls?"

Theo shifts from one foot to the other. "You can go. I just . . . I didn't know if you knew."

Josh rolls his eyes. "You can tell a lot about a person by their taste in manga, Theo. I'm not a dumbass."

"*Josh*," I say.

"Sorry." He grabs a jacket from the closet. "Can I stay over at Theo's tonight?"

Josh's casual attitude about this monumental moment between the two of them reminds me so much of Atlas.

Considerate Josh.

But his question about leaving with Theo kind of stumps me. My eyes widen slightly. I've only lived here four days. Josh hasn't asked me permission for anything before, and Atlas and I haven't really laid ground rules. "Yeah, sure. But let your brother know where you are."

I really don't think Atlas will mind. Now that we live to-gether, we're going to have to tackle things like this when it comes to Josh and Emerson. Who parents who, when, how. It's kind of exciting. I like figuring out life with Atlas.

My mother still hasn't returned with Emerson yet, so once Josh and Theo have left, the house is quiet and empty for the first time since we moved in. I've never been here alone before. I spend my alone time walking through rooms, looking in cabinets, familiarizing myself with my new house.

My new house. That's fun to say.

I go out back and sit in a chair on the deck, staring over the backyard. It's the perfect backyard for a garden. Almost unheard-of for a place this far into the city. It's like Atlas searched for a house specifically for the perfect garden space just in case I ever came back into his life. I know that's not at all why he chose this house, but it's fun imagining he did it for that reason.

My phone rings, startling me. It's Atlas returning an earlier call with a video chat.

"Hi."

"What are you doing?" he asks.

"Picking out a spot for my garden. Josh wanted to stay over with Theo, so I let him go. I hope that's okay."

"Of course it is. Did they help you at all?"

"Yeah, we got most of it done."

Atlas looks relieved by that. He runs a hand down the side of his face like he's releasing stress. It looks like it's been a busy day, but Atlas tucks it away beneath a smile. "Where's Emerson?"

"My mom is on her way back with her."

He sighs like he's sad he couldn't get a glimpse of her. "I'm starting to miss her," he says. The words come out soft and fast, like he's a little bit scared to admit he's start-ing to love my daughter. But I caught his words, and I'm keeping them next to all the other sweet things he's ever said to me. "I'll be home in about three hours. Will you be awake?"

"If I'm not, you know what to do."

Atlas gives his head a little shake, and his mouth ticks up in the corner. "I love you. Be home soon."

"I love you, too."

As soon as we end our call, I hear Emerson's sweet voice, so I immediately turn around. My mother is standing in the doorway holding her. She's smiling like she caught some of that conversation.

I stand up to grab Emerson from her, and she clings to me. Should be an easy night. When she gets cuddly like this, it means she's ready to fall asleep. I motion for my mother to have a seat next to me.

"This is cute," she says.

It's her first time here. I would show her around, but Emerson is already rubbing her face into my chest, trying to fight her tiredness. I want to give her a chance to fall asleep before I stand up.

"What a magnificent place for a garden," my mother says. "You think he chose this place on purpose, hoping you'd come back into his life?"

I shrug. "I was actually wondering that myself, but I didn't want to assume." I pause, then turn and look at her after her question actually registers. *Back into his life?* I never told her Atlas was a friend from back in Maine. I just as-sumed she didn't remember him.

I assumed she had no idea that the Atlas in my life now was anyone from my past.

She can see the surprise on my face, so she says, "It's a unique name, Lily. I remember him."

I smile, but I'm also confused as to why she never brought it up before now. I've been dating him for over six months, and she's been around him a handful of times.

I guess I shouldn't be surprised, though. My mother has always been a little hard to get to open up. I can't blame her. She spent years with a man who left her no voice, so I'm sure it's been hard for her to learn how to use it again.

"Why didn't you ever say anything?" I ask her.

She shrugs. "I figured you would bring it up to me if you wanted me to know."

"I wanted to, but I didn't want it to feel awkward for you being around him. Not after what Dad did to him."

She looks away from me, her eyes scanning the back-yard. She's quiet for a beat. "I never told you this, but I spoke to Atlas once. Kind of. I came home from work early and the two of you were asleep on the couch. Talk about a shock," she says, laughing. "I thought you were so sweet and inno-cent, but there you were on my living room sofa asleep with a random boy. I was about to yell at you, but when he woke up, he looked so scared. Not scared of me, really, now that I think about it. He looked more scared of the possibility of losing you. Anyway, he left in a quiet hurry, so I followed him outside because I was going to threaten him and tell him never to come back. But he just . . . he did the weirdest thing, Lily."

"What did he do?" My heart is in my throat.

"He hugged me," she says, her voice tinted with a drop of laughter.

My jaw drops. "He *hugged* you? You caught him with your daughter red-handed and he hugged you?"

She nods. "He did. And it was a knowing hug, too. It was like he carried this genuine sorrow for me, and I felt that in his hug. Like he was encouraging me, or comforting me. And then he just . . . walked away. I never even got the chance to yell at him for being in my house with you unsupervised. Maybe that was his plan—it could have been a manipulation tactic, I don't know."

I shake my head. "It wasn't a tactic." *Considerate Atlas.*

"I knew you were seeing him. And I knew you were hiding him from your father rather than me, so I didn't take it personally. I never interfered because I liked that you had someone, Lily." She gestures toward the house behind us. "And now look. You have him forever."

That story makes me squeeze Emerson a little tighter.

"It makes me happy to know there's a man in your life that gives meaningful hugs like that," my mother says.

"He gives more than great hugs," I deadpan.

My mother scoffs. "Lily!" She stands up, shaking her head. "I'm going home now."

I'm laughing to myself as she leaves. Then I use my free hand to text Atlas.

I love you so much, you idiot.

Chapter Thirty-Seven
Atlas

"Are you seriously about to do this?" Theo asks.

I'm standing in front of a mirror, adjusting my tie. Theo is sitting on the couch, attempting to convince me to let him read my vows before the wedding. "I'm not reading them to you."

"You're going to embarrass yourself," he says.

"I'm not. They're good."

"Atlas. Come on. I'm trying to help you. For all I know, you probably end them with something like, *It is my wish for you to be my fish.*"

I laugh. I don't know how he still comes up with these lines after two years of this. "Do you practice your insults when you lie awake at night?"

"No, they come naturally."

Someone knocks on the door and opens it a crack. "Five minutes."

I give myself one more glance in the mirror before turning to Theo. "Where's Josh? I need to make sure he's ready."

"I'm not supposed to tell you."

I tilt my head. "Where is he, Theo?"

"Last time I saw him, he was in the gazebo with his tongue down some girl's throat. He's gonna make you a grandad soon."

"I'm his brother. I'd be an uncle, not a grandad." I look out the window, but the gazebo is empty. "Go find him, please."

Josh and I are a lot alike, but he's a little bit more confident with girls than I was at that age. He just turned fifteen, and so far, this is my least-favorite age. I'm sure when he's old enough to drive next year, it's going to age me an entire decade.

I need to think about something else. I'm already nervous. Maybe Theo is right, and I should look over my vows again to make sure there's nothing I want to change or add.

I pull the page out of my pocket and unfold it, and then grab a pen in case I want to make any very last-minute changes.

Dear Lily,

I'm used to writing you letters that no one else will ever read, which may be why I had a difficult time when I first attempted to write these vows. The idea that they were going to be read out loud to you in front of other people was a little bit terrifying.

But vows aren't meant to be something you make in private. The purpose of a vow is to make an intentional promise that is witnessed, whether it's witnessed by God, or friends and family.

It has to make you wonder, though, or at least it made me wonder what the purpose is behind the need for a public vow. I couldn't stop my mind from questioning what must have happened in the past to create the necessity for love to be witnessed.

Does it mean that somewhere along the way, a promise was broken? A heart was shattered?

It's disappointing if you really sit and think about why vows even exist. If we trusted everyone to keep their word, vows wouldn't be necessary. People would fall in love, and they'd stay in love, faithfully, forever, the end.

But that's the issue, I guess. We're people. We're human. And humans can sometimes be disappointing.

That realization led me down another path in my thought process while writing these vows. I began to wonder, if humans are so often disappointing and so rarely successful at love, what can we do to ensure ours is a love that will stand the test of time? If half of all marriages end in divorce, that would mean half of every set of vows ever made have ended up broken. How do we ensure we're not one of the couples who becomes a statistic?

Unfortunately, Lily, we can't. We can only hope, but we can't guarantee that the words we stand here and promise one another today won't end up in the file of a divorce lawyer a few years down the road.

I apologize. I realize these vows are making marriage sound like an extremely depressing cycle that only ends happily half the time.

But for someone like me, that's actually kind of exciting.

Half the time?

Fifty-fifty?

One out of two?

If someone would have told me when I was a teenager that I would have a fifty-fifty chance of living my entire life with you, I would have felt like the luckiest human on the planet.

If someone would have told me that I had a 50 percent chance of being loved by you, I would have wondered what the hell I did to get so lucky.

If someone would have told me that we'd get married one day, and I'd get to give you your dream honeymoon in Europe, and that our marriage would have a 50 percent chance of being successful, I would have immediately asked what size your ring finger was so that we could get started.

Maybe the idea of love ending being a negative thing is simply a matter of perspective. Because to me, the idea that a love came to an end means that, at some point, there was love that existed. And there was a time in my life, before you, when I was completely untouched by it.

The teenage version of me wouldn't have seen potential heartbreak as a bad thing. I was jealous of anyone who had ever loved something enough to experience losing it. Before you, I had never met love at all.

But then you came along, and you changed that. Not only did I get the opportunity to be the first person to ever fall in love with you, but I also got to experience a shared heartbreak with you. And then, like a miracle, I was given the opportunity to fall in love with you all over again.

Two times in one life.

How can one man be so lucky?

All things considered, the fact that I made it here, that we made it here, to our wedding day, is quite frankly more than I ever dreamed I would get out of life. One breath, one kiss, one day, one year, one lifetime. I'll take whatever you'll give me, and I vow that I will cherish every second I'm lucky enough to spend with you from this moment on, just as I've cherished every second I've ever spent with you before this moment.

Optimistically speaking, we could live our entire lives together, happily, until we're old and frail and it takes an entire day for me just to reach your lips to kiss you goodnight. If that happens, I vow that I will be immensely grateful for the love that carried us through our life together.

Pessimistically speaking, we could break each other's hearts again tomorrow—I know we won't, but even if we did, I vow that I will be immensely grateful for the love that led to that heartbreak until the day that I die. If it's my destiny to end up a statistic, there's no one else I'd rather become a statistic with than you.

But you once told me I was a realist, so I want to end my vows realistically. In my heart, I believe we're going to leave here today and face a journey together that's full of hills, valleys, peaks, and canyons. Sometimes you're going to need me to hold your hand down the hills, and sometimes I'll need you to lead me up the mountain, but everything, from this point forward, we're going to face together. It's you and me, Lily. In good times and bad, for richer or poorer, in sickness and in health, in the past and for forever, you are my favorite person. Always have been. Always will be. I love you. Everything that you are.

Atlas

I exhale, the page trembling in my hand. They're exactly how I want them, so I start to fold the paper when Josh walks into the room. He's joined by Darin, Brad, Theo, and Marshall.

Marshall is holding open the door. "You ready? It's time."

I nod, more than ready, but before I stuff my vows back into my pocket, I decide to make one small change. I don't touch anything already written, but I do add a line to the very end.

P.S. It is my wish for you to be my fish.

Acknowledgments

It Ends with Us is the one book I have been adamant that I would never write a sequel for. I felt like it ended where it needed to end, and I didn't want to put Lily through more stress.

But then #BookTok happened, and the online petition, and the messages and videos, and I realized most of you weren't asking for me to put them through more pain. You simply wanted to see Lily and Atlas happy. When I started playing around with an outline, I quickly realized how much I needed to see Lily and Atlas happy as well. For everyone who asked for more, thank you. This book wouldn't exist without you.

I have so many people to thank, and not necessarily for the existence of *It Starts with Us*, but more for the continued support over the years that resulted in me writing a book I never thought I'd have the courage to complete. From family to friends to bloggers to readers to publishers and agents, in no particular order, I just want to say THANK YOU for your continued support, and for ensuring I continue to love writing.

Levi Hoover, Cale Hoover, Beckham Hoover, and Heath Hoover. My four favorite men on the whole planet. I couldn't do any of this if it weren't for your encouragement and support.

Lin Reynolds, Murphy Fennell, and Vannoy Fite. My three favorite women on the planet.

To the entire Bookworm Box and Book Bonanza team and board members. Thank y'all for everything you do!

To my agents, Jane Dystel and Lauren Abramo, and the entire Dystel, Goderich & Bourret team.

Thank you to my editor, Melanie Iglesias Pérez; my publicist, Ariele Stewart Fredman; and my publisher, Libby McGuire; and the entire Atria team. Thank you to the teams at Simon & Schuster UK, Australia and India for all you do for my books.

To Stephanie Cohen and Erica Ramirez. Thank you for helping make my dreams come true and always having my best interest at heart. I love you both more than words can say, and every time I walk into our office, it feels like coming home.

Thank you to Pamela Carrion and Laurie Darter for everything you do and for keeping me entertained daily.

Thank you to the team at Simon & Schuster Audio for bringing my books to life.

Thank you to author Susan Stoker for being such a champion for other authors and always keeping us in the know with your weekly messages of congratulations.

And a huge thank-you to the following for always being there: Tarryn Fisher, Anna Todd, Lauren Levine, Shanora Williams, Chelle Lagoski Northcutt, Tasara Vega, Vilma Gonzalez, Anjanette Guerrero, Maria Blalock, Talon Smith, Johanna Castillo, Jenn Benando, Kristin Phillips, Amy Fite, Kim Holden, Caroline Kepnes, Melinda Knight, Karen Lawson, Marion Archer, Kay Miles, Lindsey Domokur, and so many others.

Thank you to CoHorts, BookTok, Weblich, bloggers, librarians, and everyone who puts their hearts into spreading your love for reading.

Most of all, thank you to every single person who has ever taken the time to message or email an author to let them know what their books mean to you. You are a huge part of the reason we write.